I0517219

FATE'S VICTIM

by

ROXANE BEAUFORT

Published by **CHIMERA**
ISBN 9781903931691

Chapter 1

It was a glorious morning. The sky was a cloudless blue, the moor stretching ahead, a light breeze brushing Angela's face as she gave her mare full rein, galloping furiously, trying to outstrip Aidan. She loved to tease him, gaining confidence daily, though still hardly able to believe that he had chosen her from among the debutantes who had 'come out' that year, presented to Queen Victoria at Buckingham Palace.

He was so handsome and dashing and she thrilled to be in his presence. The mare's strong thighs rose and fell beneath her and, though seated side-saddle, she was aware of the movement causing mayhem in her lower regions. Strange feelings had begun to possess her since meeting Aidan. She was never alone with him, always chaperoned, except when, as now, they went riding. Even then a groom was not far away though, she suspected, obeying Aidan's instructions to keep a respectful distance.

The wind whipped strands of her thick, curling hair across her face from beneath the veil and top hat; essential as part of a well-turned out young lady's riding attire. Her figure-hugging jacket, cut just like a man's, clinched her tightly corseted waist. Her long skirt, worn over breeches, flowed elegantly across the mare's withers. But when she glanced over her shoulder to where Aidan was rapidly gaining on her, she had the wild desire to tear off her clothes and ride bareback and astride. She imagined the feel of saddle leather pressing against her naked female parts. The idea made a coil tighten deep inside her and she could feel dampness at the crotch of her knickers.

Her breasts tingled, the nipples hard and almost painful, and these physical manifestations alarmed yet delighted her. She knew nothing about sexual congress, had never seen a naked man. Even the nude statues of Greek gods in the art galleries to which she had been taken as part of her education, though muscular and handsome, had been discreetly covered by a carved fig-leaf when it came to the genital area. And as for knowing what would take place on the wedding night when she eventually married Aidan? This was a closed book, such matters never, ever discussed, though her companion, Miss Maude Hicks, had hinted that she must obey her husband in all things and be brave and enduring of his demands in the nuptial chamber.

Brave and enduring? These words inflamed Angela. What could they possibly mean? Would he hurt her? Somehow the notion of Aidan striking her with one of his aristocratic hands gave her those strange spasms of longing that centred below her waist. She liked to think of him being masterful, sometimes even expressing anger, but could not imagine why. The only other male contact of her own class was her father, Sir Barnaby Bayswater, and she adored him, a solitary child whose mother had died giving birth to her. He had a loud, hearty voice, sometimes lost his temper but rarely with her, a bluff, hard drinking, hard riding squire who owned Lairdland Manor and estate in this farming area of Somerset.

Angela was eighteen, used to being waited on hand, foot and finger, and being told that she was beautiful. Her hair was a rich, dark brown that gave off reddish sparks when the light struck it. Her eyes reflected her mood, blue-green and unusual. They could sparkle with mischief, become languid with desire or flash with anger. She and Aidan made a handsome couple and when the time came for them to marry, it would surely be the wedding of the year.

He caught up with her, reached across and placed a gloved hand on the bridle, slowing her horse. 'Oh no you don't,' he chided, smiling widely, his teeth white in contrast to his sun-browned face. 'You're not going to escape me, little thing. I demand a forfeit from you for even trying. A kiss at the very least.' And he kneed his mount and headed towards a copse that lay not far away, leading Angela with him.

Her heart was beating like a drum and she feasted her eyes on his profile, that hawk-like nose and strong chin, those high cheekbones and black hair and eyes that were as grey as the sea on a winter's day, yet holding fire in their depths. He reminded her of a hero from a Brontë novel, for she was an avid reader, and never more so than when devouring tales of love and romance, with mysterious heroes who concealed sinister secrets and spirited heroines who tamed them in the end.

It was shady beneath the trees, made darker after leaving the bright sunshine. Angela noticed that the groom did not follow them. The path was narrow, leading deeper into the wood, and her throat became dry with excitement and apprehension. What were Aidan's intentions? He had spoken of kisses and he had kissed her once before, when she accepted his proposal after he'd begged her hand in marriage from her father. It had been a chaste kiss, a mere brushing of lips, but she treasured the memory, hugging it to herself and reliving it, especially when in bed at night. She would dwell on it, wriggling with excitement, her secret place wet and swollen, though she never dared touch herself.

Aidan halted and, without relinquishing his hold on her mare's rein, swung from the saddle, tethered his own animal to a nearby tree, removed his gloves and pocketed them, then came across to stand close to Angela's knee. She looked down into his eyes and the expression in the depths of their black pupils made her dizzy. What did she read there? Was it true love, a deep and abiding passion that would last for all time? Or was it blazing desire, a heat that amounted to lust?

She shivered and he reached up, his large hands clipping her waist and lifting her down into his arms. He stood her on her feet but did not let go. Her breasts were pressed to his chest and she could feel something hard - she didn't know what - lodged against her belly. Without thinking she raised her arms and clasped them around his neck. His face came closer... closer still. She felt his warm breath on her lips and then the full glory of his mouth capturing her own.

Angela gasped as his tongue penetrated and tangled with hers. She knew she should draw back, refusing to permit such an intimacy, but she couldn't do it.

She wanted more and more, leaning her head against his enclosing arm and surrendering to all the wild and wicked sensations he now lavished on her.

To her intense disappointment he raised his head, staring into her bemused eyes and murmuring, 'Would you do anything for me, sweetheart?'

'Oh yes, anything,' she breathed, her hands sliding down to lie against the lapels of his riding jacket, palms flat as she became aware of the rise and fall of his broad chest.

'Do you accept that as your betrothed I am now your master, and shall be even more so once we are married?' There was a note in his voice that chilled her, and yet set her on fire, too.

'I accept it, Aidan,' she whispered.

'I shall be your lord,' he said harshly, gripping her under the elbows and dragging her closer, making her even more aware of that strange, lengthy object like a bar of iron at the front of his tight jodhpurs.

'For ever,' she vowed.

'Good girl,' he muttered, and there was a harsh note in his voice. 'And this is to be our secret. You are not to tell anyone. Do you promise?'

'I promise,' she vowed.

He released her but kept her fingers in his, and she followed him to where the bole of a large oak tree barred the way, its leafy canopy like a dome above them. Aidan pushed her against it, spreading her arms wide above her head and feasting greedily on the sight of her breasts. He took off his belt, pushed up her jacket sleeves, bound her wrists together and fastened the buckle end to a branch. He was not very gentle and the leather chaffed her delicate skin.

He stood back a pace and admired his handiwork. 'Beautiful,' he commented, then removed her hat and veil and unpinned her hair. It came tumbling down like a silken curtain part concealing her shoulders. His hands fastened on the jacket and blouse and opened them wide, tearing aside the chemise and fingering her bare, up-thrusting breasts, his thumbs caressing the hard nipples.

'Oh, Aidan... we shouldn't... I mean, we must wait until we're married,' she protested weakly.

He scowled down at her and she shivered at the sudden change in him, a cruel not a tender lover. She was helpless to stop him and he hitched up her skirt, and pulled down her breeches and cotton drawers. He cupped her mound, tangled with her dark bush and inserted a finger into the cleft, wriggling it against her little nodule that immediately hardened in response.

Angela thought she was about to die of pleasure. 'What are you doing?' she cried, unable to move and not wanting to.

'Testing your virginity,' he replied. 'I don't intend to give my name to soiled goods.'

'How dare you?' she shouted indignantly, regaining control of her wayward parts and blushing furiously at their exposure.

'I dare anything. I'm your master, remember?'

He flung off his hacking jacket and waistcoat and began to unbutton his shirt.

Angela stared, fascinated, her own discomfort forgotten. He slid the garment from his shoulders and let it fall to his waist, the tails still tucked into his jodhpurs. His chest was broad and muscular, and covered in a crisp pelt that circled the pectorals and red-brown nipples. At close to thirty he was a fine figure of a man, his body honed by riding, swimming and fencing. He had also rowed for Oxford University when an undergraduate. He was the answer to any maiden's prayer, and he knew it.

He stood spread-legged before Angela and gave her the full benefit of his impressive appearance, then picked up his crop and ran the lash through his hands in a slow, measured way.

Angela drew in a breath, embarrassed by her naked breasts and lower body, but unable to stop staring at the rod-shaped object stretching to his waist under cover of his breeches. It seemed huge, grotesque and formidable and she longed for him to unfasten so she might see it. He followed the direction of her eyes and smiled.

'You are curious about my organ?' he said. 'Ask me nicely. Say, "please, master, let me see it".'

The glade was hot, the sun captured between the high trees like a golden orb. It was a magical place and Angela's senses swam. Her body throbbed with need, her nipples hard as cobnuts and her love-bud aching for something, she didn't know what, only aware that she was dying of frustration. 'Please,' she whispered.

His face hardened and his eyes snapped. 'You have forgotten something. What did I tell you to say?'

'Please, master,' she faltered.

Still holding the crop Aidan lowered his free hand to his fly and unbuttoned. As if panting for release his cock shot out through the gap, nine inches of stiff flesh. Angela could hardly believe her eyes. It was so huge, so dark-skinned with a shiny purple helm, the foreskin stretched back, and beneath it dangled two heavy balls like ripe plums in a hairy sac. Heavens above! What was she supposed to do with such a thing?

He seemed to read her mind, smiling sardonically and saying, 'One day you will rub it for me, my dear, and take it between those precious red lips, both those of your mouth and your labia. I shall use it to wrest your virginity from you and plunge it into your welcoming sheath. I'll take your maidenhood and make a woman of you, using this mighty weapon of mine.'

'On our wedding night?' she murmured, awestruck.

'Precisely,' he replied, caressing the cock stem and head with his fingers, making it burgeon to even greater size.

'But you'll not do so now?' Half of her wanted him to, the other half was terrified. Supposing he put a baby in her, though she had little idea how this might be achieved?

'No, my dear, but I shall give you a little taste of my power,' he replied, his penis sliding in and out through the tunnel of his curled palm. He let it go and it remained sturdy as a lance, bobbing as he moved. Leaving it on show he took up his crop and, before she could even register what was about to happen, brought it down across her naked thighs. She screamed at the searing pain, jerking against her bonds. Aidan repeated the action, raising his arm, the crop whistling through the air before biting into her flesh, while his penis jerked and wept clear dew.

'Oh, oh... no more, Aidan, please!' she sobbed, and he threw the whip aside and fastened his mouth on her breasts, nibbling the nipples, sucking them into even larger and more fevered point.

His cock was wetting her lower belly, leaving streaks of moisture, and he groaned as he tongued her breasts, then let her go almost savagely, tucked his organ away and fastened up. In a few moments he was fully dressed again and wearing his low-crowned topper, the perfect English gentleman. He untied her wrists and she rubbed her numbed arms, then adjusted her clothing, pinned up her hair and retrieved her hat. Her thighs hurt and she was sure the crop had left marks, but somehow the idea of stripping off in front of the mirror in the privacy of her bedroom and viewing these stripes made her tremble.

'Are you ready, my love?' he asked politely and, when she nodded, he assisted her into the saddle, bending and cupping his hands so that she might use them for mounting.

She could hardly bring herself to meet his slightly mocking eyes. What unmaidenly behaviour! And she had enjoyed every moment of it, though was unsure about the union with his crop and her bare skin. That had hurt intolerably. Whatever was happening to her? Was she becoming a Scarlet Woman, a wanton hussy with no morals?

Calmly he led her to the bridle path where they were joined by the groom, Jacob, and equally calmly rode with them to the lodge gate that led into the grounds of Lairdland. The topmost turrets and twirled chimney pots of the ancient house could be glimpsed some way off between the trees.

'I shall call on you later,' Aidan said, bowing over her hand and raising it to his lips, placing a chaste kiss on the back of her glove. He turned to the groom, saying sternly, 'See Lady Angela safely to the entrance, Jacob. If you fail in this duty you'll have me to answer to.'

With that he wheeled his horse and trotted away, leaving her more confused than ever before in her whole life.

Jacob helped her to dismount, a sturdy youth with a winning smile, who now looked at her in a knowing manner that made her blush as she wondered if he had somehow seen and heard her recent contact with Aidan.

She tipped her head at a haughty angle and swept past him, ordering crisply, 'Daisy Belle needs a thorough rub down, and then make sure you cover her with her blanket. Give her a feed of bran-mash and don't neglect her.' She knew these instructions were totally unnecessary, but had to somehow assert her authority.

Jacob nodded and touch his forelock. 'Certainly, milady. Of course, milady.

Leave Daisy Belle to me.'

But as Angela climbed the wide stone steps leading to the front entrance she was uneasily aware that Jacob was looking at her in a bold way, as if he was imagining or even remembering how she had appeared when naked from the waist down. It was most disconcerting and she was angry with Aidan for putting her in such a position. Yet indignation was overpowered by longing as she recalled his lips on hers, his tongue tantalising her nipples and his fingers dividing her cleft. Even the throbbing of her bruised thighs did not spoil her remembrance of the encounter.

She reached the massive door under its stone portico to find it open and Jackson, the butler, waiting for her. He was a tall, stately man, very conscious of his position. He had served Sir Barnaby for years, a faithful retainer who, along with the housekeeper, Mrs Gregory, ran the household like clockwork. Now, to Angela's surprise, that black-clad, grey-haired severe lady stood by his side, both of them looking as if they were the solemn harbingers of important tidings.

Angela paused, riding crop in one hand, her skirt lifted with the other. 'Jackson? Mrs Gregory? What is the matter?'

'It's your father, Lady Angela,' Jackson replied and, to her utter astonishment, she saw tears glistening in his pale blue eyes. 'I have terrible news. He is dead, milady. His heart gave out.'

'When?' she demanded irrelevantly, unable to take it in.

'An hour ago. The doctor is on his way,' Jackson answered, and he slumped, his usually upright stance replaced by the bowed shoulders of an old man. 'He didn't suffer, milady. In the stables at the time. Just complained of a pain in his arm, and then collapsed.'

'Are you sure he is dead?' Angela was as if encased in ice, unable to register grief, fear, pain - anything.

'No doubt about that,' put in Mrs Gregory. 'Do you want to see him? They've carried him to the master bedchamber.'

Still walking as if in some terrible nightmare, Angela trailed up the stairs in solemn procession with the butler and housekeeper, aware of the unnatural hush. No more father with his noisy complaints to the staff, his sometimes coarse language, his obsession with bloodstock and thoroughbreds, his loud and rumbustious cronies. No one to pet, love and indulge her any more. But she was wrong, and her heart came to life inside her as she remembered. Aidan! Aidan, her beloved and betrothed. He would take care of her now.

Aidan strode from the stable block, through to the kitchens and the servants' domain. The cook bobbed a curtsey, the footmen bowed and pretended to be extra busy, the housemaids looked at him from beneath lowered lashes. He spotted one, a young, plump, saucy lass who was a newcomer to Compton Hall. He had already singled her out for attention. He was on fire, his cock refusing to lie down. He needed satisfaction at once.

He nodded to the girl and she met his glance - bold, ambitious maybe - eager to curry favour with her employer. 'What's your name?' he demanded, scarcely pausing.

'Lisa Depford,' she replied, in a thick, West Country accent.

She'll do, he thought, wondering if she was a virgin. There was nothing he enjoyed more than robbing girls of their maidenheads. Their fear, reluctance and pain were music to his ears. The very thought of Lisa's final submission made his penis jump, the friction with his silk underpants very nearly bringing on his orgasm. He clenched his jaw and willed the tide to recede. He was practiced at this, studying ways and means of prolonging sexual congress so that the final explosion was cataclysmic.

Aidan was a sensualist, a wealthy connoisseur of fine wines, fine food, art, books, antiquities and lovely women, although his taste ran to good-looking men as well. There were few things he hadn't tried. He was highly skilled in the dichotomy between pain and pleasure. He loved power over individuals and business associates, and delved into their backgrounds, becoming privy to their darkest secrets and using them for his own ends.

He noticed that the cook, Mrs Brabent, was eyeing him askance, arms folded across her massive bosom. She had a thick waist and wide hips. He wondered briefly how it would be to have her naked, face pressed to the crosspiece in his dungeon while he plied a whip over those quivering hinds. Would she yell and struggle, pant and sweat? Or would she howl like a cat on heat, begging him to arse-fuck her?

He outstared her, beckoned to Lisa, stalked out of the door and into the passage that connected with the backstairs, used by the staff to reach the upper floors where their duties lay. The grand staircase, leading from the great hall, was only ever trod by himself, members of his family (and these were few now) or his friends. A doctor was permitted front access, for he was likely to be from the upper classes, also the vicar, but a lawyer, like a tradesman, always came in the back way.

Aidan looked upon himself as a man of liberal views, though was anything but when push came to shove. He pulled rank, very aware of himself as liege lord descended from a long line of barons who had come over with the Normans. He looked upon it as his right to take any servant girl (or stable lad) who tickled his fancy, and today it happened to be Lisa.

'Walk in front of me,' he commanded as they approached the narrow, linoleum covered stairs.

'Yes, sir... my lord...' she stammered, blushing furiously.

As she mounted ahead of him he reached up, dove a hand under her black skirt and dingy petticoats and handled her backside through her linen knickers. As he had suspected, she was well fleshed and would prove an entertaining hour under the cane.

She paused, would have turned, but he stopped her, giving her a shove and grating, 'No, don't look at me until I tell you. You must do everything I say,'

8

and he implemented this order with an open-palmed slap on her posterior.

She hurried on upwards. Aidan could smell her, that odour of cheap soap and sweaty armpits, of linen worn just that little bit too long, of hair that was not washed often. It was the general belief among the lower orders that too much washing would weaken them. Aidan had had intercourse with duchesses, princesses, and wantons from the higher echelons, but always gained an extra thrill when copulating with common women.

They reached the corridor that connected with the bedrooms. The floor was carpeted in luxurious crimson, the walls panelled and hung with landscapes and portraits in gilded frames. There were tall windows giving views of the gardens and everywhere there was evidence of luxury and refinement. Lisa stared open-mouthed, suitably awed.

'You've been in this part of the house before, of course,' he said, favouring her with conversation.

'No, sir,' she stammered. 'I'm not a chambermaid yet. Not been here long enough. Have to finish my kitchen training first.'

'I'll have you promoted,' he said casually, unlocking the oak double doors that opened into his apartment.

She swung round, eyes shining with admiration. 'Oh, sir... could you really do that for me? What about Mrs Brabent?'

'To hell with Mrs Brabent,' he thundered, scowling. 'She'll take her orders from me. It's up to you, Lisa. Prove a quick learner today, and we'll see...'

The anteroom was furnished in grand style with period pieces handed down over the generations. Aidan took little heed of it, part and parcel of his daily existence. Logs smouldered in the grate, the brass basket resting between the white marble columns of the carved fireplace. He was much more interested in the girl he had brought there.

He pulled her towards a deeply upholstered settee, bent her over the back of it and lifted her skirts. She protested, but only slightly, and he stood behind her and spread her legs, then opened his fly and pressed his cock to the divide of her buttocks. Her drawers were in the way, but now his goal was within sight he could afford to delay.

He wanted to play, or rather his penis did. He fingered her roughly, demanding, 'Are you a virgin?'

'Not quite, sir,' she confessed, arching her spine and driving her arse against his tumescence.

He gripped her by the hair, jerking back her head and demanding, 'What do you mean... not quite? You've either been rogered or you haven't.'

'Not properly, sir,' she gasped, wincing at the pain in her scalp. 'It wasn't a lad or anyone like that after me.'

'Then who?' Aidan barked, the stranglehold on her blonde locks intensifying. 'Speak, slut.'

'It was my stepfather what done it,' she sobbed. 'He wouldn't leave me be. From the time he came courting our mother, her being a widow and all, he kept touching me up, and after the wedding he'd sometimes come into my bed at night or catch me in the fields... anywhere... and have his way with me.'

'Why didn't you tell your mother?' Aidan asked, his cock even more lively at the vision of Lisa being corrupted by an older man, her mother's new husband to boot. This was the kind of perverse behaviour that aroused him.

'She wouldn't have believed me. Soft on him, she was,' Lisa responded, wriggling her arse against him, a girl who had learned young how to give in to men and their demands.

'So you know how to please, eh?' Aidan said softly. 'You know how to obey and submit. You'll submit to me, my girl, and be glad of it.'

'Yes, sir,' she whimpered.

'Stay there,' he commanded, dragged her drawers about her ankles and pushed her face down amongst the soft cushions. She gave a muffled squeal.

He left her and went into the bedroom, returning with a rattan cane in one hand. For a moment he admired her up-thrust buttocks, the pale thighs above the thick woollen stocking tops, the fair fuzz poking from between her legs, part covering the pouting purse of her pudenda with its dividing slit. The sight was enough to addle a saint's brain, let alone a highly sexed man used to indulging his desires.

With excitement catching his breath he raised his arm. The cane whistled through the air and landed on Lisa's bottom. He restrained himself, using a small particle of his strength but it was sufficient to make her yell and squirm. He spaced out the blows, keeping her on the edge never knowing quite when the next would fall. Her flesh turned pink, then red, the mottled skin embroidered with a latticework of stripes. She writhed and tried to break free.

'Be still and take your punishment, you dirty little trollop,' he hissed.

'What have I done, sir?' she pleaded, tears streaking her face.

'You're a whore,' he shouted. 'A slut who enjoys men poking her.'

He imagined saying these things to Angela, a red mist seeming to float before his eyes. Angela, with her delicate complexion and innocence; by God he'd make her suffer once he had his hands on her. She wouldn't know whether she was on her head or her heels. He'd make her endure everything, including his infidelities, once the ring was on her finger and her dowry safely lodged in his bank. And when she had provided him with an heir, possibly two, he'd give her to his cronies to try out during one of his wild orgies.

'Get up!' he snarled.

Lisa moved stiffly, standing before him in her disarray with tears streaking her snub-nosed face. Any pleasure she might have gained through being singled out by his lordship was now replaced by fear. Aidan was pleased to see it. He had little interest in willing victims.

'On your knees,' he said with a quick flick of the cane. She flopped down, blubbering and raising her blotchy face. He was a fastidious man, and the sight of this abject misery disgusted yet aroused him. 'Come closer,' he whispered, his voice smooth as silk.

She crawled towards him on hands and knees, her bare bottom lifted, scored by the livid marks of the cane. 'Master,' she said tremulously.

'Kiss my foot.' Obediently she placed her lips on his booted instep where mud still clung from his ride. He stared down at her, a huddled, pathetic figure, but felt no compassion. She deserved everything she got - so did Angela, and every other bitch who came under his domination. 'You may look at me,' he added, seeing the taut rigidity of his engorged penis and thrilling at what he was about to have her do to it.

She knelt between his feet and stared with swollen eyes at his penis rising like a serpent before her, the glans glistening, topping that spear of power. 'It's so big,' she breathed, then remembered that he had not told her to speak. 'I'm sorry,' she spluttered, her hands flying to her sore backside.

He chuckled, always flattered by any reference to the size of his weapon. 'Do you know what I'm going to tell you to do?' he whispered thickly.

'No, my lord,' she murmured, and he lifted her under her arms so that her face was close to his genitals, the warmth of her breath stirring his dark thicket and tantalising his eager helm.

'Lick it,' he ordered. 'Do as you're told or I'll flay you alive.'

'Oh, sir... my lord... I've never...'

'Not even with your stepfather?' he mocked.

'No, sir, he took me up the bum though, as well as in the other place.'

'Now you'll learn something else. Do as you're told. Lick it.' He twined his fingers in her hair and, using it as a bridle, dragged her closer to him. A sob shook her, then her tongue came out and he felt the shy lightness of her caress, and his penis leapt, hitting her alarmed face. She whimpered and panted, her fumbling fingers finding the full ripeness of his balls and stroking fearfully at the mighty stalk. Aidan could wait no longer. He seized his cock and rammed it against Lisa's mouth. She shuddered, then opened wide and he felt the unutterable bliss of her wet cavity and that fresh young tongue flicking across his helm.

He groaned, the torrent gathering, about to erupt into a mighty explosion of spunk. He did not loosen his grip on her hair as her head dipped up and down, her wet face burrowing as she warmed to her task. She breathed loudly, every so often raising her head for a draught of air, then returning to suck and gnaw, nibble and slurp at his quivering, semen-packed tool.

It was coming. He had reached the point of no return. His control was useless now. He clamped her to him, pumped her head up and down. She panicked, as if guessing what was about to happen. She tried to pull away but her held her to the throbbing organ that had completely taken him over, the compulsion to orgasm more important than life itself as it flared and convulsed in a final welter of ecstasy.

The hot semen pumped out over Lisa's face and drenched her hair, but Aidan was not done yet - not quite. The sticky spunk continued to shoot and he was determined she should be plastered in it. She gagged, wrested her head away

11

and spat out as much as she could of that cloying emission. Aidan's legs trembled and he reached for the couch, sprawling there, momentarily satiated.

'You may go now,' he said, coldly dismissive.

Lisa sunk back on her heels, weary and gulping, rubbing her mouth on the back of her hand, trying to free her lips of his taste. She looked at him, her eyes huge and reproachful. 'You said you would speak to Mrs Brabent, sir,' she said.

'So I did,' he replied carelessly, back in control, his body relieved of the urge to ejaculate.

Lisa stood up, her hair straggling round her face, her chin smeared with his juice, her uniform crumpled. She looked every inch the drab she was. 'Please, sir...' she went on, 'I'd like to better myself. Don't want to be a skivvy all my life.'

Aidan was feeling generous, as men often are after having shot their load. 'Oh, very well, I'll see what I can do,' he promised. 'Now get out of here.'

He lay at his ease on the settee, watching her with a tigerish smile as she backed out of the room. Soon he would have Angela in exactly the same position - not a servant, of course, but his wife.

He was roused by a knock at the door. 'Come in,' he said, and the butler entered.

'My lord, there's a messenger arrived from Lairdland. Sir Barnaby has had a heart attack and died. Lady Angela requests your presence there at once.'

Chapter 2

There was so much to do, so many things to organise, Angela thought, panicking. The funeral. The wake. Meetings with the executor of her father's will.

Doctor Carmichael had examined the body and written out the death certificate. 'Natural causes,' he had said, shaking his stately silver-haired head and adding, 'I did warn Sir Barnaby that if he continued to live life at such a hectic pace, then he might shorten it.'

The Reverend Beardsley had hurried over from the vicarage, full of platitudes and sympathy. 'Trust in the Lord, my child,' he said piously, hands folded over his black cassock. '"He giveth, and He taketh away". Have you someone with you during this sorrowful time?'

'I have no relatives. Even my Godparents are no longer alive, but I have my betrothed, Lord Aidan Driscol. I've sent for him. He will be here shortly,' Angela replied, hardly able to speak through her tears. The pain inside her was like a raw wound. She knew that only Aidan's presence would make her feel better.

'It would not be proper for him to stay, you understand,' Beardsley prompted, steepling his fingertips together. 'You must be chaperoned.'

Angela was uncomfortable. His hooded eyes under their bushy brows were regarding her too closely - not only her face, but her figure. She did not care for the way in which he mouthed the words, as if relishing the idea of impropriety.

'My companion, Miss Hicks, is with me,' she replied hurriedly. 'And there are the butler and housekeeper, and other members of staff.'

'I'm pleased to hear it,' he said in the nasal, rather singsong voice he always adopted when speaking with parishioners or sermonising from the pulpit.

She recalled that her father had not had a great deal of time for him, dubbing him a canting hypocrite. How annoyed he must be to have him hovering over his deathbed, if he was aware and there was any truth in an afterlife.

'Don't worry, your Reverence, I shall be with her,' Maude Hicks said, her voice level, and Angela was so glad that she was present. It was she who had joined her in the bedchamber and supported her when she knelt there, weeping.

Maude was in her early thirties, a plain, no-nonsense woman, who had taken over from Angela's governess a year ago, employed as a companion. Though never one to mince her words she was kindness itself, more like an older sister than a paid assistant. Now she placed an arm protectively round Angela's shoulders.

'I'm glad to hear it, Miss Hicks, you must guide her through this trial,' the vicar said, and prepared to take his departure.

After he had gone Mr Pearce, the undertaker, arrived with an assistant and concentrated on the corpse, suggesting that Angela left them to their work.

'Come along, my dear,' Maude said, and Angela was thankful to lean against her. 'Your fiancé will be here soon.'

She was always neat and tidy, and was wearing a long, bell-shaped shirt with a nipped-in waist and a blue and white striped blouse, its high collar finished with a navy tie. She smelt of lavender soap and her own fragrance that wafted from her light brown hair, parted in the centre and coiled into a coronet atop her head. This emphasised her swanlike neck and willowy, almost boyish figure.

Angela walked with her into the drawing room, a lovely flower-filled place that had a welcoming air, with its panelled walls and huge fireplaces, one at either end, and its ceiling rich with cornices and plasterwork. The deep bays had box seats and diamond-paned windows. There were velvet drapes and Persian rugs strewn like colourful islands on a sea of polished oak. Angela used it more than her father. He had preferred his study, a den where he liked to entertain his cronies, there to smoke, play cards and exchange hunting talk, traduce the Government and gossip, bigger scandalmongers than women ever were.

No more! The thought struck her like a spear. No more! He was dead and she must carry on. The task seemed enormous, more than she could manage, swamped as she was with grief. She knew nothing about the running of the estate. Sir Barnaby had not believed in too much education for girls. She could read, write, add up and had a smattering of knowledge concerning history and geography. She had been taught to sew and embroider, and was a dab hand at producing pretty watercolours and pressing flowers. She could play the pianoforte competently and sing, her voice sweet and tuneful. Dancing was another attribute; one that would be useful in the ballroom. But as for bookkeeping or finance? This was beyond her comprehension, although she was bright and could have tackled it had she been shown the way.

'What am I to do, Maude?' she cried, pacing the floor, striking her right fist into her left palm. 'Do I stay here until Lord Driscol and I are married? And when this happens, do I leave Lairdland forever? And there are the funeral arrangements, and letters to write informing people, to say nothing of getting in touch with the solicitor. I don't think I can manage.'

'You won't have to do anything, dearest,' said a strong, masculine voice from the doorway.

She swung round, then ran towards him, hands outstretched. 'Aidan! Aidan! I'm so glad you're here,' she cried, and flung herself into his arms.

Peace pervaded her, the first easement she had known for hours. He held her and rocked her and she cried all over his shirtfront. She registered that he was still in riding clothes; having come directly he heard the news. This was disturbing, flooding her with memories of that morning. She looked around for Maude but she had withdrawn to the window embrasure, available if needed but discreetly giving the couple space.

'You shall stay with me until the funeral is over,' Aidan vowed, and his hands soothed and petted Angela, running up and down her spine and making her deliciously mindful of his bodily strength, even in the midst of her turmoil. The prospect of residing at Compton Hall earlier than she had anticipated brought a ray of hope. She had been certain that Aidan would care for her, and this was now being proved.

'I can't leave father, can I?' she demurred, nestling her head against his chest, wanting to stay there forever. 'He will be lying in his coffin in the Great Hall, so that the villagers and tenants can come and pay their respects.'

'Jackson and the undertaker can take care of that, can't they?' Aidan said imperiously. 'And Mrs Gregory, who will also make arrangements for food and wine at the wake. And you can drive over whenever you wish until the interment. I shall inform whoever needs to be told, including his lawyer who, I assume, is in London.'

'Oh, Aidan, thank you! You are so good.'

He released her and turned to Maude, ordering crisply, 'See that her Ladyship has everything she needs. Have her maid pack a valise. We are leaving in half an hour. Send Jackson and Mrs Gregory to me to receive their instructions.'

The carriage reached the top of the drive and the coachman turned right, taking the road that led to Compton Hall. Aidan and Angela were alone. She had been so distressed that she had forgotten Maude should be with them, and now the companion and the ladies maid, Bertha Marten, were travelling in the gig behind.

Angela felt that her whole world had been turned upside down. It was strange

14

to be in Aidan's coach like this, as if they were already married. Despite her relief at him taking charge it should not have happened for several months yet, and only after her father had led her to the altar and given her to her bridegroom with due pomp and ceremony. Now Aidan was taking her away from her home, motivated by love and consideration, and yet it did not feel right.

He was seated next to her and he turned his head and said seriously, 'Well, well, here's a strange twist of fate. I'm so sorry about your father, Angela, I truly am. But every cloud has a silver lining, it seems, and now I can take care of you. It is almost as if we are already husband and wife. I think we should advance the date of our wedding. What do you say? I'm sure it could be arranged for a couple of months' time.'

'Can this happen whilst I'm in mourning?' she answered, already attired in black from head to toe. Death was a common occurrence and every lady had suitably sombre attire in her wardrobe.

'Under the circumstances I'm sure it can be done, a much quieter affair than planned, of course. You need to be protected. You can't go on living at Lairdland Manor by yourself. I shall speak to my lawyer, and yours. Give me his address and I'll write to him with the sad news, and give the date of the funeral, once it is decided upon. Presumably he will be there to read the will. Have you any idea how your father bequeathed his property?'

Angela was startled by this question. She had not given it any thought. 'I am his only child and, as far as I know, it will all come to me, apart from a few provisions he may have made for his oldest retainers,' she answered, and a sob rose in her throat. She pressed her handkerchief to her lips.

He settled back against the plush crimson upholstery and inserted an arm behind her. Angela was glad to lean into him, like a lost child coming home. Although she needed nothing but comfort, she was conscious of his body heat through her clothing. His face was close to hers, so close that she could see the thickness of his long lashes and read - she did not know what - in his flint-grey eyes. His mouth fascinated her, the upper lip firm with a curl that showed his impatience with incompetence, and the lower full and sensual. And this wonderful man was soon to be hers and hers alone. She melted into his embrace, wanting to deny him nothing.

'What shall we do with Lairdland?' he mused, and his hand came to rest lightly on her breasts. 'We don't want to sell it, do we?'

'Oh, no,' she murmured, stunned by the electric currents coursing from her nipples to her cleft. 'It has belonged to the Bayswater family for generations.'

'Quite right, my love,' he went on, and now his hand was inside her jacket, running smoothly over the silk of her blouse and finding the jet buttons of the front fastening. 'I suggest we lease the house and the land. It should command a substantial rent and, when our sons are grown up, the eldest can take it over, combining the two estates into a powerful whole.'

'You speak so confidently,' she whispered, thrilling as his skilful fingers wormed their way inside her blouse and contacted the chemise she wore beneath it, rubbing over the fragile material and making her nipples rise into stiff peaks. 'How do you know we shall have sons?'

'Of course, we shall,' he answered firmly, and bent his head to kiss her, a mere brushing of lips that fired her and increased the wetness pooling in the secret place between her thighs.

His arm remained around her possessively. The swaying of the coach threw them into even greater contact. His thumb continued to revolve over one of her nipples and she ached with want, wishing the knot had already been tied and they were off on their honeymoon. She sighed and, almost without knowing, opened her legs a little under the sober black skirt. 'You are so sure of yourself,' she murmured. 'I wish I were more like you.'

He chuckled, indulging her, saying, 'Silly little goose. Leave weighty matters to me. You really don't have to bother your pretty head about anything. I shall take care of it. Do you trust me?'

'Of course.'

'Do you fear me?'

'Sometimes,' she confessed, but any trace of fear always heightened the desire that heated her blood.

'And this morning's introduction to the lash? Are you bruised?'

'Yes, and I'm bewildered by my feelings. You hurt me, but it served to make me love you more.'

'Love or lust?' he asked with a throaty chuckle. 'You are neglecting to call me master.'

'I'm sorry... master... but so much has happened over the past hours. Please forgive me.'

'You enjoyed what I did to you?' he muttered, and slowly lifted her skirt and the petticoat beneath. His hand slid up the silkiness of her stockings and contacted her naked thigh.

'Oh, yes... but you stopped too soon. I needed you to go on, but I don't know why.'

'Have you never played with yourself down there?' he said, an alert look in his eyes. 'Never brought on your crisis by rubbing your love-button?'

'No, Aidan... I mean, master. I w-was taught that genteel ladies never, ever examine their private p-parts,' she stammered. 'And what is a love-button?'

'I'll show you,' he growled and pressed closer, making her aware of the lump in his trousers. She vividly recalled the sight of his penis. Her heart pounded, as it had done earlier when he teased her with his manhood but made no attempt at consummation. Now he did not disturb her undergarments, merely sliding a finger into the central opening of her knickers. He insinuated a hand between her legs, finding them relaxed. His digit moved, scooping moisture from her virginal mouth and spreading it over her cleft.

'Oh... oh!' she cried, as spasms of delight shot through her. They seemed to connect with her needy nipples. Aidan bent his head and his cheeks hollowed as he sucked them greedily. With each passing second she was finding it more and more difficult to stay still and passive. Even the stripes that throbbed dully on her skin did not detract from her longing. She would even be willing to endure them again, if Aidan would only satisfy this frustration welling up within her. When his fingertip found the head of her swollen clitoris and stroked it from side to side, then up and down, sensations such as she had even known gathered and quivered through her, culminating in one irresistible surge towards ecstasy. But he knew and eased off, teasing her mercilessly.

Angela lifted her hips, chasing her pleasure, moaning her desire. 'You want more?' he said.

'Yes, yes,' she sobbed.

'And you'll do what I demand, without question. Do you agree?'

'Yes!' she cried, pressing against his hand.

He went back to his task with practiced ease, stroking her bud till nothing mattered but that this delirious feeling continued, leading her onwards... to what? She couldn't stop, languishing under his expert frottage, surrendering entirely to him, pleasure swamping her, reaching a crescendo that made her swoon.

'Oh, God, I must be dying,' she cried, regaining her senses.

He laughed again, low in his chest. 'The French call it "the little death",' he said. 'Have you really never experienced it before? This is your first orgasm?'

'I dream something like it occasionally, but never knew, never realised that such bliss existed,' she sighed, waiting for something more, wanting to feel his appendage inside her so that her inner muscles could contract around such firmness.

Aidan, however, having demonstrated his control over her, sat back and watched as she rearranged her skirt. He raised his hand to his nostrils, sniffing appreciatively. 'You have the most seductive odour,' he said calmly, and she was thrown by his cold sensuality. Embarrassed, too, unaware that men liked woman smell. Angela wanted to be cuddled. His abrupt withdrawal made her feel cheap and she could not understand why he was behaving in so cavalier a fashion. Why had he bothered to introduce her to her own carnality if he didn't intend to follow it through by taking his own pleasure?

He said nothing more and they arrived at Compton Hall in silence. Once there the footman lowered the iron step and Aidan leapt out, then gave Angela his hand. The gig disgorged its passengers and several strong male house-servants came to take the luggage.

'I shall see you at dinner,' Aidan said, bowing formally over her hand. 'Try to rest for an hour, dearest. It will put the roses back in your cheeks.'

She wasn't aware of looking pale. In fact her face felt as if it was on fire, the feelings still radiating from her lower regions enough to heat her thoroughly, and making it difficult to look him in the eye - or Maude, for that matter. Supposing she guessed what had taken place in the coach?

17

Angela was treated like a queen. Aidan could not do too much for her. The servants tiptoed around her as if she was suffering from a terminal illness. No one was allowed to upset her, and he acted as if she was made of spun glass, too fragile for this world.

She had secretly hoped that he might take advantage of the fact that she was under his roof, but they dined together formally on the first evening, attended by the butler and a fleet of footmen and he escorted her to her room later. She was moved by his gallantry, but disappointed because he made no suggestion of stepping over the threshold, giving her a goodnight peck on the cheek.

This set the tenor of her days and nights. Though she wanted to experiment with her newfound sensuality she was still too repressed to do so. In fact, by the time her head touched the pillow she fell into a deep, troubled sleep, and woke weary and unrefreshed. She told herself it would be better once the funeral was over.

She had dined at Compton Hall several times with her father, but only seen a fraction of it. One morning soon after her arrival Aidan took her on a conducted tour. The house was a huge, rabbit warren of a place and she found its atmosphere oppressive. Parts of it were no longer used, but had been kept from falling into disrepair.

'When we're married we will open up the ballroom and hold grand soirées, inviting members of the county gentry,' Aidan said, arm resting lightly round her waist as they traversed corridors and peered down stairwells sunk in gloom, opened creaking doors and stepped into rooms where the shutters were drawn across the windows and the furniture shrouded in dustsheets. 'And as our babies are born we'll refurbish the nursery wing, and the place will ring with childish laughter and hullabaloo.'

He stopped near one of the panels in a dressing room that adjoined his own chamber, pressed a Tudor rose carved into the panelling and, with a click, a low door sprang open. A musty smell escaped from the darkness beyond.

Angela took a step back. 'Ugh!' she complained. 'A secret passage? Where goes this lead?'

He looked at her strangely, and she was struck by the tight slant to his mouth. 'To the dungeons,' he replied.

'They can't be in use?' She tried to turn her sudden dread into a joke.

'Part of them are... as wine cellars and storage space. The rest...' he shrugged his wide shoulders under the tweed jacket that matched his trousers. 'I have been known to hold parties down there.'

'Whatever for, when you have so many lovely rooms above?' she asked, chillingly reminded that there were so many things she didn't know about him.

He opened the little door wider and held out his hand. 'For fun... perhaps on Halloween or new year's eve, when spirits are abroad.'

'Don't tease,' she said with a shudder, and tried to tug her hand free. 'Let's go back. It must be nearly time for luncheon.'

He laughed, took up a candle from the dressing table, struck a match and lit the wick. 'Not yet. Didn't you promise to do anything I asked you? I hope you haven't forgotten. I shall be angry. Now, come with me and stop being silly.'

He disappeared through the aperture and, bunching her skirt in one hand, she followed him timorously. The candle bobbed ahead of her and her feet encountered narrow stone steps winding downwards. 'Wait for me,' she quavered, and felt his hand grip hers.

This was better. Now she was no longer afraid of tripping and plunging into the darkness below. She tried to be brave. It was only an underground part of the house, after all, set in the foundations. No need for her to think of bats and ghosts, demons and witches and other unearthly things that go bump in the night.

He led the way silently until they emerged into a long, low-ceilinged corridor with a sloping floor. It was pitch-black on either side of that precious candle-glow that dazzled the eyes yet was infinitely comforting. Arches upheld the ceiling, and Aidan stopped outside a heavily studded door. He turned the iron key in the lock and pushed it open. He entered first and Angela hurried after him, too scared of being left behind. He went round igniting torches that stood in braziers fixed to the walls. Light flared up and she found herself in a large room, the roof supported by pillars, the walls of uniform grey stone. It was cold there and decidedly creepy. Angela shivered.

'Where are we?' she asked, her voice echoing.

'It is the oldest part, where a keep once stood when the house was a castle,' he explained, glancing at her through narrowed eyes, as if gauging her reaction. 'Do you see the cells?' and he pointed to a series of rusting iron gates, the darkness accentuated behind grilles. 'It was also the torture chamber.'

'C-can't we go now?' she protested, her lively imagination creating sounds of the distant past: the screams, the protestations of innocence.

She followed him to the far end, too terrified of being left, though dreading what she was about to see. The candle flickered as he applied the flame to a wall-hanging torch. The stronger light flared over the forbidding shape of a crosspiece. What was it for? She could only hazard a horrified conjecture. Near this was a rack complete with pulleys and ropes, cogs and winches. A bench stood close at hand with holes in various places, and a structure that resembled a pillory, also a throne with open space where the seat should have been, leaving whoever sat in it exposed below. This was not all. There were implements on hooks fixed to the walls - long whips and short crops, multiple-thonged taws, leather-covered paddles, rattan canes, belts, straps and manacles, handcuffs, gags and blindfolds, chains and restraints.

'Why do you keep these awful things?' she gasped.

He gave a crooked smile and the flickering light threw strange shadows over his face. 'Relics, my dear. A piece of history to which I have added. Some of my acquaintances find them more than just amusing.'

'I don't understand,' she began, then half-turned, adding, 'can't we leave? I don't like it here.'

For answer he grabbed her and, with one arm around her waist, carried her until she felt the wood of the crosspiece at her back. He pressed against her, making her aware of his erect penis. She was possessed with dread, yet gravid with desire. Was he about to perform the act she longed for, yet feared? He lifted her higher till her feet came to rest on a small platform. He spread her legs and she heard a metallic click as manacles were fastened round her ankles.

'That looks so pretty,' he murmured, standing back to admire his work.

'Aidan, stop, this has gone far enough,' she protested, trying to bend from the waist and free her feet.

'Not quite, my love,' he countered and, seizing her hands he pulled them above her head, just as he had done against the tree-bole, and slipped handcuffs around her wrists. Now she hung there, helpless.

Being so vulnerable was a curious sensation. He had rendered her incapable of doing anything but handing her will over to him. Her black gown emphasised the paleness of her skin. She was cold, yet a fire raged in her loins. Why didn't he take her, if that was his intention? 'Why are you tormenting me?' she gasped. 'Set me free.'

'Are you begging me?' he asked coldly.

'I am... master,' she added, remembering the rules.

'Don't try to convince me that you're not longing to experience the "little death" again,' he said harshly. 'Really, my dear, I fear for your morals, and can see that I shall have to keep a very close eye on you once we're married. I don't intend to harbour cuckoos in my nest. Say it, Angela... repeat after me, "I'm a wanton whore willing to let any man fuck me".'

'That's not true,' she cried, tears springing to her eyes. 'I love you and will always be faithful.'

'Ah, but darling girl, you're eager for your completion. I know it. I can smell it. Your bud is screaming out for its crisis. You remember how that felt? The ecstasy that swept you to the heights? The madness that brooked no denial?'

He pushed her skirt high and there was nothing she could do to prevent his invasion. His hand slipped between her flesh and her lawn drawers. She was wet, always so when in his presence, and the steady thrum of his finger on her clit was irresistible, almost painful at first then dissolving into pleasure. She forgot her weird surroundings, only knowing that she wanted him to go on, her lower lips swelling and her nodule plump with wanting. Every sensation centred on the spot between her legs. She was no longer aware of the wood pressing into her back and the restraints chaffing her wrists and ankles. She was almost there, each nerve tingling as her body prepared itself for climax.

Aidan stopped abruptly, withdrawing his finger and cranking the revolving crosspiece until she faced away from him. She stared into the shadows and then felt his hands at her waist, tucking up her skirt and pulling down her drawers. The cold air played on her buttocks and thighs.

Silence followed, though her straining ears caught his slight movements, followed by a stillness like a drawn out scream. Then the air moved. There was a whistle. Angela jerked in her bonds as a bolt of lightning streaked across her naked hinds. The agony seemed to dive into her cleft, her womb, the very heart of her. A second blow followed, even worse than the first and she shrieked, her cry bouncing back from those brutally cold walls.

'Aidan! Aidan! Master, stop. I beg you!'

A third kiss of the lash, laid on under the first two, rendered her almost senseless. Yet beneath that anguish it added fuel to the fire and that burning itch in her clitoris no way abated. In fact, it was as if she still hovered on the very edge of climax.

As the fourth blow descended, delivered so skilfully by her master's hand, she writhed madly, consumed by pain and the excruciating lust that demanded relief. She heard the whip clatter to the floor as he flung it aside, then he appeared in front of her, his trousers unbuttoned, his penis ramrod stiff pointing towards her. He gripped it in one hand and rubbed it over her throbbing delta. She felt the helm pulse and her own nubbin responded while she relaxed into dreamy warmth. She was certain her goal was in sight, the pain in her whipped posterior as nothing in comparison, an adjunct to pleasure, that extra demonstration of Aidan's strength and purpose. He was her master and she must learn from him.

She began to flow as he brought her to the edge, and then held off a little, teasing her until she begged for release. 'You want it so much, don't you?' he breathed, and she watched as his free hand caressed his cock-stem and circled the tip. The organ quivered in response and clear fluid seeped from its single eye. He rubbed harder and, at the same time, swirled his finger round her clit, then frigged it hard, bringing her to a final explosion.

She came down from the heights, aware of wetness as he poured out his libation, his cock jerking in his hand. He had climaxed and so had she, almost at the same time. Such unity lifted her heart and convinced her that they were, indeed, soul mates made for each other.

The procession of black-clad figures trailed towards the grey church. Some had walked from the village, but the well to do had driven there. Angela had been among the latter, accompanied by Aidan in the largest of the Driscol vehicles.

It was early summer, a time of sunshine and abundance, the blue sky unmarred by a single cloud. The air hummed with mingled sounds; birdsong, the rustle of branches caressed by the light breeze. A day like many another when Angela had attended St Stephen's Church with father. Now she walked behind his coffin, following the pallbearers through the lych-gate. They sweated beneath their burden, hardworking tenant farmers who had offered to honour Sir Barnaby.

Aidan's fingers gripped her under the elbow and she was thankful for his support, her knees like jelly, her mind refusing to take in what was happening. It was a charade, surely? At any moment her father would come striding across the turf between the gravestones, making a joke and demanding what all the fuss was about.

Later she didn't remember much about the ceremony, too distraught to take it in. It dragged to its mournful close and then she was standing by the ornate family mausoleum, the pillared door already open to receive the latest Bayswater. The coffin was carried inside and down the stone steps.

'This can't be the end of him, can it?' she asked, clinging to Aidan's arm.

She felt him shrug as he replied, 'Who knows? I find it hard to believe in heaven and harps and angels. Shall we go, my dear? Let's get the funeral feast over and done with and then we can concentrate on what Mr Doynton has to say.'

Cyril Doynton was the lawyer who had handled the estate affairs for years. He had arrived by train from London early that morning and intended to return by nightfall. Elderly but distinguished-looking, he politely offered his condolences and attended the service. He maintained his dignified manner when, on reaching Lairdland Manor, he joined the other guests in the banqueting hall where trestle tables had been set up, damask cloths spread and a substantial repast laid out.

Everyone was suitably subdued, speaking respectfully of the dead man, and it seemed he had been a popular figure thereabouts. The hunting fraternity was well represented, toasting him repeatedly, recounting memorable incidents in the field and laying into Mrs Gregory's ham sandwiches, slices of cold roast beef and pork pies. The Reverend Beardsley was relishing the fine port wine and subjecting Angela to the touch of his damp, flabby hands. Maude, ever watchful, even of a churchman, came to her rescue.

Cyril Doynton stood to one side, quietly observant. He had been so silent throughout, scarcely exchanging more than a few words with Angela, that she wondered. It wasn't that she knew him well, her father had been the one who consulted him, but she sensed something in the air that made her uneasy.

Some people had already gone, though others wanted to stay for the kill - the reading of the will. There was a little trace of anticipation as those left squashed into the library, facing Doynton who occupied the wide, brass-trimmed Napoleonic desk at the far end. Some sat, others stood at the back of the room where books lined the walls, their handsome spines glinting behind glass-fronted cases. Angela took a chair opposite Doynton, with Aidan standing behind her. The head servants, Mrs Gregory and Jackson, were a little way back, ready to hear their master's last bequests, each hoping, perhaps, that there would be a little something for them so they might retire from toil and each purchase a humble dwelling in which to end their days.

Doynton shuffled papers on the desk's dark green leather surface, cleared his throat and looked around. The shuffling and low talk ceased. 'Lady Angela,' he began, inclining his head towards her, then his glance encompassed the whole throng, 'and those who have gathered here at the reading of the late Sir Barnaby Bayswater's last Will and Testament.' He paused, and appeared to be disconcerted. 'I'm afraid this is not a straightforward matter.' He looked at

Angela and added, 'You should have been the sole beneficiary, my lady.'

'*Should* have been? What do you mean? Speak out, man,' Aidan butted in rudely, his white-knuckled fists clenched on the back Angela's chair.

Doynton shot him a disparaging glance. 'Have you a right to speak up on this matter?' he queried coolly.

'As her fiancé I have every right,' Aidan snapped back.

The onlookers were silent. The whole room had become one listening ear. Such an event would provide endless speculation and rumour for months to come, maybe even years. Angela spoke up, and her calmness astonished her.

'Mr Doynton, will you be so kind as to explain?' she said in a steady voice.

Doynton shook his head and then spread his hands over the paperwork in a defeated gesture. 'The truth is, Lady Angela, that your father died penniless.'

An astonished cry arose from the audience. Some said, 'It can't be true!' and others declaimed, 'But he was a rich man! There must be some mistake!'

Aidan was one of those who demanded, 'You must be mistaken. What are you playing at, man? Is this some dastardly trick?'

Doynton's face set like granite and his expression showed that he didn't much care for Lady Angela's betrothed. 'It is correct, Lord Driscol. I've been through it with a fine toothcomb and, in fact, Sir Barnaby had been to see me shortly before his demise. He was deep in debt, you see, the house was mortgaged to the hilt, and everything he owned must now be sold to pay his creditors.'

'Everything?' Angela whispered, unable to take it in.

'Everything, I'm afraid. You'll have nothing except the clothes you stand up in.'

'This is monstrous!' Aidan bellowed. 'What about her dowry?'

Doynton looked at him with a curl of his lips and replied, cuttingly, 'There is no dowry. Sir Barnaby gambled it all away. He spent money like water on high living, the card tables, an abundance of alcohol and a fondness for ladies of... shall I say? ...unsavoury reputations.'

'So I have nothing?' Angela said slowly, beginning to grasp the enormity of the situation. 'I shall have to leave Lairdland?'

'That's right. Every stick and stone will now be sold.'

'Where shall I go? Didn't he even leave me the meanest cottage?'

'No. I'm sorry, Lady Angela, but you will be obliged to fend for yourself. Have you no friends or relatives who could help you through this?'

'No, sir, but I have Lord Driscol, to whom I am engaged to be married,' and she turned and looked up at Aidan, expecting reassurance.

But what she saw astounded her. His eyes were cold slits, his brows drawn down into the blackest scowl she had ever seen on a man's face. 'I can't marry you now,' he said in clipped tones. 'You have no dowry.'

Chapter 3

There was such uproar in the hall that only Angela and Doynton heard what Aidan said. She could not believe those callous words. He loved her, didn't he? He had promised to care for and protect her!

Doynton's face was grim as he leaned forward and addressed him, saying, 'If this is the case, my lord, then I think we may be suing for breach of promise.'

'Sue away,' Aidan returned insolently, placing his hands flat on the desktop and staring him straight in the eye. 'You won't get far. Better to listen to my proposition. Shall we retire to somewhere private? This is turning into a bear-garden,' and he cast a disparaging glance at the gesticulating throng.

Doynton rose, and Aidan had a quiet word with Jackson and Mrs Gregory concerning the dispersal of the guests, and then followed Angela into her father's sanctum. She walked like an automaton. The full significance of Aidan's statement had not yet sunk in.

The room was redolent of her father, the atmosphere spiced with the aroma of cigars. He had smoked nothing but Havana's finest. There were hunting trophies staring glassy-eyed from the walls - stags' heads, that of a wild boar, a fox mask, even a snarling tiger he claimed to have shot when visiting members of the Raj in India. And she realised she had never really known him at all. He had led a secret life far removed from the genial parent he pretended to be. Was it pretence? She did not want to believe he had been insincere in his love for her. But there was that other side - the gambler, the profligate, the womaniser - of whom she had known nothing.

Her heart sank like a stone as a voice within her whispered that maybe the man she loved and to whom she had been betrothed might be of the same ilk. It was true that he was sometimes over-attentive, sometimes neglectful, keeping her on a knife-edge of uncertainty.

'Sit down, Lady Angela,' Doynton said kindly, indicating a chair. 'You're as white as a sheet. I'm sure this has been a great shock for you.'

'For us all,' grunted Aidan, perching on the edge of the table, one foot swinging, the other leg braced on the floor. 'Was there no provision made for her?'

'None at all, but this wasn't intentional. You see, along with most gamblers, Sir Barnaby was always convinced that he was about to hit a lucky streak, be it horseracing, boxing matches, a turn of the card - whatever. But he never made it and simply landed deeper and deeper in debt.' Doynton reached for the carafe and filled a crystal tumbler with water, then handed it to Angela.

'So he wasn't a wicked man?' she said, sipping slowly.

'Indeed not. Simply a foolish one,' the lawyer replied.

'Did you mean what you said, Aidan?' she asked, forcing herself to look up at him.

'About our marriage? Oh yes, I need a bride with a substantial dot, so this can no longer take place. But I can offer you a solution,' he answered, so calm that

24

she wanted to slap him across the face.

'And what, sir, is that?' Doynton cut in.

'I am going to London. She may come with me and I'll place her in the care of an acquaintance of mine, the Honourable Mrs Valerie Gail. As a renowned society hostess she may be able to find a post for Angela... as a governess, perhaps, or a companion to an elderly lady.'

Doynton frowned and cast him a distrustful glance. 'Is she a respectable person?'

'She is. I give you my word as a gentleman.'

'What do you say, Lady Angela?'

'I have no alternative, have I?' she said dispiritedly, her dreams of a future as Aidan's wife crumbling into dust. 'I'd much rather not see you again, Aidan. You have treated me shamefully. Your behaviour is far from that of a gentleman. I'd get more consideration from a labourer.'

'There's no call to speak to me in that tone. It's not that I don't love you,' he replied and, just for a moment she believed him. 'But I'm not a rich man and need a wealthy wife. You understand, don't you? I will do my best for you in other ways, and Valerie will help. Of course, you may have to dismiss Miss Hicks and your maid, unless we can come to some arrangement.'

'Arrangement? I don't understand.' She passed her hand across her brow, then addressed Doynton, asking, 'What can I take with me, sir? Some of my clothes are already at Compton Hall.'

'Pack everything from your wardrobe, and any jewels that were given to you as presents. Apart from that there is nothing,' the lawyer said, with a sorrowful shake of his head. 'Even the family gems that were worn by your mother and should have passed to you on marriage will now be forfeit.'

'My mare, Daisy Belle?' she questioned, feeling empty inside and totally numb.

'Will be sold with the rest of the stable.'

'So I can't spend another night under this roof?'

'You could, but I don't advise it. The servants will all be dismissed and the house shut up until the bailiffs and creditors arrive, which will be very shortly.'

'Can I take Maude upstairs to help me pack?' she asked Aidan.

'She will be doing it out of the goodness of her heart, for you have no money to pay her wages,' he reminded with a shrug, then added magnanimously, 'I'm sure I can sort this out.'

It was unbelievable. She stood in the bedroom that had been hers ever since she left the nursery, and assisted Maude to lift dresses from hangers and hats from shelves and underwear from tallboys and shoes from the wardrobe. Servants had hefted in two trunks and these were soon full of her belongings. The clasps were fastened, the leather straps buckled securely, and all her worldly possessions humped down the back stairs and out to a waiting cart that would bear them to Compton Hall.

She was ushered out through the front door, casting a despairing glance around her, seeing her beloved home for the last time. She was aware of being watched by unseen eyes, though none of the staff were in evidence. Aidan escorted her to the carriage and Maude was invited to sit inside with them. Doynton came as well, having been offered a lift to the railway station. The coachman cracked his whip. The horses leaned into the straps. The carriage began to move.

Angela pressed her face to the window glass, taking a final look at the house she had assumed would be home to her down the years. Then her sight blurred, the scene fractured across by tears.

'Don't unpack,' Aidan commanded. 'We're going by train to London in the morning.'

They were in the drawing room and one of the servants, a pert girl called Lisa, with corn-coloured hair and sparkling blue eyes, brought in a silver tray containing porcelain cups and saucers. A footman carried a lighted spirit stove and placed a matching kettle over the flame, so that the silver teapot might be topped up with boiling water.

Angela felt extremely embarrassed and awkward, nothing but the poor relation now, only there on sufferance. Aidan was not making it easy for her either, outwardly polite but looking at her in a strange, calculating manner. To her astonishment he had invited Maude to join them, and there had been a subtle shift in dynamics. She seemed different. Any suggestion of servility had gone, and she met Aidan's eye boldly as he said, 'Well, Maude, here's a to-do. Matters have gone apace quicker than we expected, eh?'

'Indeed they have, sir,' she answered, seated on one of the dainty Chippendale chairs, as cool and collected as a duchess, little finger extended as she lifted her cup to her lips.

'What are you talking about?' Angela demanded, uneasily aware of undercurrents that baffled her. 'You are my companion...'

'I was your companion,' Maude corrected, and helped herself to an iced fancy from the filigree cake stand. 'And happy to be so, until I met his lordship.'

'Aidan, what does she mean?' Angela could feel every vestige of colour draining from her face. She felt sick, bombarded on each side by ghastly revelations.

He was relaxed and at ease in a deeply upholstered winged chair. He smiled at the two women in his mocking way, and it was as if he was enjoying the situation. 'My dear, Maude and I have become close. It was necessary to do so, for she was your guard in my absence, and I wanted daily reports on your actions... who you had been seeing... what you had been saying. I needed to ensure that you came to the nuptial bed a virgin.'

'It was my pleasure,' Maude explained, and she beamed across at him. 'Lord Aidan is that rare individual... a man who understands women's needs.'

'But you were more like a friend than a servant, or so I thought,' Angela said, horrified by yet another betrayal of trust. 'How could you have behaved thus?'

'Lord Aidan can be very persuasive,' Maude said, smiling smugly. 'I was to remain in my position when you became his wife.'

'A spy? How despicable!' Angela cried, hardly able to bear looking at her.

'Not at all. Merely a faithful companion,' Aidan corrected.

'But that isn't going to happen now, is it? You have no intention of marrying me. What, then, do you see happening to me in the future, and where does Maude fit in?'

'As I told Doynton, I will not abandon you. Wife you may not be but mistress and slave you certainly shall.'

Angela leapt to her feet, eyes flashing, even her hair seeming to spark with indignation. 'Never!' she stormed, palm itching to smack his sneering face. 'I'll not submit to you and perform those acts that you have already tried to force on me.'

He threw back his head and laughed. 'Tut, tut! Such a show of temper! She needs a lesson in manners, don't you think, Maude?'

'As you say, master,' Maude answered, and Angela was all too aware of the title she had given him.

Had she, too, experienced the kiss of the lash wielded by his hand and known the delirious joy of him caressing her most intimate places? The thought made her want to gag, as did the idea that all the time the wretched woman had been pretending to be a prim and proper chaperone. Angela's first taste of perfidy came as a dreadful shock. She could hardly believe the evidence of her own eyes and ears.

Maude had changed visibly, too. Her hat was tilted forward at a rakish angle, and there was a trace of rouge on her cheekbones and lips. She was in mourning black, but though her bodice had a high neck it outlined her figure. Her waist was tightly corseted, accentuating her breasts, and her hips were made more pronounced by the skirt swept into a bustle at the back. And as she crossed her knees, glancing at Aidan provocatively, Angela caught a glimpse of stylish buttoned boots with high heels. Fine feathers indeed, for a companion! But then she wasn't, was she? Not any more - not at all - even in the past. She had been spying for Aidan. And what, Angela wondered, had she received as a reward?

She was not left in ignorance for much longer. Aidan beckoned Maude across and she draped herself on his lap, her hand plunging down to cup the bulge between his legs. 'I think, my dear,' he said softly, 'that Angela needs training. And you are the person to do it.'

'Why not Valerie?' Maude asked, a trifle petulantly. 'I thought you considered her to be the perfect dominatrix.'

'She is,' he agreed, and lay back further in the chair while she slipped to the carpet between his knees and started to unbutton his trousers. 'But there's no time like the present, and she should start her lessons now. Watch closely, Angela. See how Maude handles my prick so cleverly... but then you were once a member of the oldest profession in the world, weren't you, Maude?'

'That's right, my lord. I was a whore.'

'Then how did you join my father's household?' Angela demanded, though terrified of the answer.

Maude looked over at her coolly, then wetted Aidan's cock with saliva before answering, smoothing it over the fiery helm that became redder and harder. 'I heard he was seeking a respectable lady to guide you through the pitfalls of "coming out" and as a very necessary duenna, even after you were engaged to be married. I needed to leave London for a while. I'd been somewhat extravagant and my dressmaker was becoming boringly pressing with regard to my bill. A mutual acquaintance introduced me to Sir Barnaby and he gave me the job.'

'And when you met Lord Aidan, what happened then?' Angela whispered, revolted by yet envying Maude's actions as she straddled his lap, her skirts riding up to display shapely black-stockinged legs supported by suspenders attached to her corset. She wasn't wearing drawers, but had retained her fashionable hat with its osprey and frothy veiling. This added to her lewd appearance.

'Ah yes, well, he stuck his prick in me and I loved it,' Maude said huskily, raising her hips a little and angling her pelvis so that her wet, hair-fringed crack hovered just above the tip of Aidan's glans.

He grunted, pulled her over him and fastened his teeth on one bared nipple. She held her breath and he bit harder till a bright drop of blood glinted on his lips. Maude took his erect penis in her hand and guided it between her thighs, then slowly, languorously, lowered herself onto it till it disappeared from sight, lost in the seductive darkness of her body. She sat back with a long-drawn sigh and started to rock gently, finding the pink pearl of her swollen clitoris and playing with it.

Angela's own bud ached with want, and her hand dipped and found its way unerringly under her sombre skirt, parting her linen knickers and landing on her own overheated seat of sensation. She followed Maude's action; rubbing her nubbin from side to side, then up and down, circling it, wetting it from the copious dew seeping from her virgin slit, then frigging it hard. And all the while she wished that Aidan's mighty weapon was sheathed within her, jealous of the savage lunges he was making, envious of Maude's groans and the speed with which she was bringing herself to climax.

The coupling pair made a fascinating tableau; she so confident of her charms and that beautiful man as strong as a sword, and with the same ruthless cutting edge. Until today he was to have been Angela's husband, her mate for all time, her lord and master. Her heart bled because this was no longer possible. He was so handsome, fulfilling her every dream of a desirable hero. His head was flung back, his black hair brushed from his brow and curling at the nape of his neck. He had divested himself of his dark jacket and his shirt was open over his muscular, hirsute chest, his tight trousers gaping, exposing his hairy lower belly, though she could no longer see his cock, buried as it was in Maude's cleft.

'It's not fair!' Angela cried, without realising she had spoken aloud. 'I've lost him! Oh, father, why did you do this to me?'

The fornicators ignored her, too engrossed in their pleasure, and she was borne along on their frenzy. Nothing mattered but the achievement of ecstasy. Angela rubbed and rubbed, her finger flying over her clit, and all the while her eyes were fixed on the sweating, straining couple. So this was what sexual congress looked like. The mysterious veil had been torn asunder and her curiosity was almost, but not quite, satisfied. One thing remained: the loss of her maidenhead and the feeling of being well and truly shafted by a man's enormous cock.

Maude was panting. So was Aidan. His hands gripped her buttocks tightly, pumping her up and down. She started to moan loudly, and then this became a prolonged wail like a cat on heat. She clutched herself, shuddered from head to foot, gave a savage yelp and flopped forward. Aidan barked his pleasure, jerked once, twice, thrice, as he spent himself deep inside her.

This was all Angela needed to drive her over the edge of bliss. The orgasm was so powerful that it was as if she was sharing in theirs as well as enjoying her own. In the seconds' silence that followed she opened her eyes and saw Aidan staring at her. She was frightened by what she read in his glinting black pupils - cruelty, dominance, overweening pride and a fathomless abyss of lust.

He moved, tumbling Maude from his lap, seizing a handful of her skirt and wiping his penis on it. In a trice he was buttoned up and respectable again. It was as if nothing had happened. Maude took her cue from him, adjusting her attire and straightening her hat. Now they looked normal, two practiced dissemblers well versed in the art of disguise.

Angela attempted to follow suit, but she was flustered, not only by what she had just witnessed but because of her own reaction to it. A new emotion had been added to her list - she was now plagued by unmanageable passions.

'You wanted to join in with us,' Aidan said, matter-of-factly. 'It's down to you, my dear. Or rather it is down to me and my inclinations at any given moment. I will house you, clothe and feed you, and in return you will take lessons with Mrs Gail, become my hostess, entertain selected friends in any way I see fit. Maude and Bertha will continue to look after you. Do you agree?'

Angela stood before him with her chin high and rebellion in her eyes. 'This isn't what you told Mr Doynton,' she challenged. 'You said I should be found honest work.'

He threw himself back in the chair, smiling crookedly as he regarded her, and then drawing out his pocket watch on its gold chain and consulting the face. 'Doynton seemed perfectly satisfied with the arrangement. If anything, he was relieved to be no longer responsible for your welfare,' he said lightly, then stood up and shrugged his shoulders into his jacket. 'I have pressing business. Maude, take Angela to her room and begin her instruction. She's still a virgin, and shall stay that way for the moment. Her fundament is tight. Stretch it. I expect to be able to enjoy her arse in the not too distant future.'

Angela took flight, hurling herself at the door and tugging at the handle. 'You can't force me to stay! Let me go... at once!'

Aidan paced towards her, reached out and gripped her under the elbow. He drew her towards him and she was all too conscious of his nearness, her heart thudding like a drum, making her breasts shake. 'And where will you go?' he asked smoothly.

'Anywhere but here,' she panted, tugging at her arm.

'You have no money,' he reminded. 'No servants, no means of transport, no friends... only myself.'

'Then behave honourably. Do as you promised. Take me to London and introduce me to Mrs Gail. Surely you can do that much in memory of my father, and of what you and I might have meant to one another?'

He gave her a strange look and once again she was all too conscious of the power and persuasiveness of his eyes. 'You must promise me that you won't do anything foolish, like running away,' he began.

'I swear it,' she answered. 'I will do exactly as you tell me, be ready for London tomorrow and look forward to meeting Mrs Gail. You surely wouldn't force yourself on me, would you?'

'Force?' he said with his sinister smile. 'How dramatic. Very well then, let us strike a bargain, you and I. Maude will take you to your room. You will join us for dinner later, and I promise you won't be molested in any way. In return you will listen to Mrs Gail and I guarantee that one day, in the not too distant future, you will find that "force", as you put it, can be a very pleasant adjunct to pleasure. Are we agreed?'

'Yes, Aidan, and I'm very confident that I shall never, never agree to your terms... no matter what.'

There's nothing more beautiful and desirable than young male flesh, Valerie decided, stretching voluptuously among the tangled coverlets and duck-down pillows of her massive four-poster bed. She was of statuesque build, with big breasts and wide hips, the archetypal late-Victorian ideal of womanhood.

'Young man... lovely young man,' she whispered, her crimson lips pouting, her agile tongue licking over them, leaving a shiny trail of spittle.

'Valerie, mistress, goddess,' he replied, his body that of a Greek deity, his brown curls falling wildly over his smooth brow, his cock springing to attention, as it always did when exposed to her gorgeous white flesh.

'Am I your goddess, Julian, really, truly?' she insisted, teasing him, her nimble fingers working their magic on his trembling penis. It wept milky tears as if imploring her to take it into her fragrant delta. Instead she formed a tunnel of her magnificent, coral-tipped breasts and inserted his eager weapon, moving her torso up and down, driving him to distraction. He gasped and covered her hands with his, holding each globe close to his swollen, scarlet shaft. He watched the helm appearing then disappearing, and his movements became more uncontrolled. She knew precisely what he wanted but was inclined to torment him a little.

No matter how often she brought him to climax, within a few moments of spurting he was ready to start all over again. That was the advantage of youth and vigour and an insatiable appetite. Older men lost it more easily unless, like Aidan Driscol, they were exceptional, and even he could no longer sustain an erection for hours as he had once done.

'You know I adore you,' Julian insisted, rubbing against her harder. She was delighted with his progress. He had changed dramatically from the naïve lad whom she had first brought into her bed, the youngest son of a female friend who had asked her to initiate him into carnal pleasures. 'These past months, they have been a revelation,' he gasped, 'and meeting you, the most wonderful thing that has ever happened to me.'

He gave a strangled cry and bathed her naked breasts with his emission, long jets pumping from his cock-head. Valerie changed quixotically. In an instant she was bored. Julian was just too perfect and predictable. She missed Aidan with his black moods and evil temper and, above all, his sinful knowledge of how to make her walk the wafer thin line between agony and extreme pleasure. She pushed Julian away, massaged his spunk into her breasts as if it was some expensive beauty cream, then tugged at the thin gold chain that linked the rings in his wine-red nipples, making him squirm.

For a moment she toyed with the notion of having him bend over her, open her legs wide and apply his tongue to the folds of her labial wings and the tight bud of her clit. He'd do it, she knew, and this willingness amused yet irritated her. They had spent the entire night together and at first it was fun. She brought him home from dinner at the Ritz followed by a performance at the Gaiety Theatre. The roads had been jammed with private carriages, hackney-cabs and those new-fangled, noisy motorcars, that she so hankered after and was determined to purchase.

Valerie had been promising herself another sample of Julian's nubile body for some time, waiting for the right opportunity. Her elderly husband, the Honourable Dennis Gail, was in Monte Carlo with a couple of his fat mistresses who, like him, were addicted to the gaming tables, and she was spending the season in their splendid house in Chelsea. This was a much sought-after area that besides being extremely fashionable, had the added piquancy of harbouring several well-known artists, sculptors, writers and musicians, giving it an excitingly cosmopolitan ambience. It reminded her of Paris, a city of which she heartily approved.

Her maid, Viola, had already been in to pull aside the curtains and lay out coffee-cups, plates and a rack of toast. Employed by Valerie for several years she was absolutely trustworthy. Loyal servants were essential if one was to continue the outrageous lifestyle that Valerie favoured. She paid her generously and reaped the rewards.

Fired by an imp of perversity she beckoned her closer, whipped back the richly embroidered coverlet and exposed Julian in all his perfection. He did not bat an eyelid, staring up at the two women with a smug smile curving his ruby lips, sprawled at his ease, partly propped up by Valerie. His legs were slackly parted and the ribald surprise of his large blush-red balls and long cock nestled amongst his dark pubic curls made a mockery of his tender years. He had the genitals of a mature man, obscenely developed in contrast to his slender figure, graceful mien and noble aspect that resembled a Renaissance painter's vision of an Eros, or a boy David, or a young warrior.

It was too much for Valerie. She dipped down and sucked his penis. It started to lift again and his testicles tightened. Viola watched, hands on her black uniformed hips, a gleam in her eye, her breath quickening. She was accustomed to taking her pleasure among the servants, tradesmen, grooms and whoever took her fancy below stairs, the younger the better, it seemed. She was never backwards in coming forwards when it came to educating boys. Valerie and she agreed on this point, and sometimes shared the spoils. Gentlemen thought it their right to drool over pretty girls, but it was not considered proper for women to feel the same desires for youths. A male fable that all proper females knew to be absolute nonsense.

'He's pretty, my lady,' Viola whispered.

'You've seen him before.'

'Oh yes, and I thought so then and I think so now. Lady Jane's boy, isn't he? Well, well, ain't he growing into something? Never seen such a handsome prick,' and Viola swept up a basket of rose petals that lay on the nightstand and scattered them over and around Julian's parts.

The action of that light pattering of dried leaves caused his oversensitive member to stir again. It poked through the flower covering, cheekily demanding attention. Valerie leaned over and nibbled his neck where the light sprinkling of fluff had not yet been touched by the razor. Julian chuckled and exposed his throat to her teeth, just as if he was the willing victim of a vampire. It was a most erotic gesture and Valerie bit deeper. His cock was huge now and Viola seized it in her hand, running her fingers up and down the pulsing stem while jiggling his balls and tickling his anus, the crimson petals falling between his legs, leaving him fully exposed.

Valerie's boredom had evaporated, renewed lust spurred on by Viola's participation. The maid had hooked her skirts up and placed one leg on the bed, knee bent as she displayed black woollen stockings, fancy garters and a crotch devoid of covering. Valerie could smell her strong, oceanic odour that wafted out from between her slit that was hidden by a thick coating of bushy hair. It was not the first time they had shared intimacies. Many a night when neither of them was otherwise engaged in sexual congress and needed satisfaction Viola had entered her mistress's bed, both of them enjoying the experience immensely and privately wondering why they bothered with men. Women knew so well how to pleasure one another, finding the clitoris with ease and giving it just the right treatment.

Now, exchanging glances, they knew they could spend an exciting half-hour toying with Julian and, if he didn't come up to scratch, share orgasms together. No problems, no heartbreak and frustration, just perfect enjoyment. What could be simpler?

Viola was just about to join the couple on the bed when the door crashed open and Aidan swept in like an avenging angel. 'What the hell...?' he shouted.

'What the hell indeed!' Valerie blazed back, shifting the boy from her and sitting up, dragging her silk kimono around her nudity. 'How dare you come bursting into my bedroom without a by-your-leave?'

'Dare? To me?' he returned, looming over her, big and menacing. Her blood turned to ice in her veins but she continued to defy him.

'You know me, Aidan. Dare me and I'll do it! This is my house, my room, my privacy. Now get out!'

At that he laughed loudly and unpleasantly, while Viola slunk away and Julian slid from the mattress, gathered up his scattered clothing and headed for the adjoining bathroom. Valerie was really angry now. Aidan was so dictatorial, thinking he had every right to interrupt her love life and order her about. He stopped laughing, sat on the bed and dragged her facedown across his knee.

'I didn't give you permission to roger young Julian,' he began, and his face was set in stern lines. 'His mother is a particular friend of mine and I'm sure she wouldn't approve.'

'On the contrary; she asked me to initiate him,' Valerie muttered, half smothered by the coverlet, her body stretched over Aidan's lap, her skin, nerves, loins and mind anticipating his first stinging blow.

'Did she indeed. Well, it's time I had words with her,' he growled. 'She's an attractive woman, and I admire them slightly older. They are so goddamn grateful for a man's interest. Can't wait to be his slave.'

'You're a bastard, aren't you?' Valerie hissed, and although she knew full well his intention to give her a painful half-hour, her desire began to climb steeply, her sexual organs heating explosively.

'Of course, and you adore me for it,' he replied blandly, and she turned her head with difficulty and stared up at his right hand. This is what he would use to punish her and her heart was pounding so hard that it felt as if it had lodged in her throat.

He dipped between her buttock cheeks and she felt his fingers penetrating her fissure. 'Oh, Aidan,' she whimpered, despising herself for her weakness where he was concerned, yet revelling in her decadence.

His fingers plunged deeper, hurting her delicate membranes. He withdrew, raised them to his nostrils and sniffed. 'You reek of him,' he said. 'Your minge is full of his spunk. Dirty bitch!' His hand landed ruthlessly on the rounded globes of her rump. 'What are you? Say it!'

'I'm a dirty bitch,' she repeated, every word sending shivers down her spine and into her groin.

He was between her legs again and she sank willingly into his caresses and slaps. She felt the shape of his cock behind his fly buttons, the length of it reaching to his navel. She longed to see it, to touch and suck it, but knew her role. As a submissive she must wait for him to give the commands, accepting everything and keeping her own passion in check.

She wondered briefly what he was doing in London, but then he was a maverick, a law unto himself. There was a prospective bride somewhere in the offing, and lands, estates and a generous addition to his coffers. This meant nothing to her. They were not even fond of one another, simply partners with tainted tastes, enjoying the darker side of perversion, seeking unbridled sensations.

Most times he worked her flesh without thought to her soul or emotions and she was every bit as selfish, using him to ease that never-ending ache in her epicentre.

Now, stretched across his firm thighs, she wondered what form her punishment would take. His naked palm, calloused from handling the reins? The thrasher with its dozen deerskin thongs? The flat, flexible paddle? She owned the last mentioned toys, but he had not asked for them. Flesh on flesh then, his hand striking her bottom. This was quite her favourite means of chastisement, the contact almost as close as intercourse. Heady stuff, and it was this more than her upside-down position that was making her dizzy.

He struck without warning, making her jolt. Her posterior burned from the harshness of his first blow. Tears filled her eyes. Then his hand was stroking her blotched skin gently and she relaxed. A foolish move.

He struck again and she almost lost control of her bladder, drops of urine escaping to dampen his trousers before she gained control. He seemed unaware, or if he was, took pleasure in it. She did not know what to expect next. When he hit her it was with full force, her body jerking, her skin on fire, but then he would change, massaging her injured bottom and making her believe her ordeal was over, even though she longed for it to continue.

She had entered that strange, trancelike stage that always preceded orgasm when she was being treated like this. She had expected him to continue spanking her, then finger her clit until she came, after which he would take his own pleasure, either in her vagina or her fundament.

But her complacency was brought to an abrupt halt when he withdrew a small implement from his jacket pocket. It was spoon-shaped, a springy wooden object covered in leather. The effect was startling, though she knew it of old. The paddle snapped and stung and she longed for Aidan to stop and lay his hand on her reddened flesh between blows, but he was in an awkward mood, refusing respite. The tears flowed freely, dripping from her chin.

'Oh, don't,' she implored. 'No more, master.'

'I'm the one who calls the tune,' he grunted, and the paddle whacked her again. 'You want me to stop?'

'N-no...' she stammered, but couldn't believe she was saying it.

'Good. You need a lesson in humility, Valerie. I've noticed with displeasure that you've been getting above yourself lately. I have a task for you. One you will carry out to the letter.'

He flicked her again and she shrank against his thighs. 'A task? Anything, master.'

'I shall tell you about it later. Meanwhile, discipline, my dear Valerie. You need discipline.'

'Ah, yes... I do, I do,' and she wriggled, seeking the paddle, his palm, anything that would bring her closer to climax.

'You like to be mastered because you're a randy slut who needs to be kept in line,' he hissed, and spanked her harder with the flat of the paddle. 'I'm bringing you a pupil. She is Lady Angela Bayswater.'

The name rang a bell and even in her semi-hypnotised state of painful pleasure, she had wit enough to ask, 'Isn't she your betrothed?'

He smacked her so hard that she bucked against his thighs frantically. 'She was, but the marriage is off. Her father died recently and he was declared bankrupt. Everything has gone; the house, the lands and Angela's dowry.'

'So much for true love,' Valerie observed cynically and earned herself another vicious spank. Twisting against him she tried to fling herself to the floor, but he was strong and kept her in position with one hand at the nape of her neck. With the other he continued to rain blows on her crimson, bruised buttocks.

'I don't believe in love,' he growled. 'She shall be my mistress, my submissive. She has no one else, is quite alone in the world. I shall bring her here after lunch and you will train her. She's proud and defiant, but I'd see her brought low and humble and begging me to be her protector.'

Valerie was hardly listening; her mind absorbed his words but her body was a thing apart as he spanked her to higher and higher peaks of sensation. Her skin welcomed the pain and her guilt needed the humiliation, and her sex needed the stimulation.

He flung her onto the bed, forced her legs apart and found her clit poised on the edge of coming. He rubbed it mercilessly and sprawled across her, his released cock plunging into her.

'Oh yes... yes!' she squealed, coming just before he did, her inner muscles clamping round his cock as he, too, reached his apogee.

He did not collapse on her when he had finished, simply rolled to one side and left the bed.

She lay with her eyes closed, but when she finally raised her lids it was so see him sitting in a chair, smoking and staring at her.

'You'll do as I say,' he observed, taking another pull at the cigar, the grey-blue smoke drifting upwards to the ornamental ceiling.

'Of course,' she answered lazily, feeling limp and fulfilled despite her aching buttocks and the remembrance of his punishment.

'I'm determined to break her,' he went on, and reaching over to the occasional table, squashed out the stub in a soapstone ashtray.

Valerie stretched like a sun-warmed cat and asked, 'Why this one, in particular?' He scowled and she wondered. Was he perhaps disappointed that he had lost his bride? She hardly thought this likely. Aidan was one of the least sentimental men she knew. Nothing seemed to move him.

He stood up and shrugged, then reached for his coat. 'She's beautiful and will prove an interesting experiment, hotter than she realises, covering her urges with a ladylike gentility. I want her to stay here with you and be introduced to all the byways of passion. Do you understand?'

'Perfectly, Aidan,' she cooed, so content that she could have lain there all day.

'Don't disappoint me,' he warned, looming over her. 'You know that I don't take kindly to disappointment.'

'Leave her to me. I'll soon have Lady Angela pliable and bendy, willing to pleasure you in every way possible,' she promised, but to her surprise even this did not seem to please him.

'Don't break her spirit,' he ordered. 'I like the fire that burns in her. It excites me, challenges me, and makes me swear to be the only one to tame her.'

Chapter 4

Angela was no stranger to London. There was a family mansion near Hyde Park, but this had now gone, along with everything else. It was there that she stayed when her father was called on parliamentary business. There she had shopped and been groomed by a fussy, elderly aristocratic lady whose job it was to prepare young girls for their 'coming out'. She had attended concerts in the Albert Hall, passionate about music and, gifted in this direction, had played and sung at soirées, and visited the theatres, too. Another life, it seemed, another existence entirely. She had been carefree then, beholden to none save her father.

She huddled in a corner of the Driscol coach, with Maude on one side, Bertha on the other (privileged, as she was but a humble maid), and Aidan opposite her. The traffic was thick and progress slow. She wished it would take forever, reluctant to be introduced to Valerie Gail. True to his word Aidan had not interfered with her last night, though Maude took her to task, spoke freely about sexual matters and instructed her as to what would be expected of her. Her meals were served in her room, the same one in which she had stayed as his guest during the dreadful days after her father's passing. Bertha was there; a solid, comforting link with her recent past. She said nothing, it was not her place to pass comment, but Angela was grateful for her silent sympathy.

The train journey had been uneventful. They travelled first-class, and Maude had been seated with them. Keeping up the pretence that she was a respectable young lady, it would have been unthinkable for Angela to occupy a railway carriage alone with a man.

It was all so much nonsense, she thought angrily, staring out of the window as they left the station, seeing the dirty London scene with its mish-mash of people and jumble of vehicles, brewers' drays, coal-carts, cabs and horse-drawn omnibuses and private equipage. The sky was overcast, hazy with chimney smoke, and the air rank with the conglomeration of smells from tanneries and factories, abattoirs and gasworks.

They reached his mansion by hansom cab. There she was given little chance to recover from the train journey, bundled into Aidan's coach and off to call on Valerie Gail. He was in a mocking, sarcastic mood, ordering that she should leave her baggage and not bother about taking anything with her. Valerie would provide for her wants. Maude was to go too, so was Bertha who had been ordered to make herself useful. Angela had bad feelings about all this. It did not bode well.

The scene changed, still crowded, but they were entering the West End where the thoroughfares were broader, the pedestrians smartly dressed, the shops magnificent emporiums, and crossing-sweepers keeping the streets clear of horse manure. Soon they reached the River Thames and the beautiful Regency architecture of Chelsea. Obviously Aidan was a frequent visitor for his coachman drew up the team outside one particularly impressive house. Its pillared frontage faced on to a square in the middle of which was a fenced-in area of neatly mown grass and bushes and trees, for the use of the residents only.

A footman appeared at the top of a flight of shallow stone steps. He was dressed in a black uniform and came down to open the carriage door. Aidan made no attempt to get out.

'You will stay here, Angela, while Valerie prepares you. Don't cause trouble, or it will be reported to me,' he said, and he leaned across and she flinched as he placed his lips on her cheek.

Marshalling her courage she rested her fingertips on the footman's arm as she alighted, and was conducted up the steps and under the shell-shaped portico. She was aware that Maude and Bertha were behind her, each carrying a piece of hand luggage. They had not been prevented from bringing their own belongings, it seemed. Then why her? What was so special about her grooming that it necessitated a complete transformation?

'Mrs Gail expects you in her private apartment,' the footman said, a fine figure of a man, very conscious of the importance of his position. He stared into the middle distance, just above Angela's head. 'Please come this way.'

Though wary as a cornered animal, Angela was impressed by the terracotta and white tiled floor of a large hall complete with Greek statues on plinths and landscape paintings in immense gilt frames. Light flooded from a cupola, the stained glass scintillating with red and blue and green and gold designs. The graceful staircase curved upward and Angela mounted it in the footman's wake, her gloved hand on the ironwork balustrade. Reaching the top she passed along corridors with many closed doors, and long windows that gave impressive views of the garden that surrounded the house. She glimpsed stables and outbuildings and caught the flash of a greenhouse roof. This was in London's very heart, and yet it had all the attributes of a gracious home, as had her father's city property, to say nothing of Lairdland.

Tears stung Angela's eyes, but she did not break down, too proud to let anyone see her misery. She waited quietly as the footman paused and tapped at a double cedar wood door. It was opened at once and Angela blinked, unable to believe what she was seeing.

A young man stood there, naked to the waist. Small gold hoops pierced his nipples and he wore a spiked collar around his neck from which chains stretched, attached to the rings. His baggy, oriental pantaloons should have preserved his modesty, but they were open in front, displaying a large cock that sprang from a nest of brown curls. As he turned Angela saw his backside was also bare, and that a whip had embroidered crimson welts on his skin.

She didn't know where to look, though he seemed not in the least concerned, bowing and smiling and saying, 'Welcome, Lady Angela. My mistress awaits you.'

'Bring her at once, Julian!' commanded an imperious voice, and Angela and her companions were ushered inside.

Such a room! Stunning, fantastic and bizarre, like something out of *The Arabian Night's Entertainment*.

Exotic artefacts were in vogue, inspired by India and Japan and China. Liberty's famous store produced fabric and clothing and furniture. Angela was familiar with all this, yet Valerie's boudoir was beyond her wildest imaginings. The air was aromatic with incense smouldering in metal holders shaped like writhing serpents. The hangings were of silk, the cushions and bolsters too, and the occasional tables were of beaten brass, the lamps miniature temples complete with minarets. Music wailed in the background, the weird sound of pipes and tambours reproduced on a gramophone with a large trumpet-shaped horn.

But the most striking feature of all was the woman who reclined on a divan in an alcove. She rose, a beautiful creature in her early thirties, her glorious legs shamelessly displayed through a diaphanous skirt, her breasts squeezed high by a tightly-laced black leather basque designed to divide and separate each large globe. She had flaxen hair that tumbled about her shoulders and halfway down her back. Her arms were covered to above the elbow by close-fitting gloves fastened with minute pearl buttons, and this had the effect of making one even more conscious of the parts of her that were exposed.

'I'm Valerie,' she said, gliding forward. 'And you, I suppose, are Lady Angela. Good afternoon, Maude. We have met before.'

'Indeed we have, Mrs Gail,' the woman replied smugly, and Angela wondered when and where, appalled to think of the deception that had taken place behind her back.

'And you, girl? Where do you fit in?' Valerie demanded, pacing round Bertha on her high heels, her skirt floating open, showing her stockings and fork - naked of pubic hair, bare and smooth and infinitely alluring.

'I'm Bertha Marten, Lady Angela's maid,' Bertha replied staunchly in her broad Somerset accent, facing her full square, a plain girl with a snub-nose and freckles and sandy hair. 'I were her maid when Sir Barnaby were alive, and I'll serve her for as long as she needs me.'

'Will you, indeed?' Valerie said, her eyebrows arching significantly. 'Then you'll need to follow my rules. I shall want you dressed more becomingly.'

She reached for a hand bell and its tinkle was answered directly by a young woman who appeared from a far door. She wore a starched white cap with streamers and a frilly apron. Her breasts were naked, the coral nipples peeping over the edge of an exceedingly tightly laced red satin corset. Her pink tulle skirt stuck out like a ballerina's, very short and full, dipping and lifting as she walked, showing her plump arse cheeks and stomach, for she was entirely naked beneath it. Like Julian, she bore the marks of a recent whipping.

Bertha gasped and drew herself up, eyeing the girl with scorn. 'You'll never get me making an exhibition of myself like that,' she said pithily.

'That's what Trisha said once, wasn't it, slut?' Valerie said, and implemented her words with a resounding slap on her maid's backside. 'If you don't comply, Bertha, then I'm afraid you and Lady Angela have come to the parting of the ways,' she continued calmly.

'I won't leave her,' Bertha vowed, on the edge of tears.

'There's no question about it. Do as I say or get out. The choice is yours.' Valerie turned away, peeled off her gloves, beckoned Julian to her, slid a hand into his breeches and started to play with his genitals.

'It's all right, Bertha. Go. I shall survive. I have no choice, but you do. Will you go home?' Angela asked with a catch in her voice, putting her arms round the maid, who started to weep.

'Yes, milady. I've enough for the fare back, but oh, I feel dreadful abandoning you like this,' she sobbed, and Angela realised just how much she had depended on her stalwart presence. Soon there would be no one she could trust and rely on. She could not watch as Bertha, still crying, left the room. Now she was alone with the enemy, for this was how she thought of Aidan and his associates.

Valerie, still working on Julian's swollen penis, gave a cold smile and said, 'Let us get started. There is much to do to turn you into the mistress Aidan requires.' Unable to control himself, Julian spurted into her hand. She slapped him sharply and wiped her fingers on his curly locks. 'Disgusting little beast!' she scolded. 'Did I say you could come? I shall have to think of a suitable punishment. Meanwhile, flat on your face at my feet.'

He flung himself down, his attitude one of abject misery, yet there was an air of excitement about him that Angela could not fathom. Valerie stood above him and drove one of her spiked heels into his neck. He groaned, though more in pleasure than in pain, then with a final savage kick she left him and strolled towards Angela. 'Don't be afraid,' she said soothingly, and trailed a finger against Angela's cheek, down to her throat, parted the black jacket and touched the blouse beneath where her nipples protruded, so stiff with arousal that they lifted the soft material.

The caress of those experienced fingers, still fresh from Julian's dew, caused a deep disturbance within Angela. To her dismay she could feel juices wetting her knickers and suddenly yearned to have Valerie fondle her intimately and perform those fascinating acts that Maude had described last night. Her erstwhile companion's words had roused her and she'd been unable to sleep, tossing and turning, needing to pleasure herself but afraid to indulge lest Maude or Aidan found out.

Valerie left her and sashayed over to an elaborate cabinet, rich with marquetry and gold leaf. From it she drew a large album and laid it flat on the table, gesturing to Angela to join her. 'Photography,' she said, her eyes shone and her crimson lips smiled. 'What a wonderful invention. And they are experimenting with moving pictures, too. Imagine it. One day we shall be able to see couples fucking over and over, whenever we like. All we shall need is the equipment to reproduce sexual scenes.'

Angela knew about having her photograph taken. Sir Barnaby had this done after she'd dipped a curtsey to Queen Victoria, and there was a copy in a silver frame among her possessions. She was holding herself stiffly, obeying the photographer's orders not to move. She looked very young and innocent, an angel in white wearing the family heirlooms, a diamond necklace, earrings and tiara which had now gone the way of all the Bayswater possessions.

It had never occurred to her that the camera could be used to capture other aspects of the human condition - that of couples in intimate acts - and photos of their genitals for all to see. This is what immediately struck her as Valerie started to flip over the pages. The album had thick leather covers and was ornately scrolled. It could have been a Bible or a book of innocent country views, but it contained nothing like this and Angela found it immensely disturbing.

Not so Valerie. 'This collection was compiled in France,' she announced, and turned the pages quickly, adding, 'And I'm in it. Look. Of course I kept my face part-covered, using a pair of binoculars, you know, but anyone who is familiar with my pussy would recognise it immediately, though I've since had it depilated.'

It was her all right, lounging on a low, armless chair, naked from the waist down and hiding behind the opera glasses. Her legs were spread wide and her labial wings parted, fringed with golden fuzz, and her excited clitoris peeped forth, of larger than average size, as if she had been stimulating it.

'How could you do that in front of a photographer?' Angela gasped, but she was leaning closer, mesmerised by the shot that Valerie proudly showed her.

'It's easy, once you know how,' she answered. 'You just have to stay still, that's all. I like being admired, and though the man behind the camera is a professional, more interested in angles and lighting than a woman's minge or a gentleman's erection, it makes me horny.'

'It's so rude!' Angela protested, though unable to tear her eyes from the picture.

Valerie gurgled with laughter. 'That's why it is such fun! You'll see. Aidan wants photos of you...'

'I won't pose like that. Never!' Angela averred.

'Not even like this?' Valerie teased, and showed her another in which she was perched on the back of a sofa, skirts up, feet and ankles encased in black buttoned boots, her legs splayed and bent at the knee.

She was holding her sex lips open, and smiling down at a mature lover with fiercely twirled and waxed moustache, dressed in a red military jacket. He reclined below her, gazing up at her juicy cleft surmounted by her enlarged clitoris. His white breeches were rolled down to meet the tops of his shiny black boots and he was clasping his stiff cock.

'It's like a ramrod, isn't it?' Valerie mused, and scratched a fingernail over it. 'He's a goer, that one. Stiff as a pikestaff and off like a rocket. I still see him sometimes. Would you like to meet him? He's one of Aidan's cronies.'

Angela shuddered and went to move away. 'No, I don't want to meet him. Whatever next? How could I face someone when I've already seen a photo of his private parts.'

'There's not much private about it,' Valerie chortled. 'He can't wait to flaunt his dick as publicly as possible. Renowned for it.' She shut the album with a snap, clapped her hands at Julian and said, 'Time to start. Add perfumed oil to the bath, Julian. Maude and Trisha, help Lady Angela to undress.'

'What? Why? It's not yet time for dinner, is it?' Angela burst out, backing away.

'I want to look at you and see what must be done to enhance your beauty,'

'And if I refuse?'

'Then you shall have a lesson in discipline. Aidan instructed me to take whatever action I deemed necessary.'

Hemmed in by Maude, the hard-faced Viola and the brazen Trisha, Angela unbuttoned her jacket and laid it aside. Beneath it she wore a high-collared white lawn blouse with leg-of-mutton sleeves. Her skirt was swept to the back, and her hand-span waist emphasised by a wide belt. She stood there like a doll as Valerie turned her this way and that, admiring her figure.

'I'm still in mourning for my father,' Angela said, not knowing how else to respond to this scrutiny. 'And shall be for a year.'

'That's not essential in the circles in which you will now move. No one will know who you are, and certainly not associate you with the aristocracy. You'll simply be known as Angela. A pretty name, don't you agree? That of an angel, but a fallen one in your case. Now no more hesitation. Off with the rest of your clothes.'

There was no help for it. Angela undid the mother-of-pearl buttons all the way down the front of her blouse and Trisha eased it from her shoulders and arms. She could feel the blush spreading up from her neck and into her cheeks. Julian was present. Though young he was still male and she had never

41

undressed in front of a man before.

'Can't I go behind there?' she asked, pointing to a lacquered Japanese screen with delicate panels painted with scenes of Mount Fuji and pagodas and little figures crossing bridges over water where golden carp lazed.

'No,' Valerie answered crisply, and Angela could almost feel the snap of the short-handled leather whip she had picked up and was now running through her fingers.

Maude came to assist Trisha. She had already removed her hat and coat, and it was as if she had mentally rolled up her sleeves ready for action. Angela made up her mind: she wasn't going to give them the satisfaction of having to forcibly strip her. She would do it herself.

'I don't need help,' she said tersely.

'You will with the lacing of your corset,' Valerie reminded, as she stood there smiling and swishing the whip playfully.

This was true; most stays fastened at the back. Angela felt the cool air raising the fine down on her bare arms and shoulders. Her nipples crimped, and she untied the ribbons of her chemise and lifted it over her head. The corset remained, made of cream cotton, an unyielding garment reinforced with whalebone. Some said it was designed to make ladies aware of their frailty and help them maintain self-control, whilst others looked upon it as a necessary adjunct to high fashion. Angela had never thought about it before, accepting it as part of her underclothing. Yet staring at Valerie's waist-clinching basque, she could see that such restriction had a certain allure.

'Let me help you,' Valerie said, standing just behind her.

Angela felt her deftly ravelling the lacing. The corset began to open. She could breathe deeply once more, filling her lungs with air. Valerie freed her entirely and she was left wearing the thinnest of camisoles. She massaged her ribs and stretched her arms, relishing the freedom. Her bustle consisted of a horsehair pad attached to a petticoat and Valerie loosened the strings. It fell to the floor and Angela stepped out of it. She was trembling in her drawers and skimpy top, folding her arm over her breasts and covering her crotch with her free hand.

'This has gone far enough,' she mumbled, though there was nothing but admiration in the eyes feasting upon her.

'Not yet,' Valerie rejoined, and lifted Angela's resisting arm aside and took the pointed nipples between her fingers, tweaking them through the silk. 'Such perfection,' she sighed. 'Aidan was a fool not to marry you, but that's his business. He may be the one to deflower you but I shall enjoy your bounty before taking you to his party tonight.'

'Tonight? So soon... I didn't realise... imagined I should be here for several days...' Angela gasped, pleasure shooting from her breasts to her clitoris even as she panicked.

'Oh you will, darling, for there is much for you to learn,' Valerie said, her eyes smoky as if she understood Angela's need, her hand going down to enter the slit in the cambric knickers and cup the damp, heated mound.

'Ah... oh, yes... yes...' Angela breathed, and wished that she and Valerie could be swallowed up and transported to some secret spot where she, the novice, could be satisfied by those knowledgeable fingers.

'Later,' Valerie promised, her voice a seductive murmur in Angela's ear, her tongue circling the rim and adding to the desire raging in her pupil's loins. 'You've felt the kiss of Aidan's crop? I know you have, for he has told me, and you still bear faint bruises.'

'That's true, I'm ashamed to say,' Angela confessed, pressing against that invasive finger.

'It is a good thing that you experience shame, for the pleasure is doubled if one feels that one is being punished for sin.'

'He took me to his dungeon at Compton Hall.'

'And?'

'Tied me to the crosspiece.'

'Ah, you were privileged.'

'You know the place?' Angela was beyond caring, her single goal that of reaching completion.

'I have been a guest there, and his London house is even more finely equipped, as you will soon discover.' Valerie withdrew her caress and Angela gasped in disappointment and tried to finish herself off, rubbing her cleft, but prevented from reaching climax by Valerie. 'You must save it for tonight. I want you as hot as a fiddler's bitch. Time to prepare. Come along, Maude and Viola. Let's do it.'

The décor of the adjoining bathroom was as decadent as the rest of the apartment. Obviously Valerie's husband doted on her and gave her free rein with his bank account. Following the Eastern theme the walls were lined with Islamic tiles and the large oblong bath was sunk into the centre of the polished marble floor. Candles blazed on glass shelves, reflected over and over in mirrors, and there was the strong scent of flowers standing in large urns or scattered on the water. The atmosphere was that of a sultan's harem.

'Sit down, my lady,' said Trisha, obviously familiar with the routine.

Angela occupied a small carved stool and the maid knelt and took off her shoes and rolled down her stockings, then, 'And the rest,' ordered Valerie.

Julian was leaning over, swishing the water as he added scented oils, but Angela was no longer conscious of him. It was as if Valerie had injected a potion into her veins, a powerful aphrodisiac that made her oblivious to everything except satisfying her lust. If she pleased Valerie, then perhaps she might take pity on her and relieve her frustration.

Angela unpinned her hair and tossed it round her shoulders, then slipped off the fragile camisole and dropped her knickers. With a boldness that was no longer a façade she stood before Valerie, hands clasped on top of her head, one knee relaxed, defying her to fault the grace of her pose or the symmetry of her body.

Valerie had no inhibitions, wriggling out of her basque and skirt, and Angela stared, entranced, as the lovely form emerged. Trisha crouched at her feet and removed her high-heeled boots, and then barefoot Valerie padded across to the tub and descended by way of a narrow step, till the water crept up her thighs and immersed her. She lay back like a wanton mermaid, her hair floating round her, nipples poking above the water.

'Join me,' she ordered, holding out a dripping hand to Angela. 'Don't you just love all these modern inventions... electricity, and hot water on tap... it's brilliant. Not so readily available in the country. I was disappointed in Compton Hall, so old-fashioned. I told Aidan that he must have the place updated, and he said he would as soon as he married you, his bride with a large dowry. But that never came to pass, did it? And now you are dependent on his whims and fancies... his slave, as it were.'

'I'm nobody's slave,' Angela countered defiantly, but edged towards the bath.

'Of course not,' Valerie said with a quirky smile. 'It's sometimes impossible to tell who is the slave and who the dominator. We play games all the time. Even in our ordinary lives.' She held up a hand, stopping Angela from slipping down into the water. 'Wait, let me look at you. What a luxuriant bush you have. I'm wondering whether or no to have Julian shave it. Presumably Aidan has already looked his fill of it. Maybe he would prefer your mound to be smooth as silk. He enjoys mine,' and her hand crept down to her groin, fingering her satiny mons.

'I don't want to be shaved,' Angela returned smartly, and lowered herself under the warm, deliciously perfumed water. 'Goodness, I've never even considered it.'

'You will find you'll be doing many things you've never dreamed of,' Valerie continued. 'We will leave it for the moment and see what Aidan says. Julian, wash me,' she commanded.

He crouched at the rim of the bath, but this did not suit Valerie. She reached up and pulled him in. His lithe body glistened with water, his hair streaming and his pantaloons clinging like paste to every angle and bulge. Valerie had him take up a large sponge, soap it generously and apply it to her body. She stood up, almost purring as the sponge dribbled and foamed and covered her with lather. Julian turned her, attending to her back, his hand disappearing into the valley between her buttocks. She opened her legs so that he might attend to the rosebud moue of her anus, her perineum and the plump labial lips. She threw back her head, long hair streaming as the sponge rubbed against her nodule.

'Do it!' she hissed, and Julian squeezed and moulded, wetted and sponged the seat of her pleasure until she suddenly jerked, stiffened and clung to him with her hands on his shoulders.

Angela watched and ached and shook off Maude when she attempted to wash her. 'I can do it myself,' she grated, and longed to seize Julian by the scruff of the neck, pull him down on her and have him deflower her with his large prick. Instead she washed herself very thoroughly, including her hair.

Valerie and Julian had already retired to the bedroom by the time Angela finished her ablutions, left the bath and was swathed in a large towel by Trisha. She wound another, turban-wise, round her head and, wondering what was to happened next, was escorted into Valerie's inner sanctum where she entertained her favourite lovers of either sex, and plotted her deepest mischief.

This was an even more elaborate room, again with an Eastern ambience, the walls hung with yellow silk, the ceiling tented in the same material. The focus was on the bed, wider and longer than usual, piled high with cushions in rich and sombre hues and spread with a coverlet of matched jaguar pelts. The carved head was inlaid with mirrors and the tester above it draped like a Bedouin prince's tent.

Valerie and Julian lay beneath it. Her legs were lifted, her feet resting on his shoulders while he pumped away in her depths and she squealed like an alley cat. Angela was gravid with desire, reaching beneath her bath towel for her fulcrum of sensation. Valerie caught her eye and, with a final shriek, reached fulfilment.

She recovered at once, saying, 'Come over here, Angela.'

As if in a trance Angela dropped the towel and lay on the bed. She could smell costly perfume and damp skin, Valerie's female essence and the strong, musky odour of Julian's genitals, sweat and spunk. It was an overpoweringly sensual brew.

Someone pressed her back against the fur quilt and Maude and Viola were working on her nipples, the delight echoed in her eager bud. She closed her eyes and lips, sucking at each eager peak, replaced the fingers, and Angela's hands clenched as wonderful sensations racked her and she was mewling like a kitten. It was no longer Maude and Viola servicing her, but Valerie and Julian.

'Spread your legs,' Valerie murmured, lifting her mouth from Angela's right teat. 'I want to examine you closely and find out if you are a virgin and how much pleasure you've already experienced.'

She made no protest, peeking through her lashes and seeing Valerie lean over her parted legs, moving her hands along the insides of her thighs and landing unerringly on her exposed delta. Angela shivered and relaxed. Julian was there, holding her lips apart, and Valerie's middle finger explored the pink cleft and lingered on the pearl-like nodule. Angela moaned her need.

'You know what to expect, don't you?' Valerie said softly, increasing the friction on the quivering clitoris. 'You've brought yourself off, and Aidan's done it for you. Isn't this true?'

'Yes,' Angela whispered.

'But you're still a virgin,' and Valerie sank a fingertip into her vulva, not enough to break the seal but to ascertain that it was in position. 'You are indeed a virgin,' she concluded, 'and you're ripe for deflowering... eager and ready for it... so very wet. Your lower lips are swollen with longing, red with desire, and your bud is near to bursting and your shapely arse is crying out for punishment.'

'Then do it, bring me off, don't tease me any longer,' Angela begged, willing to accept the cane, the rod, the whip, if only she could be released from such torture.

Maude was standing by the bed and Viola was kneeling between her legs. She had pushed back the black skirt and lifted it to waist height, and her face was buried in Maude's dark, hairy fork. The sight of her once-companion being brought to fulfilment increased Angela's lust, and Julian was paying attention to her nipples, moulding them into peaks, the three-fold pleasure of tits and clit driving her to the edge but not quite sufficient to push her over into bliss.

Then, as she was about to peak, all touch and movement ceased. She opened her eyes to see them looking down at her and, desperate with disappointment, her clit pulsing, she begged, 'Why have you stopped?'

'I'm obeying Aidan's orders. He said you were not to reach a climax until he was with you. I was to prepare you, arouse you, but leave the rest to him. Do you understand?'

'No, I don't, only that he's a selfish bastard,' Angela complained, her eyes flashing angrily. Then her hand dropped to her crotch and her finger started to palpate her love-bud. 'If you won't bring me off, then I'll do it myself.'

Valerie moved like lightning, bringing her hand down across Angela's in a vicious smack. 'You won't.'

'How will you stop me?' Angela challenged, but sat without moving, her hand smarting and tears running down her cheeks.

'We shall be with you at all times. And if you persist in this obstinate attitude, then I shall fetch the chastity belt. Don't fret, my dear, the evening will be here soon enough and you'll have more cock and orgasms than you can cope with,' Valerie told her, suddenly an ice queen capable of any cruelty and vice.

Chapter 5

Jacob Taylor stood on the arrival platform of Paddington Station and stared around. The crowds, the noise and bustle were astounding and he drank it all in.

Trains belched forth steam and smoke as they chugged in or departed. The stationmaster waved his flag and blew his whistle. Brawny uniformed men heaved at sack trucks. Passengers, some experienced and cool, others lost and flustered, found their connections or waited, ensconced in the restaurant, reading magazines. Some stared up at the large clock that took pride of place centre stage, or attempted to get hold of porters to take their bags and find them cabs.

The biggest city Jacob had ever visited was Bristol. To travel to London was a great adventure, one inspired by boredom with being a groom and the chivalric urge to assist Lady Angela, for whom he had long harboured a secret passion.

A short time had passed since Sir Barnaby's funeral and the collapse of the known world, in the shape of the Bayswater estate. Rumour had been rife. The very efficient grapevine that existed backstairs had reported that Lady Angela was no longer betrothed to Lord Driscol. He had, however, carried her off to Compton Hall and from there proposed to take her to London and place her in the care of a Mrs Valerie Gail, wife of a politician, to be trained for suitable employment. This had scandalised the servants. Lord Driscol was pronounced a cad for not honouring his promise, but they had problems of their own - the chief of which was finding work.

After saying goodbye to the mare, Daisy Belle, Jacob had formulated a plan. He obtained his Lordship's London address from one of the Compton stable lads. This was good enough for him. Packing a few belongings in a holdall he kissed his mother and left the cottage where he had first seen the light of day. He had relatives in the city; an uncle on his father's side who had tired of rural life and gone there to seek his fortune, setting up his own grocery business. Though Will had never met him, Arthur Taylor had kept communication open and let it be known that if ever his nephew wanted to visit, or find a job and live there, he would be more than welcome.

This was Jacob's destination, and he headed across the platform to where a row of cabs stood, and then decided that he'd better take a bus. He had money but knew he must make it stretch. Employment might not be instantaneous, although he was prepared to turn his hand to anything. His uncle was not aware of his imminent arrival. No time to send a letter; he would probably have reached the grocery store before it. He was taking potluck and hoping that the gods were smiling favourably on him.

Not celestial beings, perhaps, but he was certain he had aroused the interest of at least two of the gaudily dressed woman who were leaning on the barrier near the cab rank. 'Hello, darlin',' one of them called across in a cockney accent. 'Lookin' for a good time?'

'Not exactly, miss,' Jacob replied, doffing his cap and setting his bag on the ground. He did not suffer from shyness, and had never had difficulty in making contact with the opposite sex. He had always found them friendly, so modest himself that he did not realise it was his charm that won them over every time. They wanted to mother him and copulate with him, to take him under their wings and keep him from harm.

'Ooh, a country bumpkin. You're not from around 'ere, then?' said the youngest of the pair. Wearing a considerable amount of rouge, her flaming auburn hair was piled high under a wide-brimmed hat that flaunted purple ostrich plumes.

'Somerset, miss,' Jacob answered promptly and, although his heart was Lady Angela's, he was a red-blooded male in his prime, and the dress, style and cheap perfume of these streetwalkers appealed to him.

His cock twitched and he wondered if they might invite him home with them. What would they charge? He had heard the footmen talking about prostitutes, but never really thought he might meet one. He tingled with lust and enthusiasm, always the optimist and certain he had done the right thing and that

London was paved with gold. He would never forget his goal, that of offering his services to Lady Angela, but could not imagine that she might return his feelings, as far above him as the moon and stars.

'And where are you goin'?' asked the redhead, tickling him under the chin with the end of her feather boa.

'To a mansion in Mayfair,' he said, bringing out this prestigious address with as much ease as if he owned it.

'Oh, listen to '*im!* What a masher! Ain't that so, Doreen?' she teased, addressing her companion who was dark and sultry, with a scarlet gash of a mouth and hooded black eyes.

'Right enough, Tilly,' she replied, leaning towards Jacob, her full breasts bulging over her low-cut neckline, and the tip of her tongue poking out suggestively while her agile fingers ran down his jacket and waistcoat on their way to his flies.

His cock was stiff as a board, and he was afraid to move a muscle in case she disappeared like a mirage. He had never seen such alluring creatures, though he had taken his fill of maidservants and the girls who pulled pints behind the bar of the Red Lion, a public house in the village.

There had been three older women who had treated him to their favours, married women who were tired of their husband's infidelities and seeking solace in young, virile arms. But in spite of these dalliances he had remained true when it came to Lady Angela. He had envied Lord Driscol, watching him in the woods when he'd been seducing her, whipping her and playing with her cleft, making her moan in delight. Hidden behind the bushes, Jacob had undone his riding breeches and brought himself to a climax, roused beyond endurance and fired by the sight of her curly pubic hair. Ever after, that scene was his favourite masturbation fantasy.

"Ee's a fine big chap, ain't 'ee?' Tilly agreed, arching her brows at Jacob and letting her hand stray down to his prominent package. 'Want to come with us, deary?' she whispered. 'I'll bet your dick is burstin' with spunk. Bet it dribbles all day and all night, don't it? You got a girlfriend?'

'No,' Jacob returned, his cheeks reddening under his tan, her words going straight to his loins. 'But there is someone I admire greatly.'

'Ain't she the lucky one?' Doreen sneered, already looking beyond Jacob at several gentlemen in top hats, fur-collared greatcoats and pinstriped trousers who were regarding her and Tilly speculatively, as if they were slaves on the auction block. 'Come on, Till,' she added, 'stop messin' about. We got punters. Sorry, boy, but there's a livin' to be made and we needs the money.'

'You got anywhere to stay?' Tilly asked, while giving the interested males the eye. 'What's your name?'

'Jacob Taylor, and yes, I'm going to my uncle's in Soho.'

'I thought you said somethin' about Mayfair.'

'I'll go there later. I'm looking for someone.'

'This woman you fancy?'

'Maybe,' he said cagily. It did not seem proper for Angela's name to be bandied about.

'Right, I likes you, I really do,' Tilly said, reaching up to kiss him. Her breath smelt faintly of gin, reminding him of the barmaids and setting his pulse aflutter. 'You're a change from the old rams what usually want to tupp me,' she went on. 'Wait 'ere while I go round the back with that bearded granddaddy over there. He won't take long to do. I'll give 'im an 'and-job.'

And Tilly swaggered off about her business with such aplomb that Jacob could do nothing but admire her. Doreen disappeared too, and he was left there alone. 'I feel like a spare prick at a wedding,' he grumbled to himself, his body on fire. There was no privacy in which he might seize his throbbing cock and give himself relief. He doubted that Tilly and Doreen would come back, though the flame-haired one had seemed keen on him. Could one trust a whore, or was she so used to putting on an act that it came to her automatically? He waited, watching as other harlots went across and propositioned the gentlemen. Some were rejected but others drifted away with their clients, seeking a secluded spot.

This was torture. He was exceedingly uncomfortable and about to grab up his bag and find a bus that would carry him to his destination, when Tilly returned. She looked remarkably cool and was stuffing coins into her purse. There was no sign of Doreen.

Her eyes alighted on Jacob. 'You still 'ere?' she remarked, while he waited as mesmerised as a rabbit with a snake. She thrust her hand inside his shirt, almond-shaped nails seeking his nipples as she added, 'You want to fuck, darlin'?'

'I can't afford to pay you,' he confessed, as she ferreted about amidst his chest hair and pinched his sensitive flesh.

'We'll talk about that later,' she replied softly, her voice no longer waspish and strident.

She was a common harlot, crude and coarse, selling herself to almost anyone and yet Jacob wanted her, needing the relief that orgasm would bring. His heart was hammering, his cock throbbing painfully and threatening to make him come in his trousers. There was not much they could do on the platform, but she seized his hand and led him through the throng and past the cabs and omnibuses into the wet street. It was drizzling and umbrellas had sprung up like mushrooms everywhere. Tilly did not have one, and her feathers were soon drooping.

They walked for some time and then she took him through a gate and down a dark alley. It was cobbled and smelt of boiled cabbage and cats' urine. Rubbish lay thick in the gutter. She opened a door and they went up a steep, rickety staircase and she unlocked the door of a room at the top. Dim light filtered through the grimy windows and she took a match to an oil-lamp, and Jacob looked round at the dingy attic. It was untidy and dirty, littered with articles of clothing, and unwashed plates and empty beer bottles.

'You live here?' he asked, though none of it mattered compared to the driving urge for release.

'Yes,' she answered with a careless shrug. 'Live, sleep an' work 'ere. I bring punters back sometimes. Don't always do it in dirty stinking alleys. Depends 'ow much they wants to pay.'

'That's just it,' he mumbled, but reached out for her, 'I haven't much money.'

'I'm feelin' generous,' she said with a smile, then rubbed her body against his. 'I needs a little fun, you know, and I fancy you, Jacob.' His hands closed round her behind and he tried to kiss her, but she turned her head away. 'No, deary. Much as I likes you, we 'ave a rule that we never give kisses, only to close friends and relatives and kiddies.'

She pulled him down on the double bed, the blankets and pillows sour-smelling from innumerable encounters with clients. His hands closed round the breasts that she bared for him, and he sucked her puckered nipples, set in large brown circles. She hoisted her skirt and dingy white petticoats and displayed the thick bush between her legs. He could smell her sweat and the salty odour of her pussy. He fingered her hot wet sex, and tried to control his lust as he played with her bud, using foreplay he'd learned from one of his married lovers.

'Ah, so you knows 'ow to please a woman, do you?' she crooned, snuggling into him and working her clit against his hand. 'I 'ad a feelin' you might, lover-boy, that's why I brought you 'ere. Who taught you to finger-fuck? And I'll bet you can tongue-fuck, too, and take a girl up the back way.'

It was almost too much responsibility, that of pleasuring this experienced women who had probably had more men than Jacob had had hot dinners, but it gave him a feeling of pride. He would show her what a country lad could do, just as long as he could prevent premature ejaculation. He lowered his head and kissed her mound, then parted her labia with his tongue, finding the hard pink gem hidden within the folds. She started to jerk and moan and dug her nails into his scalp, holding him to his task. He felt her spasm and an extra gush of fluid covered his lips.

She moved then, sinuous as a snake, and he plunged his cock into her, wanting to lose himself in her darkness forever, to breathe in her salty odour, revel in her coarseness and he thrust fiercely, holding her buttocks so he might penetrate deeper and longer and harder. It did not last long. In a few vigorous thrusts he was there, coming in a surge of feeling that tossed him high and then dropped him down. For a second he was aware of nothing else, lost in blissful sensations. It blotted out the memory of the woman he had come to London to find, but this lasted only a moment.

He slid out of Tilly, who sprawled on her back, eyes closed as she sighed contentedly. Now all Jacob wanted was to leave. He found his clothes but was unwilling to appear churlish. He bent over and placed a kiss on Tilly's brow, whispering, 'Look here, I like you, I really do. Can I see you again?'

She opened her eyes. They were ringed with smudged black kohl. A warm smile curved her lips, and she said, 'You don't 'ave to say that, though it's sweet of you. You'll find me in the Bunch of Grapes pub most nights. I may be busy

50

with a bloke, but we can work somethin' out,' and she turned on her side and burrowed into the pillow, closing her eyes again.

Jacob let himself out. He looked up at the grey sky and was warmed by the thought that it not only stretched above him, but Lady Angela as well. He was sure he would see her soon.

There was more titivation before they were ready to drive to Temple Grove where Aidan was holding his party. Angela was relieved at Valerie's decision to leave her mound unshaved. She prayed that Aidan would not demand this sacrifice, for she was proud of her pubic floss that somehow symbolised her emergence into womanhood. However, it seemed that she had little say in what was to happen to her.

The theme for the night was Eastern. Valerie was enthusiastic, exclaiming, 'The costumes are so seductive... transparent and flattering, and there are jewels galore! Come here, Angela, and let me attire you.'

She was dressed like Cleopatra, in a very revealing white pleated skirt, slit up the front to her fork. Her waist was emphasised by a scintillating girdle with red sequins, and it had a panel that hung down between her thighs. Every time she moved it swung to one side, giving a flash of her hairless mons. Her fine breasts with their puckered tips and dark aureoles were bare beneath a wide, lavishly ornamented collar. Her hair had been crimped and adorned with a bejewelled headdress. Gold sandals encased her feet and drew the eye to her bare, beautiful legs. Angela envied her, and wished she had her insouciance, poise and exceptional looks.

In spite of her reservations about the coming event, a quiver of excitement gripped her as Valerie and Maude helped her on with her outfit. The long pier-glass threw back her reflection and as each piece was added so her former self seemed to slip away, replaced by an odalisque... a harem slave whose only task was to pleasure her master, bow to his every wish and submit to the lash if he thought she needed correction. Somehow Angela no longer found this idea repulsive. Valerie's views were brushing off on her. But how would she feel when she actually faced Aidan?

She looked every inch the *houri*. Her legs gleamed through the pale pink chiffon pantaloons embroidered with gold thread. The garment hung low on her hips and her navel was bare. 'Hmm, that needs piercing, then you can wear a ring in it, or a gemstone,' commented Valerie. 'I shall speak to Aidan about it.'

'But I don't want it done, neither do I want my nipples pierced like Julian's,' Angela protested. 'I think it is barbaric.'

'And you really believe that your opinion is worth spit?' Valerie replied unkindly. 'It will be better for you if you cooperate, although, come to think of it, Aidan does like a rebellious victim. Says this affords him more enjoyment than a weak and willing one.'

'I've never met such a decadent crew,' Angela snapped, and then yelped as Valerie slapped her hard on her bottom, the thin trousers offering no protection.

51

'Keep still,' ordered Maude, a threatening figure in a black burnous that opened over tight trousers. She was naked to the waist, her full breasts crowned with prominent nipples, and she wore several chains round her neck that dangled down to her waist.

Angela stood like a waxen image as they dressed her in a flimsy chemise and a tiny velvet bolero that did not conceal her assets. She gasped and could not control the stab of desire as Valerie pinched and rolled her nipples, making them stand out.

'Oh you're ready for it, my dear,' she murmured with a vulpine smile. 'I was right to keep you waiting. Don't you agree?' And she dipped a hand between Angela's legs, cupping her mound and pressing a finger into her damp cleft through the thin material.

Angela did not stir, passion rising hot within her. Valerie gave a knowing smile and withdrew her caresses. Then Angela slipped her feet into slippers with turned-up toes and let them fasten a necklace of semi-precious stones round her neck with earrings and bracelets to match. A veil was fixed to a circlet on her hair, and arranged so that it drifted over to part cover her face.

'Gorgeous!' Valerie said, standing back to view her handiwork. 'What do you think, Julian? Do you want to roger her?'

'Yes, mistress,' he answered, bowing low before her, 'but you are my goddess. I need no one but you.'

'Then you're a fool,' Valerie retorted crisply. 'Tonight you won't get the choice. Aidan will have planned what he wants you to do. I should imagine that you will be in demand. A pretty young man like you is sure to appeal to the more adventurous among his guests.'

Angela was given a velvet cloak to drape over her and the party moved towards the door, down the staircase and out to where a coach waited.

It was full dark by now, though gaslights illumined the thoroughfare that was wide and tree-lined, a far cry from the slums. It was busy, a constant stream of vehicles conveying their occupants to dinner parties or restaurants or theatrical performances. It was a world to which Angela was accustomed and made her momentarily forget her misfortune.

They skirted St James's Park and turned into an avenue flanked by impressive houses set in spacious gardens. The coach swung through the gates of one, its wheels crunching on gravel as it circumnavigated a short drive and halted before the front door. There were footmen waiting to assist the ladies out, and each one was handsome and well blessed, wearing breeches and tailcoats.

'Aidan likes to surround himself with beauty,' Valerie explained, wrapped in a cloak identical to Angela's. 'You won't find anyone remotely plain in his entourage.' And she familiarised herself with one of the servants' genitals while he stood there, impassive, as if well used to this intimate treatment.

Angela was led through the hall and out by way of a conservatory filled with exotic plants, palms and banana trees, and jungle orchids that emitted a strong perfume.

Valerie was on one side of her and Maude on the other. Julian had been sent ahead. The house was quiet and this surprised her as she had expected it to be filled with people and noise, but now she was taken through French doors and along a colonnade. Ahead of her she saw the dazzle of light streaming from a rotunda with many windows and a domed roof.

'Where am I?' she asked anxiously.

'This is Aidan's playground, where he loves to entertain. It was added to the original house by one of his ancestors a hundred years ago,' Valerie replied.

As they drew closer the circular building loomed over them, eclipsing the stars with its brightness. Music came from within, and the sound of voices and laughter. Angela's cloak had been removed and she shivered in her thin garments and took one reluctant step after another. Valerie and Maude were uncloaked too, their costumes or lack of them suitably shocking, their attitude bold.

They stopped at a pair of doors that opened as Valerie knocked on them. A crimson curtain separated them from the interior, but this was pulled back with a jangle of rings on brass poles. With her heart pounding like a drum, Angela entered the room beyond, lit by electrified chandeliers with sparkling crystal drops that radiated light on the crowd below. She had eyes for only one, however. Aidan occupied a divan in full view of his guests. It resembled the throne of a potentate. He was wearing a brocade robe with a sable collar, and holding a goblet between his hands and staring straight at her.

'Ah, there you are, my dear,' he said, while all conversation ceased. He held out a hand and beckoned her closer, addressing the throng as he did so. 'This is Angela. She is a virgin, gentlemen, but don't let this excite you, for I shall be the one to deflower her.'

Good-natured cries of 'Shame!' greeted this, and Angela felt herself to be the cynosure of all eyes.

The invited gentry reclined on cushions on the benches surrounding the central space dominated by the divan. Some were dressed as pashas or sultans, while others were in evening suits, with a flash of diamond cufflinks and jewelled orders. Several wandered around, fingering the girls who wore black stockings, satin stays and high-heeled shoes or outrageously brief harem outfits. These were not ladies, but women who offered their services for payment. Wine flowed and champagne corks popped. The girls shrieked and giggled and were coquettish, leading the men on. Some of them were not so young, middle-aged harlots steeped in every vice, their breasts bulging over the tops of their corsets, their large backsides bare and their hairy clefts displayed wantonly.

Not only female prostitutes obliged. Angela was surprised to see good-looking young men accepting advances, and some who she at first took to be women dressed in fine gowns, but on closer inspection proved to be too tall, too broad-shouldered and too narrow of hip. Men disguised as women? What was this odd world into which Aidan was introducing her?

There were slaves of both sexes chained to pillars, heads drooping, naked and vulnerable and subjected to the lash, helpless to defend themselves or avoid the hands that made free with their bodies. Murals of a scandalous nature ringed the walls, mythological legends carried out with no thought for modesty. Goddesses frolicked with satyrs who had goats' legs and horns and enormous phalli. Armour-clad warriors raped enemy women. Gods took their pleasure with human females. And there were photographs in another section, enlargements of the kind shown her by Valerie. The air was filled with music, sensual Chopin nocturnes played by a man with a shock of white hair and strong hands who was seated at the grand piano with an admiring group around him.

Aidan drew Angela down beside him on the divan and gestured to a servant. The man was immediately at his elbow with a silver salver holding a champagne flute. 'Drink, Angela,' Aidan said, leaning closer to her. 'This is a rare vintage and it will relax you.'

His robe fell open and the sight of his naked body, so muscular and hirsute, with the large cock rising from the black thicket, caused a stab of lust to pass through her. Valerie leaned over the back of the couch, eyes heavy-lidded, mouth pouting as she said, 'Have I done well, master? Is she all you desire?'

He scowled and shook off the hand that would have descended to his lower belly, snapping, 'She looks well enough but it is too early to tell how much pleasure she will give me. If she fails, then you will be punished.'

Valerie looked more excited than frightened by this threat and Angela wondered what lay between the two of them. Was she his mistress? Or was it deeper even than that?

She sipped the wine. It was red as blood, with a bittersweet aftertaste. It burned her throat and settled like fire in her belly. Within seconds she felt dizzy, Aidan's smiling face slightly out of focus as she managed to gasp, 'What is it?'

'That's for me to know and you to accept,' he replied, his voice seeming to come from a distance. 'Drink up, my love.'

By now she was less conscious of being watched by dozens of prurient eyes, less conscious of any threat from him, only aware of his attraction. Even the frisson of fear she always experienced in his presence was arousing. So why was she still reluctant to surrender to him? In spite of the drugged drink, there was a stubborn core within her that clung steadfastly to her principles.

He held her closer to his nude body, enfolding her in his robe. His phallus was like an iron bar pressing into her. He opened her chemise and palmed her breast. She was fuddled by the drink, but in control enough to say, 'What are you going to do?'

'Enjoy you,' he answered huskily and his cock jumped in anticipation.

'Not here, not in public...' she protested, attempting to draw back, but his grip tightened, demonstrating the power of his well-honed muscles.

'And why not? It won't be the first time they have witnessed my virility,' he

54

said loudly. 'And you will comply, willingly or not.'

'Have you no respect for me?' she cried, all too aware of the solid thigh placed between hers and unable to resist working her pubis up and down on it.

He chuckled wickedly. Her protests delighted him, it seemed, adding zest to the encounter. He feathered his fingers over her breasts and down her body, past the exposed navel and into the top of her pantaloons. His touch was that of an expert, sliding over the downy mound and finding her wet furrow, then concentrating on the tip of her swollen clitoris.

'Respect, dearest? How can I respect someone who let me down so badly?' His voice rang in her ear as he tongued the sensitive lobe, sending spasms to her nipples and sex.

'What do you mean? I loved you and thought I was to be your wife. I didn't mean to harm you,' she whimpered, angry and tearful at the injustice of it.

Aidan continued to rub her, and the feeling was mounting uncontrollably. 'But you did... or rather, your gambler of a father cheated me out of your dowry,' he muttered, and his fingering grew harsh and dry, causing her more discomfort than pleasure. 'This left me somewhat embarrassed,' he continued. 'My creditors were none too pleased, and now I have to go to all the boring trouble of wooing another insipid virgin with a wealthy father... really wealthy this time. I shall have my accountant go into his affairs with a fine toothcomb before I commit myself.'

His words pierced her heart like a dagger, and his harsh handling of her most sensitive organ made her writhe away, trying to avoid him. 'So this is what it's all about; revenge,' she hissed, making the onlookers concentrate on the drama taking place between their host and his latest victim.

'You could say that,' he agreed, and hauled her against him again. 'But you'll make it up to me.'

'How?' she asked, beating against his chest with closed fists.

'Like this,' he laughed, seizing her wrists in one hand. 'Fight me, vixen. Don't make it easy. I want you to hate and despise me and, by God, you shall!'

He snapped his fingers and a curtain whipped aside. A cheer went up from those who recognised the purpose of the small, neat man with a waxed moustache who was adjusting a machine that stood on a tripod. Horrified, Angela knew what it was, and guessed Aidan's diabolical purpose. His fingers fastened vicelike round her upper arm and he propelled her forward. They stopped close to the photographer.

'Undress,' Aidan commanded. 'Unless you want me to do it for you.'

'No!' And she started to move. Her fingers flew to take off the bolero and find the chemise buttons. Now she was naked to the waist, apart from jewellery.

'Stop,' Aidan ordered and she paused, turning gracefully to look at him. There was a pop and a flash.

'Beautiful!' exclaimed the photographer. 'What a lovely model. Collectors will be clamouring for copies of this, my lord.'

'Better ones to come,' Aidan promised, and loosened the drawstring at the top of her harem trousers. They slid down to her feet and she shook them off, along with her slippers. She was naked, apart from the veil attached to her hair. He motioned her to the couch. 'Sit there with your legs wide open, hands behind you, breasts thrust out and your head lolling back.'

There was a moment's hush as the photographer, with the help of his assistant, moved the camera forward and prepared the lighting. He took several shots, and it was easier than Angela had thought, though uncomfortable holding the pose for so long.

The spectators were losing interest in the proceedings, seeking the greater stimulus of caning girls and buggering men, though they paid attention when Aidan said to Angela, 'Now on your knees with your legs spread.'

She took up this position on the divan, and it was only because she had been imbibing in the potent drink that she could bring herself to do it. She hollowed her spine and raised her bottom and her secrets were fully exposed for everyone to see, the plump purse split like a luscious fig, the crease that divided her buttocks, the tiny, puckered mouth of her anus. The air was cool on her fevered parts and, face buried in the cushions, she heard the click over and over, and knew that, successful development in a darkroom permitting, her sexual attributes would be captured there for posterity.

'Just one or two more,' Aidan said, stage-managing the whole thing. 'Angela, lie on your back and masturbate for me.'

It was easier to obey than to argue. She was so hazy and filled with mixed emotions that she did as he ordered, warmed by the velvet beneath her, forgetting the crowd, the photographer and even Aidan as her fingers explored her cunt, gathering juice to lubricate her clitoris. She circled it, rubbed and played with it, and pinched her nipples with her other hand. The photographer was flashing away busily and Angela raised her hips and moved her pubis against her fingers.

She yearned to reach a climax before anyone stopped her. Valerie had deliberately frustrated her and now it was likely that Aidan might do the same, for his own twisted amusement. Perhaps she could cheat on them, have it quietly and secretly before anyone knew. But she was too tense for this to happen.

Aidan flung off his robe and stood above her. From that angle he looked enormously tall, wearing an undeserved halo of light around his head. She shuddered with almost superstitious awe as he addressed her. 'The time has come, Angela, and what more fitting way for you to lose your maidenhead than in front of a camera. We move with the times, my dear.'

'You can't be serious,' she objected, staring up into his smiling eyes.

'Oh, but I am,' he assured her. 'I rather fancy being photographed while I'm fucking you. It will be something you can show your grandchildren in years to come.'

'What a disgraceful idea.' She was really alarmed; lust withering under the cold blast of reality. He was hell-bent on doing it, and nothing she could say

56

would stop him.

Everyone was watching now, and the photographer most of all, though concealed under his black cloth. His assistant was ready to ignite the flash. Angela struggled, but her arms were pulled back and her wrists held by Valerie on one side and Julian on the other.

Aidan gripped her legs and forced them apart, then positioned himself between them. Flash, click went the camera, catching him whilst he paused. He lowered himself on Angela, and she felt the pressure of his cock against her entrance. She muffled a scream, even then unwilling to admit that she was terrified. After one photo her arms were released.

The photographer was behind Aidan, so that his face was concealed but not hers. Aidan hitched her legs up round his waist and pushed, inching into her. She clenched her muscles but it was useless. The pain was excruciating and he gave her no respite, sweating as he wrestled to rupture her hymen, his arms bracing his weight. A murmur rose from the spectators.

'Look at me,' he demanded harshly, and she let herself drown in the darkness of his eyes. Then he took his penis in hand and wetted the end with her juice, then rested it against her vulva again and, with a push, sank into the depths of her virgin passage.

She shrieked and the watchers expressed their delight in the show. 'Go it, Aidan!' some of them advised. 'Bring tears to her eyes!'

The camera flashed again but this was of no significance to her as the pain started to melt into pleasure. Aidan moved slowly and his cock was hot and long and solid, filling her completely, nudging against the gateway to her womb. He thrust again, getting faster, and she was so wet that now he was sliding in and out easily, but no matter how she wriggled the root of his prick missed her clitoris and she longed for a finger or lips to make her come. Aidan paused momentarily, as if aware of her need, but he was beyond the point of no return, thrusting harder, gathering momentum, and she clung to him with her arms around his neck, praying for release but not quite reaching it.

He was oblivious to everything except his own satisfaction, lying full length now. She was crushed beneath him. Unable to reach the peak she sobbed as she begged him to bring her to completion. He kissed her savagely and his passion roused her, his dominance exciting her as she dug her nails into his back and shoulders, leaving long red scratches.

He drove his loins against hers, his pubic bone chaffing her love-bud, his balls in their scrotal sac brushing her inner thighs. Angela had never known a sensation like it, her inner muscles clasping him, her clit yearning to be rubbed. She welcomed his possession now, the heat and ardour of him, the masculine intensity that drove him to take her and use her and experience his climax.

He threw back his head and barked his release. She felt his cock pulse inside her and then the flood of his milky tribute. There was a second's pause, and then thunderous clapping. The photographer took a final shot of Aidan rising from the prone girl, godlike and triumphant.

'Well done, old chap!' his friends enthused.

'I say, you were right; she was a virgin. No longer, though, thanks to your mighty todger!'

Angela sat up painfully. Her thighs were sore, her tender female crack, too. And for what? Was that it then? This act that was talked of as the be all and end all? She had longed for love, or at least fulfilment, and had neither if these from Aidan.

He looked at her and said, 'Now you are no longer a greensick girl. I have transformed you into a woman.'

'Don't flatter yourself,' she remarked coldly and got to her feet, even though the room was swaying. She reached for her clothes, but Maude was there preventing her.

Aidan scowled, then gave a sinister smile. 'Still rebellious?' he sneered. 'I can see that you require further training.' He turned to Valerie, cupped her breasts in his hands and added, 'I think a spell on the crosspiece is in order. See to it.'

A cheer arose from his guests, and wild excitement reigned as they followed Aidan into another part of the rotunda where only the closest of his companions were permitted to go.

Chapter 6

'No... please no!' Angela cried, as she was lifted by two of Aidan's near-naked footmen and taken, not to the whipping-post, but to where a tangle of leather and chains hung from a hook in the ceiling.

She began to tremble, knees turning to water, her thighs bathed in Aidan's spunk and her virgin blood. The footmen handled her intimately, her cunt was explored and her breasts and she could do nothing but endure. Indeed, she was in such a frustrated and high-strung state that even their caresses were welcome. One bent his head and sucked her nipples, drawing them out to strawberry points. The other smiled darkly and snapped a collar round her neck, fur-lined so that it did not damage the skin, and metal cuffs were closed round her wrists before they were raised high above her head and fastened to the chain above. A rigid bar was placed between her feet to keep them apart. It was clamped to her ankles tightly and she was immobilised.

Aidan's friends jostled each other in their eagerness not to miss a moment of this entertainment. Some were intoxicated on wine, but in the main Aidan's performance and the promise of further examples of his dominance over his latest slave aroused them to fever pitch. The whores were doing a roaring trade, albeit that they had already received a substantial wage from the host for their services that night.

He swaggered in. He had changed into black leather breeches and top boots, stripped to the waist, the light playing over his magnificent torso and muscular arms. Even the harlots gazed at him in almost drooling admiration, and they were as hard-bitten as they come. He carried a short whip in one hand, striking it against his thigh as he walked over to where Angela stood between her guards. He stared at her long and hard, then gestured to his helpers.

Before she could protest a ball-gag was thrust into her mouth, her teeth jarring against its rubber surface. The last thing she saw was Aidan's sardonic smile before a blindfold was settled over her eyes, its ties tangling in her hair. Locked in darkness and discomfort she could not stop the tears welling up. This was a far cry from the wedding night she had once dreamed about. Aidan had treated her like an animal, using her, abusing her, and there was more to come.

'Oh father, father, how could you have left me in such dire straits?' she mourned inside. 'What price your gambling against a daughter's affliction?'

No answer came from beyond the grave.

She gave a muffled cry, swaying in her bonds as someone hauled on the chain, lifting her so that only the balls of her feet touched the floor and there was a fearful ache in her stretched arms. Someone's fingers were on her pussy, steadying her, then whoever it was started to rock her. She hoped it was Aidan, but there was no way of knowing. Hands were crawling all over her now, sweaty hands or dry ones, male hands, maybe female. They toyed with her nipples, pinching or caressing, and slipped into her cleft, finding her clit and rubbing it till she was on the brink of ecstasy. She moaned into the gag and writhed in her restraints, and voices murmured encouragingly or taunted her maliciously. Someone trailed his penis over her thigh, leaving a wet smear.

'Stop that!' Aidan shouted angrily, and the cock was withdrawn.

So he cared if she was molested, she thought. Or could it only be done at his command? Was that the power he wanted over her? She sensed his presence and felt his body positioned between her splayed legs. His hands, and she was certain they were his, fondled her intimately. No part of her was safe from his examination. The crowd had fallen back and the silence was absolute. It was as if she and Aidan were alone on a mountaintop. He left her and she sobbed. The stillness was intense, her hearing extra keen because she could neither see or move. There was no way she could know what was going to happen to her.

Then she heard a swish and he struck the first blow.

She gasped at the impact, agony firing up from her lower belly where he had chosen to begin her torment, the lash biting into her mons. The breath rushed back with the burn of agonising pain, and her bound body arched and her limbs twisted but she could not escape. Groaning into the gag and waiting in fearful suspense for the next stripe she heard him behind her. There was the sound of something hitting the air, not the whip. Then what?

She did not have long to wait. The implement disturbed the space in front of her. He held it under her nose. She could smell the freshness of the outdoors, and it transported her back to the country where birch saplings awaited man's need to transform them into means of punishment. Love juice seeped from her and her clitoris throbbed, joining the scalding heat of her welts. As if well aware of this her master pressed the switch into her labial folds, concentrating on that swollen nodule. She could not resist seesawing against it, begging for more with each tell-tale lurch of her hips. She heard him chuckle, and there was no doubt that it was Aidan. He stroked the rod up and down her delta, softly at first, then harder and harder till she was gasping her passion, unable to cry out in pain and rapture.

He moved round to her backside. With a whistle the birch cut the air and she gave a strangled scream as it connected with her tender derrière. The unseen audience could no longer contain themselves, breaking into wild whoops and cheers. Aidan picked up speed, the sapling rising and falling till she was sure there could not be an inch of skin left unmarked.

Then, just when she felt her senses slipping away, he stopped. His hands removing the ball-gag and others were releasing her bonds. She would have fallen had he not held her firmly against his chest. His fingers were at the back of her head, undoing the blindfold. The light dazzled her. There were leering faces all around and couples at every stage of fornication. Aidan's face blazed above her like a dark comet and she was shocked by her desire to fondle his body and kiss his lips after he had abused her so savagely.

'Well, Lady Angela Bayswater, I think you enjoyed that almost as much as I did,' he mocked. 'My cock is hard as a broom handle. Look.'

She stared at his leather-covered crotch and could see the shape of his erection straining against the fastening. She yearned to spring the buttons and take it between her lips, tasting the salty flavour of him, sniffing his testicles and the wiry hair coating his pubis. Most of all she wanted his fingers to bring her off, then his mighty weapon plunging into her vagina. 'Why are you so cruel to me?' she sighed, and could not help rubbing her palm over that solid bulge. 'I would have loved you for ever, Aidan.'

'I'm demonstrating that there are depths within you that you didn't know you had,' he answered, and she felt his cock twitch. 'As for love? I think you still love me. Which is your greater emotion... love or hate? Both are opposite sides of the same coin.'

Angela's senses swam. She was so confused she could not answer this riddle. In that mad moment she did not care what he did with her. He glanced round at his panting, eager guests and gave an ironic smile, then he gathered Angela to him and picked her up, one arm beneath her shoulders, the other under her knees.

'Oh, ah!' she moaned, her bruised body aching.

He looked down at her, supporting her without effort. 'Are you sore, little one?' he murmured, then moved towards a door. 'Don't worry. I have salve to soothe you.'

'Where are you taking me?' Angela said, nuzzling against his bare chest.

'To my bedroom,' he replied.

'Are they coming?' She indicated his quests.

'You ask too many questions. Wait and see,' he teased

He left the rotunda, using a private way that included a spiral staircase leading to the upper floors and his private apartment. Angela marvelled at his strength, for he bore her as easily as if she was made of thistledown. They encountered no one on the way, and arrived at last at a corridor leading to a panelled door set in an architrave carved with acanthus leaves and vines, with the Green Man's face peering between them. Aidan set her down momentarily and inserted a key in the brass lock. The door swung open and she was enchanted by the dim lighting within and the gorgeous smell of incense wafting towards her. He kicked the door shut, swept her up again and carried her across the thick carpet into the bedroom.

It was the most extraordinary chamber she had ever seen; the first impression was one of sombre grandeur. The walls were draped in purple and black, interspersed with large paintings of nude, big-bosomed woman and well-endowed men locked in obscene embraces. Not only males with females, but every other combination, too. The furniture was heavily embossed and gothic in style, the fireplace a monument to the architect who had designed it to rear ceiling-wards, made of black marble with columns and cornucopia, the mantel upheld by statues of Hercules and Atlas. Coal burned in the ornamental basket and gleaming fire irons reflected the glow.

Aidan did not put her down until he'd reached the bed. This in itself was daunting, with its extra width, length and towering posts, its ebony curtains and coverlet. To Angela's embarrassment she saw that the tester supported a mirror that reflected everything taking place below it.

He laid her on the soft mattress and smiled at her consternation, saying, 'We shall be able to watch ourselves in the throes of love.'

She shuddered and attempted to draw a portion of the silk quilt over her. 'Have you no shame at all?' she said bitterly.

'None whatever,' he rejoined, and the whole situation seemed to be according him a great deal of amusement.

'This room!' she exclaimed, and noted that, as in the rotunda, there were copies of those scandalous photographs everywhere. 'It's monstrous! How can you sleep peacefully in such a place?'

'Easily. I sleep like a babe,' he answered, and poured himself a snifter from the cut-glass decanter on the nightstand. 'What's worrying you? The photographs? My dear, those taken of us this evening will soon join them, I can assure you.'

'You wouldn't...' she countered.

'I do anything I fancy,' he remarked, and the mattress sagged as he sat down beside her and kissed her neck, his breath faintly tainted with whiskey. 'Those pictures will make me a handsome profit, too, when I offer them on the underground market. There are plenty of gentlemen who would give their eye-teeth for a copy.'

'You have no heart... no conscience...' she said, trying to pull away from his arm that circled her waist, but he would have none of this, putting down the glass, and with a toe against the heel, removing his boots. His breeches followed and he stood there, legs astride, staring at her in all the fine glory of his masculinity, his cock jutting forward proudly. Its size was daunting, even though she had already experienced it inside her. She wanted him to do it again, but he had other ideas.

'Look up at the mirror,' he said, and laid her back. 'Open your legs. Watch as I pleasure you.'

She raised her eyes and saw the astonishing spectacle of herself lying there with her legs spread. Nothing was sacred any more. Under the tangle of damp public floss her sex stood out blatantly, the lips pink and swollen, the slit engorged and the clitoris looking like a small version of a penis, and equally hard.

'I'm sore,' she complained, attempting to cover herself.

Aidan pulled the quilt off so that she lay on the black satin sheets, the paleness of her body starkly emphasised. Nowhere to hide. He opened a drawer in the bedside cabinet and took out a jar. 'Be still,' he said, 'and enjoy the view,' and he took off the lid and commenced applying a sweet-scented ointment to her bruises, beginning with those on her belly and mons.

She wanted to protest but his touch was magical, the salve a potent spell that removed pain. She went limp as he massaged it into her skin, not only on the bruises but other parts as well. She sighed deeply and relaxed, even peeked at herself in that unbelievably abandoned pose, with a man's hands roaming all over her. And such a man, too! His penis was growing bigger, if that were possible, astounding her with its length and girth.

He sat at her side, careful not to block her view of the mirror, continuing to apply the salve and spread it even further. He reached down and let his slippery hand enter her cleft. He parted the outer and then the inner lips, and the sensation of those agile, slippery, experienced fingers palpating her was nothing short of bliss. She wanted to watch now, and could see her sex, shiny and pink and wet, glistening like some exotic jungle flower, her love-bud, her labia, the entrance to her vagina.

His eyes met hers in the mirror, the little laughter lines deepening at the outer corners, his sensual lips parting over even white teeth. That arrogant smile angered her. It was as if he was sure of victory, confident that she would be his creature forever. It was degrading to watch herself responding to his caresses, but she could not resist it or stop her hips from rising a little, pressing against his fingers. There was no time now for loathing or hatred. She wanted him, for good or ill. The mirror threw back a vision of his muscular shoulders and taut hips, the hollows in his flanks, the long thighs. And then she could no longer see her pubis as he lowered himself between her legs, his face buried in her mound, his tongue licking her clitoris.

He reached up and rolled each nipple between thumb and forefinger, tripling the acute sensations of pleasure. And all the time he kept up a relentless nibbling and sucking, and she buried her hands in his hair and murmured incoherent love-words, unaware of what she was saying. Her orgasm rose, higher and higher and she peaked, crying out, and then clinging to him, trembling. He raised his head, slid his body upwards, threw a leg over her thighs and dug a knee between them. Watching the couple in the mirror she brought up her legs and rested them on his shoulders while his cock-tip rubbed against her vulva. Then, with a push, he thrust his prick inside her.

This time it did not hurt, though it felt warm and huge and she wriggled against it, taking it even deeper. Because he had satisfied her she was willing to accord him the same pleasure, her passage fully lubricated, her muscles demanding this large object to clench round. Even the pain of her birching was no longer significant. If anything it added to her desire to subject herself to this forceful man.

She wanted to belong to him through all eternity, delighting in her slavery. She would indulge him and, in the end, he would love her as she had once thought and make her his wife. Whether this was true or a result of the aphrodisiac she had drunk there was no way of knowing, but whatever it was, Angela was in heaven.

She raised her legs, digging her nails into his back, hugging him closer to her. By now he was no longer in control, bucking wildly as he chased his climax. He reached it, grunting and thrusting, his libation spurting from him. He fell on top of her and she revelled in his weight. It made her feel complete, conquered and enslaved.

She was utterly replete, cuddling him in her arms when he finally rolled off, and pulling the quilt over them both. He slept, his eyes hidden beneath thick, curling lashes, the lines smoothed from his face, making him look almost boyish. The house was now silent, the revellers either having taken their departure or snoring where they had fallen in the rotunda.

They could still be happy together, she thought, then it would all seem like a bad dream, and worn out by their excesses, she dropped into oblivion.

Angela was in the Lairdland Manor grounds, running across the lawns and into the little copse, making towards the lake. She was happy and light-hearted and her father was not far away. He had gone fishing and she was to join him. She could hear the sound of water and splashing and laughter. He wasn't alone, then? She became anxious, pushing her way through bushes and undergrowth that clung stubbornly to her skirt. It was as if they were trying to stop her reaching him.

In her dream she began to cry and woke sobbing in Aidan's bed. She was disoriented and it took a few seconds for reality to take hold. Her eyelids flew open. There was the tester with that great mirror that had reflected her impure actions. There were the curtains, the rude paintings and photographs, and a servant had been in to tend the fire. But it was the sounds that had brought her back from the dream world, similar sounds to those she'd thought she heard coming from the lake - splashing, laughter, girlish cries. They were issuing from an adjoining room.

Angela sat up and swung her legs over the side of the mattress. She was completely naked and her clothing, such as it was, had been left in the rotunda. A robe lay across the foot of the bed. She stood up and reached for it. One of Aidan's, obviously. It was very grand, made of rich brocade in dark hues, with a sable collar and a girdle with twelve-inch tassels. She shrugged her shoulders into it and wrapped it round her. It was too long and tripped her feet, and the sleeves fell way below her hands, but she folded them back and made towards those intriguing noises.

The door was ajar and daylight streamed through the gap, whereas the curtains in the bedchamber were still closed. Curiosity overcoming trepidation, Angela crossed the threshold. She was in a spacious bathroom, with a massive tub supported on claw-feet. It even had a shower arrangement at one end, and the taps were solid gold. There were padded benches here and there, and a china washbasin that matched the bath. The walls and floor were tiled, and the water and iron radiators heated from a system lodged somewhere deep in the bowels of the house. It was apparent that Aidan never stinted when it came to luxury, or anything else for that matter.

Angela was brought up short by the sight of him performing an act that stunned her. Julian was lying on his stomach across one of the benches, facing her, and Aidan was behind him, gripping him firmly round the hips and driving his penis in and out of the young man's fundament. Julian was groaning and it sounded as if he was enjoying the experience. She remembered how Aidan had done it to her and how painful it had been. Julian must be accustomed to this. But Aidan! Her once betrothed whom she was thinking might be reconciled to his monetary loss and marry her even now, how could he do such a thing?

'Dear God!' she exclaimed, and four pairs of eyes switched to her. Valerie and Maude were in the bath, washing one another, their hands caressing breasts and cunts. It was a scene of such depravity that Angela wanted to turn tail and flee.

'Ah, awake at last, my love. Come and join us,' Aidan said, unperturbed, even though his violent pumping movements indicated that he was reaching a climax.

'I won't!' Angela shouted, and the fragile hope that had blossomed in her last night crumbled into dust. He didn't love her! He loved no one but himself and took his pleasures where he willed.

'I thought you'd tamed her, master,' Valerie said, her body arching, head back, eyes half closed as she rubbed her crotch against Maude's fingers, the water sloshing.

'I have. The girl loves me. Ain't that so, Angela?' he averred, but his face was contorted with the extreme pleasure of Julian's anus closing round him.

'You fiend!' she cried. 'What do you want with me? Why don't you let me go?'

He stared at her, and his expression was contemptuous. 'No one is stopping you. Leave when you like, but remember that you have no money and no friends, except us. Remember, too, that I shall find you wherever you hide. You can't escape me.'

'I can manage alone,' Angela declared, blinded by tears of rage and disappointment.

It seemed that none of them were interested in anything but their own orgasms, and she slipped away, running from the apartment and finding the guestroom allotted to her. Her belongings were there, still unpacked. She flung open the cases, rooting through their contents and finding underwear and a blouse, also a simple black skirt and jacket. She used the toilet, washed quickly and pinned up her hair, then dressed at speed, afraid that Aidan might arrive at any moment and demand that she stay. Disgusted by this latest example of his sexuality, and hurt beyond reckoning by his callous treatment and the way in which he had wrested her virginity from her without caring, she packed more clothing into a valise and added her jewellery. She had hardly any money and was determined to find the nearest pawnshop and turn her trinkets into cash.

Ready at last she peered into the passage. It was deserted and, lugging the heavy travelling bag, she found the head of the main staircase and descended. The servants were obviously taking advantage of Aidan and his guests' delayed awakening, though the smell of fried bacon and newly baked bread drifted from the direction of the kitchen, reminding her that she was hungry.

There was no one on duty at the front door and she succeeded in getting it open. It was nine in the morning and the sound of traffic was like music to her ears. The world was out there, and opportunity to escape from the tyrannical Aidan. Angela made her way down the steps and into the front garden in the direction of the gates.

Suddenly a figure stepped from behind a tree and her heart nearly stopped beating. It was a man and, though he was vaguely familiar, she was petrified. 'What do you want?' she quavered, clasping her reticule tightly.

'Don't you know me, milady? I'm Jacob. Jacob Taylor, who used to be your groom. Oh, I'm so glad to have found you. I came to London looking for you, just to see if you were safe, that is,' he answered, and she recognised his boyish face and earnest eyes, his straggly brown hair and sturdy frame.

'The groom,' she said, voice shrill with relief. 'Hello, Jacob, and how is Daisy Belle?' And the tears rose up as she remembered her mare.

'Fine, when I left,' he assured her. 'But what about you? Are you living here? I've been hanging around for ages trying to find out.'

'No longer,' she said, shuddering. 'I've had to leave but I don't know where to go. I need to pawn my jewels to raise some cash.'

'I'll help you, milady,' Jacob said, and his loyalty was heartening. 'I can even find you somewhere to live while you sort yourself out. I'm working in my uncle's shop and we live above it. He won't see you homeless. Come on, let's get away from here in case Lord Driscol comes chasing after you.'

He lifted her bag with ease and together they hurried down the drive to the road beyond, and there boarded an omnibus. Jacob paid a penny each for their tickets and they sat on the slatted wooden seats and Angela felt as if a great weight had been lifted from her. She had no idea what the future might hold, but it seemed that her guardian angel was keeping watch over her and that Jacob had been heaven-sent.

It was a fine store, one of which any self-made man might be proud. Arthur Taylor rose early each morning, with the exception of the Sabbath, of course, when he went to church, and paced through the upstairs rooms and down the stairs and unlocked the connecting door. He took his time strolling among the goods on display before opening the shop and welcoming in his first customer of the day.

He sold everything for the housewife's cupboard, including sugar, tea, cocoa and coffee, all in large tins or sacks, ready to be weighed out on the big brass scales. A baker operated down the street but Arthur stocked bread, cakes and biscuits, also candles, nightlights, gas mantles and matches, cigars, tobacco and cigarettes. He kept a few items of haberdashery - pins, needles, sewing thread and darning wool. There was no need for the working class women who lived in that area to go further afield.

His employees had to be skilled in measurements and mathematics, and he was a stern taskmaster, giving them a hard time. They started work at seven-thirty and the shop did not close till six, sometimes later on special occasions, like the run up to Christmas.

Despite his success and comfortable bank balance, Arthur had never married. Years before a village girl had tried to slap a paternity suit on him, but he wriggled out of it, blackening her name in the process and leaving for London. Since then he'd had several other narrow escapes. There had been a middle-aged spinster who fancied himself and his shop. Also a ruthless widow who let him know that if he became husband number two she would turn a blind eye if he wanted to seduce her seventeen-year-old daughter. But even the bribe of a young virgin did not sway him. He was tight-fisted and parsimonious. Money was his god. It was his ambition to move from this humble area and open an emporium up West, maybe in Oxford Street, or Regent Street. It was not beyond the realms of possibility.

He was fond of his nephew, Jacob, and pleased he had come to join him. It seemed unlikely that he would have children of his own, and he had resolved to teach the boy all the tricks of the trade and eventually let him take over. In his mind's eye he could see the frontage of his grand West End establishment emblazoned with the words, A & J TAYLOR, *by Royal Appointment*.

He studied the clock. Seven-fifteen. The first of his workforce would be arriving any minute. They lodged in a house next-door that he also owned, and this made them obligated to him on several counts. And where, he wondered, was Jacob? He heard the lad go out early. What was he up to? Arthur scratched his balls thoughtfully, easing what he termed his 'family jewels' into a more comfortable position in the crotch of his long-legged, white flannel combinations.

This caused a stirring in his loins, sluggish, but there nonetheless. He

66

ruminated as to whether the maid-of-all-work had arrived yet. She did not live in, which he considered a pity for she was easy game, but arrived most mornings around this time. If he went to the basement now he might be able to finger her before anyone started bothering him with business matters. He could almost smell her strong odour and imagine those rough-skinned hands rubbing his cock. He left the shop, escaping down the dark stairs to the lower floor, encouraged by the rumpus she made raking at the kitchen range.

Angela had never before ridden on a bus, nor walked through narrow streets or rubbed shoulders with commoners. It was not that she was a snob, simply that she had never been called upon to be any other than a titled lady, with all the perks this entailed.

The busy people going about their errands would have alarmed her had she not had her hand in the crook of Jacob's elbow. Street cries dinned her ears, where hustlers strove to sell their goods, either from stalls or trays that they carried on a strap round their necks. They sold everything from medicine to bootlaces. The language used in this part of the city was ripe. Angela had never heard so many expletives, and they seemed to be adopted in ordinary parlance, to illustrate a point or draw attention to a bargain, not necessarily in anger or abuse.

'Take no notice, Lady Angela,' Jacob said. 'It's just the cockney way of expressing themselves. There's rhyming slang, too... apples-and-pears for stairs, syrup-of-figs means a wig, like they might say, "he's wearing a syrup". Whistle-and-flute, for a suit. There are loads more, and I haven't been here long. Met a couple of girls, though, and one of 'em taught me some. Her name's Tilly.'

'Are you walking out with her? Will you introduce me?' Angela asked, swinging along by his side, gaining confidence with every step.

'No, milady, I'm not, and she isn't the kind of person you'd want to meet, not really,' Jacob replied, and he flushed to the roots of his hair. 'Come along. We're nearly there. Uncle Arthur will be pleased to see you.'

'The pawnbroker first,' she reminded.

'Of course, though there's no need; I have money,' Jacob stated.

'I want to be independent,' she said, as kindly as she could. He was already doing too much for her.

A bell clanged as they stopped outside a pokey little shop with grimy windows. Objects of all kinds could be seen through the dimpled glass, once belonging to proud owners but now in hock. Jacob held the door opened for her and she preceded him. The interior smelled musty and was lit by a single, flickering gaslight. Its proprietor crouched behind a counter protected by a metal grill. He was a bearded, wizened man wearing a skullcap, and he gazed at Angela shrewdly, summing up her neat appearance and cultured voice. She handed over her jewels and he pawed at them, but delicately, as if bewitched by anything of grace and value. He made an offer. Jacob argued. Angela accepted, and left the pawnbroker's with sovereigns in her purse and her heart filled with the firm resolution to redeem her baubles as soon as possible.

They turned along Fleet Street and followed the road. It had shops and dwellings on either side. Jacob paused before a large, double-fronted building with plate-glass windows where goods were on display. There were customers coming out and going in and trade seemed to be booming. He took her down a side alley, and opened a door.

Angela stepped into a dingy passage. It was behind the shop and smelled strongly of cheese and coffee beans, carbolic soap and beeswax. Just for an instant she wondered bleakly if this had been such a good idea.

'Let's find uncle,' Jacob urged, and poked his head round a door behind which the commercial activity was taking place. 'Oi, Bob!' he carolled. 'Is Mr Taylor about?'

'Gone to have his lunch,' a ginger-headed youngster replied, pausing in working the bacon-slicer, catching a glimpse of Angela and staring.

'Upstairs,' Jacob said, smiling at her and leading the way. 'That's where we live, apart from the basement where Kate sometimes cooks, though mostly we have meals sent in from the pie shop.'

'Kate?' Angela questioned, bemused.

'She "does" for us, cleaning and scrubbing and that. Though we take our washing to the Chinese laundry down the street.'

It was lighter on the landing; the walls had been given a coat of white paint, though it looked as if this was done some years ago. Jacob entered a room in front, calling out, 'Uncle Arthur? Are you there? I've brought a young lady along.'

He ushered Angela into the parlour. It was stuffed with florid furniture, and had garish wallpaper and a brightly patterned carpet. A man slumped in a wing chair by the fire, a newspaper covering his face, obviously snatching forty winks. He jumped, snorted and snatched the paper away, scowling at his nephew.

'What? What? Who's there? Ah, it's you, my boy,' he said, coming awake and blinking at Angela. 'You've brought a lady visitor? You might have warned me, lad.'

'Sorry, uncle, but I wasn't sure. You see, I've been looking for her since I arrived. She was staying with a toff in Mayfair. Don't you remember her? She's Lady Angela Bayswater of Lairdland Manor. I told you that her father died recently, didn't I?'

'You did indeed,' Arthur said, struggling to his feet and bowing over Angela's hand. 'I can remember your birth, your ladyship, and how there were celebrations in the village, then I left shortly after. I'm sorry to hear Sir Barnaby has passed over. God rest his soul. And you are visiting here, perhaps? I see you are still in mourning.'

'And shall be, sir, for at least a year,' Angela stated flatly, taking a dislike to this stout individual with his receding hair, bushy moustache and brows like untrimmed hedges.

His suit was black and well pressed, his shirt collar and cuffs pristine. Even so, there was something unwholesome about him. The look in his beady eyes, the way his pursed his thin lips as if wanting to taste her, and those stubby fingers with the none-too-clean nails. How horrid to imagine them making free with her.

'Of course, my dear lady. It does you credit. How may Jacob and I help you?' he said, his obsequious manner doing little to endear him.

'No doubt Jacob told you that I have lost my inheritance,' she stated coolly, and when he pulled out a chair for her, perched on the edge, unwilling to give the impression that she intended to delay there long.

'He did, indeed. I was shocked and very surprised,' Arthur answered, sitting down again.

'Not as much as I. There had never been any indication that he was financially embarrassed. I was engaged to Lord Driscol, but unfortunately when I lost my dowry he lost interest in matrimony,' she said. It no longer hurt so much, though Aidan's latest example of his sexual inclinations still appalled and puzzled her. That he should prefer Julian to Valerie or Maude seemed the height of perversion. The men had been performing lewd acts together at the party, but it had never occurred to her that he would take part. How little she knew him! And now there was Jacob who, kind though he was, no doubt had his own agenda where she was concerned. As for his uncle? She wouldn't trust him as far as she could throw him!

'What a pity,' he said, staring at her with watery blue eyes. 'How could he be so unkind to such a, dare I say it, beautiful young woman?' Then he changed tack, turning to Jacob and saying, 'Ring for Kate. Lady Angela would like some tea, I don't doubt.'

Jacob did as he was told and within a short time a slatternly woman appeared at the door, took her orders, sniffed loudly and disapprovingly and humped off to the kitchen. 'She is your wife?' Angela asked, though sure this was not so.

'Oh, no, I'm not married,' Arthur said with a laugh. 'She works for us.'

'I need to work,' Angela put in. 'I'm seeking a post as a teacher, perhaps a governess or companion.'

'I'm certain you'll find something.' He grinned at her ingratiatingly and laid a presumptuous hand on her knee. 'Meanwhile, you are welcome to stay here with Jacob and me. We'd be honoured. Wouldn't we, Jacob? He's my heir, you know, and will come into the business when I'm gone.'

Tea arrived and there was cake as well. Angela wasn't hungry, as Jacob had already treated her to lunch. The conversation was stilted, though Arthur was trying to impress her, and Jacob appeared to admire his achievements.

'He did it all by himself,' he put in, when Arthur drew breath and poured some tea into his saucer, then slurped from it. 'That's something, isn't it?'

'Very commendable,' she commented, averting her eyes from Arthur's tea-stained moustache.

'And now, my lady, what would you like to do tonight? Shall we go to a music hall?' he suggested, smiling roguishly.

The idea of spending an evening in his company appalled her, but she did not want to appear rude, so, 'I'm rather tired, Mr Taylor, I had a restless night,' she said, and glanced appealingly at Jacob. 'If you could show me where I am to sleep, then perhaps I might lie down for a while.'

It was no sooner said than done. Jacob carried her luggage to a room on the right of the corridor. 'That's mine, over the way,' he explained. 'But I shall be in the shop this afternoon, helping out. It's my job, you see, and he pays me and is offering me prospects.'

The room in which he left her was clean but sparse, cold, too, for no spark blazed in the black iron fireplace. The atmosphere was damp and musty, and Angela went across and fought with the window catch until she could get the casement open. Even then the air was not much better, comprised of city odours. She took off her hat and laid it on the plain pine dressing table. Her heart was like a stone inside her. Oh, she had escaped Aidan, but what on earth was she doing in this dreary place?

She opened her jacket and lay on the lumpy bed. This also exuded damp, and the pillows smelt fusty. Despite herself she could not help remembering Aidan and the way he had of making love. Her bruises ached, and this did not detract from the heat that warmed her loins. If only he could have shown her respect and kept her as his one true love? But this could never be so, and she was not prepared to settle for less.

Nonetheless, she could not help undoing her bodice and toying with her nipples, then sliding her right hand down and gripping the hem of her skirt, lifting it high and then letting her fingers find her labial wings, part their damp folds and play with her clitoris. She relaxed, giving a little moan of pleasure, and began the wonderful game that would lead her to heaven. She could do it quickly or very, very slowly, but the end would be the same - perfect bliss and satisfaction.

Arthur retired to his room, too. There he closed to door carefully and slipped the bolt, then went straight across to the wall opposite, lifted down a copy of the painting called, *The Light Of The World*, and applied his eye to a hole in the plaster. It gave an interrupted view of Angela sprawled on the bed, masturbating.

'I knew it,' he said under his breath. 'Fine lady, my arse! She's a trollop, like all the rest. By God I'll have her bare-breasted and bare-bottomed, serving me any way I demand. Kate can get out. I deserve something better than her worn fanny.'

As he watched Angela lifting her hips and rubbing her slit he opened his trousers and took out a small, stubby cock. It was not long but it was thick. He handled it lovingly and, still viewing Angela, started to fondle it, pressing down the ring of foreskin and baring the shiny red dome. It did not take him long to catch up with Angela's frenzy and, as he saw her jerk and heard her give a cry, so his organ spasmed and shot forth his spunk, hitting the wall and running down to drip on that quasi religious print.

Arthur was sure he had kept very quiet, but found that Angela had her head turned in his direction, as if she could see him through the lathe and plaster wall. He shrank back and put his cock away, then tidied himself in the mirror. She mustn't suspect, mustn't know anything - not yet.

Chapter 7

Aidan never gave up. If he was convinced that something belonged to him then he would fight, and fight dirty, to keep it. He was furious beyond measure because Angela had left him. How dare she? And he gave Valerie a bad time, blaming her and taking no responsibility for his own actions.

'Bitch!' he grated, after several days had passed with no word from the fugitive. 'What did you say to her? What did you do to make her think she could be so damned independent?'

Valerie was bare-bottomed across his knee and he slapped her hard with almost every word. 'Nothing, master,' she vowed. 'I did what you ordered, but she's a stubborn minx. Ow! Aaah! Do it again! Do it again!' And she writhed against his thighs, grinding her hairless mound as she strove to reach fulfilment.

He tumbled her off and she landed in a heap on the carpet. 'I want her found!' he shouted, eyes flashing and face stormy. 'See to it, and no excuses.'

'And if I find her?' Valerie sat up and rubbed her arse ruefully. It bore the imprint of his hand.

'Report to me,' he answered, standing to his full impressive height and staring down at her with no offer of helping her regain her feet. 'If you fail in this, then I may have to seriously think about whether to continue our friendship. Do you understand?'

'Yes, master,' Valerie replied humbly. She might have Julian, Maude and Viola, and a dozen other lovers, but no one took her to hell and back, thrilled her to the marrow and catapulted her to the stars like Aidan.

She dispatched her spies out and about with instructions to search for the missing Angela and not to return without information, perhaps not on pain of death, but certainly instant dismissal.

Angela found herself in an awkward situation. Arthur refused to take money for her board and lodgings and she hated being beholden to him. Jacob, too, was becoming an embarrassment with his puppy love and adoring eyes, treating her as if she was porcelain, whereas she had proved to herself beyond all doubt that she was made of sterner stuff. Once she had longed for Aidan to show such dog-like devotion, but now discovered something within her psyche that responded to being misused by a man. Aidan had taken her on a journey down the dark pathways of passion, and she would never be the same again.

71

She had unwittingly made an enemy in the Taylor household. Kate did not hide her resentment. At first Arthur hinted that Angela might like to act as housekeeper for him and his nephew and, when Kate got to hear of this, she went into a sulk. In vain Angela tried to reassure her, declaring that she would not be there long and was simply visiting until she found a suitable live-in post. It took her a while to realise that Kate, implausible though it seemed, was enamoured of Arthur and possessed by the green-eyed monster.

'As if I'd look at him twice, let alone encourage him,' Angela said to herself, trying to make the best of an uncomfortable position, for there was no doubt that Arthur fancied her. She was forever avoiding being alone with him, or passing too close on stairs and passageways.

She broached the subject with Jacob but it was awkward, for he had put his uncle on a pedestal and would hear nothing against him. Besides, he was looking at her through rose-coloured spectacles, hardly listening to the context of her conversation, too engrossed in the fact that she was there, living under the same roof, and he was acting as her Sir Galahad.

One evening, terribly restless and unwilling to spend another night in Arthur's odious company, she said to Jacob, 'Would you like to take me out? You haven't yet introduced me to your friend. Tilly, is it?'

He cast her a sheepish look, pushed away his dinner plate and refolded his napkin. 'I could, I suppose, though she frequents public houses and ladies don't go to such places.'

'That's true,' put in Arthur, who had not been asked to voice his opinion. 'I don't think you would enjoy it.'

'Pish!' she responded crossly, irritated because Kate was hovering around, deliberately clashing china together as she cleared the table. 'I'm not a baby, you know. I'm certain Jacob wouldn't go anywhere disreputable. Would you, Jacob?'

'Huh!' exclaimed Kate, pushing back a lock of her lank hair and glaring at Angela. 'I'd not be too sure about that.'

'Who asked you to put in your penny worth?' Jacob retorted rudely. 'All right, my lady, if that's what you'd like to do, we'll go to the *Bunch of Grapes*. It's an old hostelry, used to be a coaching inn before the railways took over. You'll find it interesting, and we needn't stay long. Let's go early before it gets too crowded.'

Having got her way, Angela began to wonder why she had bothered. She had explored the area and it was apparent that she stuck out like a sore thumb - too refined and genteel, too well dressed, though wearing plain black. This is what Kate disliked about her. She was a cut above the rest of them.

'Thank you, Jacob, I shall enjoy a change of scene,' she said, and went to get her hat and cape.

It was a fine evening with the promise of spring spicing the air, lighter, too. They walked to the public house, passing families heading for the parks, parents and children heralding the warmer weather and getting away from the mean, overcrowded streets. One little lad wearing a sailor suit bumped into Angela and nearly dropped the paper bag he was hugging.

'Goin' to feed the ducks,' he announced, before being hauled away by his mother with instructions to say 'sorry to the nice lady.'

'It's all right,' Angela assured her, and she would have liked to be accompanying him, throwing bread to a greedy congregation of waterfowl, just like those who had resided on the lake at Lairdland Manor. Homesickness swept over her.

'Lots of parks in London,' Jacob vouchsafed, proud as a peacock to have her on his arm.

Soon they left the pleasant verdure and budding trees and took a side road at the end of which stood the old inn, its sign depicting purple grapes. The door of the public bar stood open, and Angela caught a glimpse of the gas lit interior with its oak panelling, brass, etched glass, benches, sawdust-strewn floor, and tables where several regulars were playing dominoes. Jacob guided her in and found seats for them on a settle near the big open fireplace where logs smouldered on the hearth.

'What can I get you to drink?' he asked.

'I don't know,' she answered truthfully, never having been in a tavern before. 'What do you suggest?'

'Port and lemon,' he replied, and she could only assume that this is what Tilly might imbibe. She wished Jacob's friend would hurry up and put in an appearance, for she was causing any amount of unwelcome interest amongst the customers.

Several rough-looking men wearing flat caps and spotted neckerchiefs propped up the bar, quaffing pints of ale and staring at her. There were others, too, better dressed but with that same predatory look in their eyes, as if wondering if she was an honest woman or perhaps one of those 'ladies of the night' of whom she had heard. There were women present, but mostly gin-soaked crones huddled in corners gossiping and dragging their threadbare garments about their skeletal frames to keep the cold out of their bones. It was altogether an unprepossessing hostelry, and even when Jacob returned with the drinks she was ready to leap to her feet and say she had changed her mind and wanted to leave.

A man took his place at a battered upright piano set against one wall, plonked his pint glass on the lid and started to thump out popular songs. The crowd joined in, keeping time by banging empty tankards on the round marble tabletops. Their rendition of these bawdy lyrics owed more to alcohol than talent. No one, it seemed, could pitch a note accurately. Angela cringed, her musical ear offended.

Jacob looked uncomfortable, saying, 'Well this is it, I'm afraid. Not what you're used to, milady, but the best I can offer. I did warn you.'

He looked so miserable that Angela placed her hand over his where it rested on his thigh. 'That's all right, Jacob. You were only trying to help.'

Impulsively he covered her small fingers with his broad ones, and the contact was far from unpleasant. He was young, nearer her age than Aidan, and there was a freshness and sincerity about him that was appealing. Angela felt a jolt within her, and a spasm that reminded her of the feelings her ex-betrothed engendered. She had never been with anyone like Jacob and wondered how it would be if he were to kiss her, or touch her breasts or even slide a hand under her skirts. A commoner! A stable lad! Dear God, what would her father have said?

The port wine was potent. Her senses swam and she was aware of the scenes taking place all around her. As the drink went down so customers lost their inhibitions, and a cheer arose when the door was suddenly flung wide and half a dozen flashily dressed women flounced in.

'Tilly, how are your parts?' one of the men roared at a girl with flame-red hair, wearing a big feathered hat and an emerald-green dress with an exceedingly low bodice. She slued to a halt before him, arms akimbo.

'Smelly, as usual,' she retorted, tossing her head. 'And 'ow's your dick? Got any bigger, 'as it? I seen more impressive things on the winkle stall.'

This sally was greeted by whoops of laughter and another woman joined her, slinging an arm casually around Tilly's shoulders. She was dark-haired and dark-eyed, dressed in crimson with a great deal of flash and plumage.

'I knows 'im,' she put in, red lips curling contemptuously. 'Not exactly a stallion, is 'ee? Newborn nippers 'as got bigger cocks.'

'Aw, shut your mouth, Doreen, you pox-ridden bawd,' the man snarled, thoroughly nettled by their scathing reference to his marriage equipment.

'Well, bugger me, don't you be so saucy to my mate,' Tilly chided, reaching out and squeezing his nipples through the coarsely woven shirt. 'Whose a naughty boy, then? Want me to tell your missus?'

Jacob was shifting uneasily and Angela had already caught the redhead's name. 'Is that your friend, Tilly?' she asked.

'Yes, that's her,' he said, with a show of nonchalance that did not deceive her one whit. To prove just how debonair he was he called across the smoky bar, 'Tilly, come over here. There's someone I want you to meet.'

Tilly turned her head and stared down her nose at him. 'In a minute, laddie. Take your turn. Get me a whiskey in,' she said imperiously and turned back to teasing her victim.

'She likes to have me on a string,' Jacob explained uneasily to Angela. 'So much attention goes to her head.'

'Are you serious about her?' Angela was surprised for Tilly, though beautiful, was common as muck. He deserved better than that.

'Serious? Like wanting to get engaged?' he said, and nervously squeezed the hand she had not removed from his knee. 'Oh no, milady, I just sees her sometimes, that's all. She kind of befriended me when I first came to London and didn't know anyone. Uncle's not exactly a bundle of laughs.'

'So I've noticed,' she replied, becoming more and more curious about Tilly and her sloe-eyed companion. Were they shop girls out for the night or maybe secretaries working those recently invented typewriters? They seemed so confident that she was sure they were in some position of authority. Perhaps they might help her to get work.

Their appearance in the pub and that of the women who'd entered with them had exacerbated the atmosphere of licence. They downed drinks, and clearing a space on the floor shouted to the pianist to play the can-can. Four of them whirled in that mad, Paris-inspired dance, posturing, kicking their legs high and then turning their backs on the audience, whipping up their skirts and bending over, displaying their naked buttocks. The men shouted and stamped and attempted to join in. There was the overpowering smell of hops and sweat, trampled sawdust and rutting heat.

Now the men were fondling the women and they were getting to work, letting them handle their breasts and dribble beer down their cleavages, licking off the droplets. Hands disappeared under skirts, but here the whores called a halt; they did not grant favours for nothing. Several of them disappeared into dark corners, engaging in monetary transactions, or took their clients into the back yard of the inn. Tilly decided to stroll across to where Angela and Jacob sat.

He moved on the bench to make room for her. 'Tilly, this is Angela Bayswater,' he began. 'I've told you a little about her.'

'The ladyship,' Tilly said, her face expressionless.

Such world-weary eyes in so young a person, Angela thought. What could have happened to make her hard? She could not avoid seeing how Tilly wound her arms round Jacob's neck and pressed her breasts against his chest. Was this how one should behave to enslave a man? It had not been thus with Aidan. He preferred a fight and an unwilling prisoner.

'I'm no longer privileged,' she said hurriedly. 'I need a job. Can you help me?'

Tilly looked surprised, her carmined lips opening and those kohl-outlined eyes becoming wider. 'You want to work? Ain't you got no money then? Did your pa really leave you 'igh and dry?'

'It's true,' Angela sighed, while Jacob went to the bar for more drinks. 'And the man who had promised to marry me, Lord Aidan Driscol, wasn't interested once he knew I had no dowry.'

'What a sod!' Tilly said vehemently. 'Typical bloke.'

'He wanted to own me, to make me his slave, but I couldn't settle for that. I intend to make something of myself, to show him that I don't need him,' Angela vowed, but there were tears beneath her anger.

'Bully for you,' Tilly said, and waved to Doreen. 'This 'ere young lady wants a job,' she continued when, in a flash of paste gems and a wave of pungent perfume, the gypsy-looking one strolled over.

'Do she now?' Doreen remarked, casting an eye over Angela. 'What's wrong wiv' 'er? Why you done up in black, darlin'?'

"Er dad croaked not long ago,' Tilly supplied, and snatched up the glass that Jacob set before her. 'Get one for Doreen, there's a love,' she said, dispatching him again.

'Black, eh? Could catch on, I guess. There's those pervy blokes what are into nuns or dead bodies. Or, on the other 'and, she could scrap the mournin' and get into brighter duds, corsets and garters and stockings and all the gear what makes 'em randy.'

'Why should I do that? I want to be a teacher, a secretary or a governess,' Angela brought out fiercely. Two port and lemons had given her Dutch courage.

'Oh, lah-di-dah, pardon me for breathin',' Doreen said nastily. 'Then why are you talkin' to a couple of whores like us?'

'I didn't know you were whores,' Angela answered, but now it suddenly became glaringly obvious.

'What did you think, then? That Jacob comes around to see Tilly to play cards or somethin'? He pokes 'er. Or didn't you know?'

'That's enough, Doreen,' Tilly warned. 'If you don't shut up I'll bottle you. Jacob and me are friends.'

'Bollocks!' Doreen snapped. 'Just 'cause he knows 'ow to diddle your minge.'

'I told you to shut it!' Tilly repeated, and the look in her eyes made Doreen back off.

'What's up?' Jacob wanted to know, heaving his shoulders through the mêlée, holding a tray aloft then setting it down on their table.

'Nothin',' Tilly replied coolly. 'Just Doreen openin' 'er trap. Gord, 'er mouth's as big as 'er cunt.'

'Cow,' Doreen retorted blithely. 'Come on, gal. There's johns waitin' to be milked of their spunk, and their soddin' cash.'

'So there is,' Tilly said, getting up. 'I'll see you anther time, Jacob. And you, Angela, you just find me if you're ever in trouble. I lives down Friggle Lane. That ain't far from 'ere.'

They disappeared into the milling, drinking, fornicating throng. 'How does the landlord allow this?' Angela asked, staring askance at one of the women who lay across a beer-stained table, her legs raised and hooked round the shoulders of a navvy in corduroys and sweaty shirt, his cock buried in her dark slit. A flashily dressed gent was fingering her anus, and two others were playing with her nipples that poked above her stays, while she palmed their cocks, then kept one in her hand and opened her mouth and sucked the other.

'He turns a blind eye. It's good for trade and he has someone on the look out for the rozzers. Anyhow, the police don't give him much trouble. They're open to bribes. Shall we go? Have you seen enough? What do you think of Tilly?'

He talked non-stop as they left and strolled back to the store through the dusky streets. It was quite romantic and Angela wished with all her heart that Aidan and she had never been set on this course that had ruined her life. A lesson to be learned? Undoubtedly for her - she would never have known Aidan's true nature had this not happened. She would have married him in ignorance of his association with Valerie and his interest in bondage and domination and wild orgies. By the time she did find out it would have been too late. She might have had children by then and the divorce laws were harsh. It was possible that if she had brought a case against him, she might have had her little ones taken away from her and put in their father's care. In any case, no matter who was to blame in the breakdown of a marriage, a divorce cast a slur over the innocent party who would not be received in polite society. She told herself that she'd had a lucky escape, but could not help picturing his strong frame, devastatingly handsome face, flinty-grey eyes and the way he had of raising her to a fever pitch of desire.

She could tell that Jacob was longing to pluck up the courage to kiss her goodnight at her bedroom door, and she almost wanted him to do so. Then they parted after a single clasp of hands and both slept alone, and she was troubled by the evening's events and wondered if she would see Tilly again, and under what circumstances.

'So, it'll be just you and me, keeping each other company,' Arthur announced complacently at breakfast several days later.

'What?' Angela said, her heart sinking.

'Uncle's sending me on a business trip Manchester way,' Jacob stated, and he was grinning, well pleased with himself. 'I'll be visiting the retailers, looking at stock and ordering it, too. It's a responsible job.'

'You'll do it well, my boy,' Arthur said, tapping his boiled egg with a spoon, slicing off the top and dunking the bread 'soldiers', as Angela's nanny used to call them, in the golden yolk. 'You look the part, I must say. Very smart, ain't he, Lady Angela?'

She nodded and bit into a thin slice of buttered toast. Jacob looked more mature, attired in a neat dark suit, with a white shirt whose collar and cuffs had been crisply starched. His hair was no longer ruffled, but slicked back with macassar oil. He wore a sober tie, and his shoes had been buffed to a high sheen.

'You could see your face in 'em,' he enthused, looking down at his feet. 'I used plenty of spit and polish. Do you think I'll pass muster?'

'Oh, yes,' she said encouragingly, though terrified of his departure.

'And you, milady?' he asked anxiously. 'Have you decided to go to one of those employment agencies who might find you suitable work? Or considered answering adverts in *The Times?* Don't do anything hasty till I return. I'll only be gone a couple of days.'

'I've already visited two,' she reminded, trying to avoid Arthur's penetrating gaze. 'I told you about it, Jacob. I didn't have any luck with either of them. It seemed I was too well educated for some posts, and too ladylike for others. Neither fish nor fowl, apparently. The ladies in charge were not very helpful. I think my speech and breeding offended them. They have said they will be in touch if anything turns up that might suit me, but I've a feeling they won't bother.'

'Don't worry your head about it,' Arthur said expansively. 'It is a delight to entertain such a charming young woman. 'My house is your house, as I'm told they say in Spain.'

Angela nodded and lowered her eyes to her plate, then said, 'But we shall be living here alone, Mr Taylor. It's hardly proper.'

Arthur slapped his thigh and laughed. 'Don't you fret about that. Why, we're surrounded by folk all day long. Don't you trust me?' And he gave her a smile that was supposed to be winsome. Angela looked away.

'It's not you, Mr Taylor,' she lied, 'but what other people may think. I have my reputation to consider.'

'I'll ask Kate to sleep in, if you prefer,' he offered.

This was an even worse alternative than being confined to the house with him. 'No, no, don't bother,' she said hurriedly, knowing she would have to put up with him, but soon he would go back down to the shop, there to keep an eagle eye on his staff and be patronising and pompous towards his customers.

After breakfast Jacob picked up his travelling bag and a briefcase, slung his overcoat over one arm and carried his trilby hat.

Angela leaned over the stairs, watching him descend. 'Goodbye,' he called, looking up at her. 'Take care. I'm sure uncle will be like a father to you. I'll see you at the weekend. I gave you the address of the boarding house where I'm staying, didn't I?'

'You did,' she said, smiling as she remembered him repeating it like a mantra several times, as if by so doing he might bridge the gap between Manchester and London. As for Arthur acting the surrogate parent? This did not bear contemplating.

The day passed in its customary dull fashion, made more so by Jacob's absence. Angela went to the market, rummaging round the second-hand stalls, interested in the china and figurines, bric-a-brac and lengths of silk. This amused her for half a morning, but she was bored and lonely. She contemplated visiting one of the agencies again, but did not feel confident enough to face those sour-faced women who ran them. She had the feeling that they were secretly triumphant to find a lady of her background seeking employment, and would not put themselves out to help her.

She sat in the park for a while, but was uneasy. Used to being chaperoned she did not know how to comport herself alone. The sunshine was warm, and the scene almost bucolic. Just for a while she pretended she was home again. She closed her eyes, and then became aware of a shadow between her and the sun. Warning bells clanged in her brain. Lifting her lids she saw a man standing there, staring down at her.

He tipped his hat, a tidily dressed person of middle years. 'Are you by yourself, miss?' he began. 'May I join you?'

Angela got to her feet, a blush colouring her cheeks. 'No, sir, I'm about to leave,' she said levelly. 'I'm meeting my mamma for lunch.'

'Really?' He raised a sceptical eyebrow and, as he took a step closer she caught a whiff of his breath. It was unpleasant and she noticed his teeth were stained and uneven. 'I beg your pardon, but I imagined that you were here in the way of business, as it were.'

'I d-don't understand,' she stammered, drawing her black cloak more closely about her.

'No?' There was mockery in his small brown eyes, and a lop-sided grin on his narrow lips. 'D'you mean to tell me that you're not touting for trade? Come here, girlie,' and he put his arms around her and dragged her behind a tree.

Angela struggled, freeing her hands and slapping him across the face. 'How dare you?' she gasped. 'I'll scream if you don't leave me alone.'

'Scream away,' he said, unperturbed. 'No one will take any notice. This is a spot that trollops often use, picking up men and selling themselves.'

'Can't you see that I'm not one of them?' she panted, for now he had her trapped with her back against the tree bowl and his arms braced either side of her, his sour breath nauseating as he brought his face nearer.

He was pressing his loins into her belly, his hardness very apparent, and Angela knew she was in real danger of being raped. Even when with Aidan she had never felt so helpless, cursing her weak woman's muscles that made her no match for this man's strength. She squirmed and tried to lash out with her feet, but was hampered by her long skirt.

'You don't speak like a tart,' he agreed, using one hand to flick open his fly buttons. His cock shot out like a freed serpent, long and mottled and thick. 'No matter who you are, rub this for me and I'll give you a half sovereign,' he added huskily.

This was a tidy sum of money and her cash from the pawnshop was dwindling fast. Just for a moment she was tempted. Why not? He was a complete stranger and she need never see him again. She could use her hand on him, then wash and wash and wash till every trace of his nasty emission was gone. But the thought made the bile rise into her throat, and unable to stop herself she turned her head, leaned over and vomited.

He threw her from him, enraged, snarling, 'Draggle-tailed slut! Do I disgust you so much, or are you ill or with child?'

Groaning, Angela doubled up, handkerchief pressed to her lips. When she next looked the man had gone. She ran back to the shop like a scared rabbit and went to her room and slammed the bolt. Throwing herself on the bed she sobbed as if her heart would break, cursing fate that had brought her so low, cursing Aidan for his callousness. That she could have even contemplated touching that vile man's penis! Shame flooded her, warring with the common-sense argument that she would have been half a sovereign richer. She began to understand Tilly and Doreen. All one had to do was get over that first hurdle.

She woke into the headachy heat of early evening. She consulted her fob watch and was surprised to find that she had been asleep for so long. The room was becoming more and more shadowy. There was silence all around. The shop must be closed by now and the staff gone home. Where was Arthur? She slipped from the bed, tidying her hair, finding her shoes, and then unbolting the door.

Her first port of call was the lavatory. Throne-like, with a flowered porcelain bowl, it had a mahogany frame, seat and lid, and a high water cistern operated by a chain. She used it, and then rinsed her hands in the basin.

Still no signs of life. She decided to go down to the kitchen and made a pot of tea. There was a gas jet alight at all times, throwing a yellowish uncertainty over the treacherous stairs leading to the basement.

Angela disliked this place; it was too gloomy and threatening and probably spider infested. Besides which, Kate ruled supreme, and the last person she wanted to meet was the disagreeable maid.

With no thought save completing her mission with all speed and retreating upstairs, Angela moved quickly, her feet making no sound.

Then she became aware of noises issuing from the kitchen itself that lay at the end of a short corridor. They filled her with dread, for she recognised that they were made by the impact if leather against bare flesh. Someone was using a whip, or belt or flogger on some unfortunate. Her skin tingled in sympathy, though her emotions were muddled, fear mingled with a grain of envy.

Her legs were shaking but she forced herself forward and now those formidable sounds were joined by sobs and moans and Arthur's voice growling, 'D'you want me to gag you, Kate? I will if you don't stop that caterwauling.'

'I'm sorry, master, but I can't help it. My pussy's that sore with you slashing at it.'

'Then mind your manners to Lady Angela,' he shouted, and Kate shrieked as another blow found its mark.

Steeling herself, Angela pushed open the door and was met by the sad sight of Kate strung up by her wrists from a hook set in a beam. It should have been used for sides of bacon or cooking pots, but now it held human cargo. Kate was naked, a slack-bosomed, heavy-bottomed woman past her prime. Both of these sensitive areas were red as fire and bore a zigzag of stripes.

Her feet were tethered to iron rings set in the flagstones, about twelve inches apart.

Not realising that Angela was watching from the doorway, Arthur, in his shirtsleeves, continued Kate's chastisement, sending the merciless length of leather singing through the air. It landed on her belly with a crack, the tip winding round to sting her buttocks.

'Oh, master, have mercy! Let me lie with you tonight. I'll do anything you want. You can thrust it up my arse, anything, but please, please don't whip me any more,' the wretched woman begged, tense in her bonds, jerking when he lay on another blow.

Angela could no longer keep silent, 'Mr Taylor, stop it at once!' she commanded.

He swung round, but did not drop the whip. 'And what brings you down here, milady?' he asked in a sibilant voice, his eyes narrowing as he leered at her face and body.

'I would like a cup of tea,' she said, advancing calmly though her heart was racing. 'I didn't expect to find you punishing Kate. Pray, what has she done to merit such severity?'

'She is insolent towards you, and I'll not tolerate her rudeness,' he bellowed, emphasising his words by another slashing blow, this time to Kate's breasts. She screamed and Angela's own nipples crimped as she imagined the pain.

'Don't beat her on my account,' she insisted, and hung on to his arm, marvelling at her boldness. 'Can't we forget this unfortunate incident?'

'Forget?' Kate cried, her face working with fury. 'Why don't you mind your own damn business, Miss High-and-Mighty? Arthur and me have an arrangement, see? We don't needs you interrupting.'

Angela was almost struck dumb. There was something going on between the two of them, something unhealthy and rooted in sexual desire. Kate was looking at him like a woman in love! How could anyone love that loathsome creature? That he was aroused, too, was apparent by the huge erection distending his trousers.

Sickened, Angela turned to leave, but he snapped, 'Don't go. The tart and me have finished for the time being. Get out of here, Kate,' and he untied her feet and released her arms. She fell to the floor then scrambled up, gathered her discarded clothing and limped out, but not before giving Angela a glare that should have killed her.

'You treat her shamefully,' she railed, turning on Arthur like a she-cat.

'Don't waste your pity on the likes of her,' he advised, and there was a gleam in his eyes that made her sharply aware that there was no one within earshot. It was even worse than when the man in the park tried to take advantage of her.

She decided to remain cool, walking across to the range and shifting the black kettle so that it stood over the hob. Then equally calmly she fetched the brown earthenware pot and spooned tea into it from the metal caddy. She hoped that such everyday actions would ground him, but one glance told her it was in vain.

He was coming towards her, unfastening his trousers en route. He rummaged inside and lifted out his large, curved, pinkish-brown cock. The action of showing it to her seemed to excite him more and he was breathing quickly, enjoying her disgust. She backed away, seeking the door, but he followed, stroking his upright phallus, wetting the stem from the dew leaking from the tip.

'Stay,' he croaked, closer now. 'Don't leave me in this state, Lady Angela. You must know by now how much I admire you. Is it beyond imagining that you might accept the hand of a grocer? I'm a man of means and you'd want for nothing. I know a thing or two about women's desires, too, and will play with your love-bud till you come, screaming for me to do it some more.'

'I can't, this will never be,' she cried, unable to drag her gaze from his tool as it bucked in his hand. 'If you don't let me pass I shall tell Jacob on his return.'

'You're so cruel to me,' he complained, but continued to masturbate, his fingers grasping his shaft, working at it eagerly, pulling the foreskin back and forth in his frantic haste to achieve his goal.

'You have no right to expect anything of me,' she said, angry now and despising this sorry little man. 'Let me pass.'

'Not yet,' he panted, breathing fast. 'Not till you've seen me come.' His hand flashed over his helm, his eyes bulged and his mouth was agape and he grunted deep in his chest as he released his semen in a creamy spurt that spattered Angela's skirt.

'Oh, God, you're revolting!' she cried, seized the handle, yanked open the door and flew up the stairs, never stopping till she reached her room and locked herself in.

Chapter 8

Without pausing to think or change her mind, Angela packed her bag. It was dark by now but she did not care. She had to get away from Arthur. Putting on her coat and hat she opened the door, picked up her valise and peered nervously into the passage. He was nowhere to be seen, so she crept down the stairs and let herself into the side alley via the back way.

She could hardly believe that she had been so lucky, anticipating trouble with Arthur, but either he had taken himself off to the nearest public house or was slumped at the kitchen table with a bottle of whiskey. Either way she did not give a hoot, just as long as she escaped him. She contemplated leaving a note for Jacob, then decided that she would post one, making sure it did not fall into the wrong hands and that he received it on his return. She had formulated a plan and walked swiftly, head held high, seeking her destination - Friggle Lane.

London by night was daunting, particularly for a female. There were still a number of people about, returning from work or setting out, doing late shopping or making their way to the taverns or music halls. Angela remembered that Friggle Lane was not too far from the *Bunch of Grapes*. She was pinning her hopes on Tilly, who had seemed good-natured enough, but she was not so sure about Doreen. In any case she had little choice, apart from returning to Aidan, and the very idea appalled her. She feared her own weakness where he was concerned. It would be fatally easy to succumb, sink herself into him and lose her self-esteem, her independence, even her very soul.

She passed on the other side of the road to the inn. It was noisy, filled with loud voices and raucous laughter and it frightened her. She recalled Tilly pointing down the street and went that way, coming to a narrow alley with a lop-sided sign that she could just about read in the flickering streetlamp. *Friggle Lane*. This was it. There was no turning back. She straightened her spine and set off into the gloom.

The smell was disgusting, that of damp and bad drains. She lifted her skirt, trying to keep the hem out of the mud. There were several doors on either side and she finally came to a dead end, facing another door which, when pulled open, gave access to a shadowy hallway that led to a staircase. She mounted it, thankful for the pallid gaslight. On reaching the top she was faced with more doors. From inside one of them came the strains of a popular song.

She knocked and, "Oo the bloody 'ell's that?' came a voice recognisable as Doreen's. 'You expectin' anyone, Tilly?'

'Nah! Open up, you lazy mare,' was Tilly's instant response. 'An' put that bloody phonogram off! Gets on my nerves, it does.'

'Oh, fuck you!' Doreen growled, and there was a sickening scrape as the needle was dragged across the record, followed by silence. The door was yanked back on its hinges and Doreen was framed there. She stared at Angela and Angela stared back. 'Jesus Christ Almighty!' Doreen exclaimed. 'If it ain't Lady Muck 'erself!'

Tilly appeared at her elbow, shoved her aside and held out a hand to Angela. 'You in trouble, miss? Come on in.'

'Thank you,' Angela said, filled with trepidation, and relief, too. The room was squalid. It was obvious that they lived, ate and slept in it and - she shuddered - probably carried out their illegal profession there as well.

'Cup of tea?' Tilly enquired, dressed in long drawers with frills above the knee and a pink satin corset from which her breasts rose, beautifully sculpted half-moons of pleasure and sustenance.

'Thank you,' Angela murmured again, resting her bag on a rickety chair.

Doreen planted herself in front of her, demanding, 'What you doin' 'ere?'

'I had nowhere else to go,' Angela explained. 'I had to get away from Mr Taylor, that's Jacob's uncle. He wouldn't leave me alone and Jacob's away, and I shouldn't be staying there without a chaperone, and tonight he tried to take advantage of me.'

Doreen grinned, relinquished her role of interrogator and slumped on the battered old couch. 'Worth a bob or two, ain't 'ee? You missed your chance there, gal.'

'I can't bear him anywhere near me,' Angela declared. 'He's a horrible, slimy little man.'

'"Beggars can't be choosers",' Doreen opined sagely, shrugging her shoulders. Her grubby dressing gown fell open over her olive-skinned breasts, crowned with prominent brown nipples. 'You should see some of the scum I 'as to wank off. Men are plonkers. That's why we gals like to make love to one another.'

Angela listened and absorbed this information, remembering Valerie and her close companions - Maude, Trisha and Viola, and the way they had caressed and toyed with each other's genitals. Her own feelings, too, had been ambiguous - her breasts had tingled and her cleft ached and she had wanted to touch Valerie and be touched in return. Was this what Doreen referred to? Did women really enjoy sexual congress together?

Tilly poured tea from an earthenware pot placed on the trivet in front of the meagre coal fire. She added milk from a chipped jug and sugar from a grocer's dark blue packet, gave it a twirl with a dented spoon and handed the chipped china mug to Angela.

'Sit down,' she said, indicating the tumbled, unmade double bed. 'Take your 'at off, an' your coat an' make yourself at 'ome. Tell us all about it and why you've come 'ere.'

'As I've said, I can't bear to be anywhere near Mr Taylor. I have a little money and will pay for my lodgings, if you can suggest anywhere decent where I might stay.'

'You a virgin?' Doreen interrupted, sprawling on the mattress, drinking gin, not tea.

'No,' Angela replied. 'But I'm not married, haven't left a husband or anything like that.'

'Then 'ow come you're 'ere, in this dump?'

'I've run away from the man who wanted to dominate me. He made me call him "master".'

'Oh, one of *them*. I knows the kind. Uses the whip an' that. Wants slaves. 'Ow d'you get mixed up with 'im?'

'It's a long story.'

'An' you don't want to tell it?' Tilly cut in, giving Doreen a warning glare. 'Jacob's told me some of it. That's all right. We've all got our secret's 'ere. You can kip with us, till you find somethin' better.'

'Thank you for the offer,' Angela said, and sipped the strong tea and wondered what would happen next. There was no knowing which way the girls would turn, particularly the volatile Doreen who now leaned against Angela's shoulder and started to unfasten the buttons at the front of her black bodice, exposing her lace chemise.

'You're pretty,' she murmured. 'I could fancy you. Ever tried it with a gal?'

'No,' Angela said, sitting stock-still, wanting her to stop, longing for her to continue, gasping as Doreen traced a line down between her breasts and, bending forward, brushed aside the lacy undergarment and opened her mouth to a nipple, not touching it, simply warming it with her gin-sweet breath.

'Time you did. You're ripe for it. Ain't she, Tilly? Let's show 'er what she's bin missin', eh?'

Tilly came to the bed and stood there spread-legged, with her knuckles resting on her hipbones. She spoke directly to Angela, asking, 'Would you like that, miss?'

'I don't know,' Angela said, her voice breaking. 'I'm so weary that my thoughts are jumbled.'

'Lie back an' stop frettin',' Tilly coaxed. 'I'll be with you, an' so will Doreen.'

'That's it,' Doreen agreed, kissing Angela's earlobe. 'Let yourself go. Learn from us, and besides enjoyin' it you'll find out about what the men likes, too - yes, deary, one of their pet dreams is to see gals bringin' each other off. Two or more pairs of tits an' arses rubbin' together an' their cocks will be spurtin' like geysers.'

Her coarse words were as nothing compared to the pleasure tingling through Angela, that tongue-tip dipping inside her ear, causing tingles down her neck to her spine and fanning out at her lower back. She sighed and trembled and lay limp and the women undressed her, just as if she was a wax doll without life-blood or animation. Still shy, though her nudity had been seen and enjoyed by many people now, she wanted to place a hand over her pussy and an arm over her breasts, but Doreen would have none of this.

'No,' she said bossily. 'I wants to see everythin'... teats... muff... arse'ole... the lot.' She looked down, mouth loose, eyes hot as she examined Angela visually. Then she turned her over onto her front, and her tone changed immediately. 'Blimey, you poor bitch! Look at the state of you! Was it 'im what done it to you? Arthur Taylor?'

'It was my master,' Angela replied, her body blossoming under Tilly's gentle handling.

'The one you ran away from?' Tilly asked, cuddling against Angela, one leg thrown over her thighs, cambric knickers rubbing against that sensitive, curly-haired triangle crowning Angel's naked fork.

'Knows 'is stuff,' Doreen commented, peering closely at the bruises then, as if inspired by such skill, bringing her own hand down, palm braced, against Angela's bare bum.

'Watch out,' warned Tilly. 'You nearly 'it me then. What you tryin' to prove?'

'That we gals knows better than those cock-happy males, an' can bring a sister off far quicker than the lot of 'em glued together,' Doreen challenged and, swooping over Angela, wrested her free from Tilly. Holding her flat on her back, arms twisted above her head with steely fingers around each of her wrists, she lowered her raven-hued head and worked her tongue between the thickened pink line of Angela's labia.

Angela jerked at the shock of so much pleasure all at one time, and bucked her hips against that wonderful mouth and agile, knowing tongue. She was aware that Tilly was pulling at her nipples, making them stand up stiffly and communicate pleasure signals to her rock-hard clitoris. Doreen let her go for an instant and stripped. So did Tilly. The sight of so much female flesh, the fragrance of their body odours, the delightful touch of their fingers on and in her most sensitive places, roused Angela as never before. She forgot the vows she had made to be good, truthful, modest and blameless. What did any of this matter now?

As if to prove their words the two women lavished pleasure on her. Tilly gently kissed her mouth, then penetrated it, her tongue coiling round Angela's that responded in a dance of desire. At the same time her nimble fingers flicked and pinched and rolled Angela's nipples. Doreen was prone between her spread thighs, concentrating on her slick wet labial wings and the eager clitoris that swelled at the top of them. Angela threw back her head, her face contorted like that of a saint undergoing martyrdom. The sensation was almost too great to be borne. And it did not stop, rising in wave upon wave till she finally peaked, screaming and mindless and plunging into unconsciousness for a split second.

When she regained her senses it was to find Tilly on her knees on the floor, arms resting on the bed and Doreen bending over her. Angela propped herself up on her elbow, staring bemused at the erect and lifelike mock phallus that jutted from Doreen's pubis, fastened there by a harness that clinched her hips and ran between her legs and up her bottom crack. She reached round and manipulated Tilly's love-bud, and then anointed the dildo with juice scooped from her vulva.

Holding her close, she inserted the skilfully moulded cock into her partner's pouting hole and worked it in and out, using the force of her pelvis just as a man would do.

At the same time she kept up the friction on Tilly's clit and appeared to be reaching a climax herself, stimulated by the mighty rubber cock.

Wailing like banshees they came almost simultaneously. Doreen unbuckled the *godemiche* that glistened with Tilly's dew. She threw it to one side and drew her paramour down on the fusty mattress, wrapping them both in the quilt, Angela, too.

'What is that thing?' Angela asked.

'It's a strap-a-dick-to-me,' Doreen answered with a throaty laugh. 'A toy, one of many. Want to try it?'

'Not now,' Angela said, snuggling down among the pillows, too tired to notice how dirty they were.

She slept for a while and was awakened by Tilly and Doreen getting ready to go out. 'Work to do,' Tilly said, smiling at her in the flyblown mirror as she stuck hatpins into her elaborate feathered headgear. 'You'll be safe enough 'ere. Don't let no one in. We'll talk later. Bye,' and both of them rustled out in a cloud of cheap perfume.

Aidan hoped that the entertainment organised by Valerie would relieve his continued ennui. He had never felt so lacking in drive, passion or ambition. He laid the blame at Angela's doorstep, frustrated at being unable to forget her, furious because she had defied him.

The party was being held at the home of a renowned brothel house madame, Mrs Priscilla Wallace. She resided in a large mansion on the outskirts of Mayfair and her clients were mostly gentlemen of standing, politicians, ministers of the church, and revered advisors to Queen Victoria. Priscilla was the soul of discretion, and such a policy paid off. She was reputed to be enormously rich. Valerie had hired her staff and services for the night. Invitations had been sent out, mostly by word of mouth in the Whitehall clubs.

It was not Aidan's first visit, and he walked across the opulent hall and into a reception room that contained billiard tables, around which stood several men in evening suits, chalking cues and eyeing up the balls. There were girls with them, Priscilla's votaries of love, wearing jewelled g-strings and high-heeled shoes and stockings upheld by garters. Some were watching play, others distracting the players. One was massaging the long member of a gentleman who was trying to line up for his next strike. She ignored this, rubbing his cock till it stiffened.

Aidan was aware of noise coming from the conservatory. The glass was steamy and it was not until he walked into this place redolent of palms and fig trees and other imported blooms that he could see what was taking place. A shallow tank had been set up in the centre. It was surrounded by sweating men, all eagerly betting on their favourites as two strapping ladies, naked as the day they were born, mud-wrestled in the container. Aidan was fascinated. The splendidly formed contestants were covered in the gluey substance, slipping and sliding, giving no quarter, hitting, scratching, biting and pinching. It was difficult for them to get a purchase and they were constantly falling down, adding another layer to their skins. They grabbed at each other's matted hair, screeching invective and insults. Blood started to flow and one girl's right eye was partly closed. The other's lips were swollen to twice their normal size.

The observers were in a high state of excitement, fired by the sight of such nudity and violence. Aidan felt his own prick responding, but unable to get through the crowd for a closer view, wandered into another room where the walls were lined with mirrors. There was a bar with waiters serving a variety of alcoholic beverages, and several couches, including one covered in white leather that looked like a massage bench, apart from the straps dangling from it, along with chains and handcuffs. Aidan imagined Angela stretched out there, could almost feel the plaited handle of his whip clenched in his palm, and see her writhing in her bonds, pleading, whimpering, begging him to release her from her agony and take her to heaven.

He needed relief for his throbbing cock that kept reminding him of the thrill that would be obtained by entering one of the muddy Amazons. He looked around for further diversion and sat on one of the deeply cushioned settees, then beckoned over a nervous looking girl. With any luck she would be a genuine newcomer, not an experienced whore pretending to be unschooled. It would cost him more, of course, but what did that matter compared to the joy of corrupting innocence?

He signalled to one of the older women who was prowling around, making sure no punter got away without paying for his jollies. She came over, tall and magnificent, in control, wearing a black leather corset sparkling with sequins, and split crotch bloomers. Her stilt-heeled boots increased her height.

'My lord, what do you need?' she questioned, using his title sarcastically, without the slightest deference to his rank. To her he was nothing but a man with an urge that needed fulfilling without delay.

'Send her to me,' he commanded, pointing to the girl. 'Is she a virgin?'

'Yes, sir, no more than sixteen,' she averred. 'She'll cost you.'

'I don't want full intercourse, only her mouth.'

'In that case you can have it for a guinea.'

'Daylight robbery,' he grumbled, yet thrilling at this transaction that reduced every contact between the sexes to the most basic, low-grade lust - sans tenderness - sans respect - sans love.

'Night time robbery, my lord,' she reminded, and her eyes flashed, betraying her dislike of men, the game and the whole degrading business.

She gestured to the shrinking girl who tiptoed across to where Aidan lounged with his trousers unbuttoned. His large organ protruded through the gap and he was proud of it, so stiff and ready, a proof of his virility. He felt strong waves of excitement as she stared down at it, her eyes wide with fear and disgust. She was a dainty blonde, wearing a simple white cotton dress that added to her naïve appearance.

'Do as the gentleman requires, Bethany,' ordered the senior whore. 'And you, my lord, will pay.'

'Of course,' he said impatiently. 'Tell Mrs Wallace to add it to my bill.'

She flounced off, flinty eyed as she sought other clients, determined they should get nothing without it costing them deep in the purse. Bethany stood there with her eyes cast down and her shoulders drooping. Aidan gave a tight smile and caressed his thickened tool. 'I want you to kiss it,' he said.

Bethany blushed and gasped, 'Sir... I've never... I can't...'

The thought of this being her first excursion into fellatio almost made him come. He gritted his teeth and pressed hard on the base of his penis, preventing the disaster of a too early explosion. 'There's a first time for everything,' he pronounced thickly. 'Thank your lucky stars that I showered before I came out. You might have been doing it to someone who wasn't so fastidious. Don't you like me, Bethany?'

'I don't know, sir. I'm not here to like or dislike customers,' she said shyly.

He did not doubt that she was speaking the truth and lay back against the cushions and smiled up at her, saying, 'Come along, dear. It's time you learned your trade.'

She knelt between his legs and her dress slithered up, giving him a quick flash of a bare and scarlet bottom. Someone had been chastising her. He wished he'd had the privilege. She glanced up at him once and the pleading in her blue eyes would have moved stone, but Aidan's heart was harder than the toughest granite. 'Please, sir,' she whispered on a sob.

'Get on with it. Suck it. Lick it. Bring me off. If you don't I'll flay you alive. The beating you have already had will be as nothing compared to what I shall do.'

Her tears fell and mingled with his wiry pubic hair as she leaned closer. He could feel her warm breath on his helm, and the fact that she was trembling and afraid made the sensation even more acute. He had rarely been so aroused. His prick rose like a serpent before her terrified gaze, the foreskin stretched back, the slit in the dome shining with jism.

Sobs shook her body, and she timidly poked out her tongue and he felt the nervous lightness of her first attempt to pleasure him. His balls tightened, his cock leapt into her face and she recoiled instinctively. He grabbed her hair and refused to let her go, inexorably pulling her back to her task. Her tears aroused him, and so did the feel of her soft fingers gingerly touching the hairy scrotal sac and smoothing the shaft that reared like a spear. It prodded her cheek, determined to penetrate her lips.

'Is she giving you trouble, my lord?' asked the glacial voice of Priscilla Wallace. A stately figure in velvet and diamonds, not tall but commanding: many likened her to the queen.

Aidan looked at her through slumberous eyes, on the verge of climax and wanting no interruptions. 'She has a freshness that delights me,' he answered truthfully.

Mrs Wallace glared at Bethany, saying sternly, 'Obey the gentleman or you'll receive a thorough thrashing and,' her cynical gaze locked with Aidan's, 'he shall give it to you.'

'Yes, ma'am,' Bethany gasped, and set to work, opening her mouth wide and taking the thick penis inside as far as she could without gagging.

Mrs Wallace withdrew though Aidan was hardly aware, head back, eyes part closed, groaning as his hips lifted to meet Bethany's act of slavery. His fingers tangled in her blonde hair, strands falling forward every time she dipped to her task, the fine golden floss tickling his groin as she worked busily. It seemed that she was warming to it, perhaps even excited by having the cock of this fine gentleman in her mouth. Freeing one hand he sought her fork, feeling it damp and hot through the thin cambric dress. He imagined her sparsely furred pussy and rubbed harder.

She moaned and slurped at him busily. His crisis was not far away. His cock grew that much harder and started to pump. Bethany, realising what was about to happen, tried to draw back but he refused to let her go, holding her to him with both hands, pushing his fiery, needy prick to the back of her throat as it jerked and pulsed and gave forth its milky tribute in a final rush of ecstasy.

She coughed and spluttered and forced herself free, starting to retch. His spunk was in her hair, over her face, dribbling down her chin. He relaxed but the girl stared at him with revulsion, trying to wipe herself clean of his cloying emission, gulping and trembling. She watched as his monstrous member started to shrink, till it lay limply across his thigh, then she spoke, her voice shrill with indignation.

'How would you feel and what would you do, sir, if someone did that to your daughter?'

Aidan frowned and sat up, tucking his penis away. Her question surprised him. 'Do?' he said, a savage edge to his tone. 'Do? I'd bloody well kill him.'

'That's men all over,' said the tall, foreign-looking woman who sidled up to the couch. 'One law for them an' one for us.'

'Good evening, Doreen,' Aidan replied, running an eye over this coarse but attractive woman, whose swarthiness hinted at a touch of the tar-brush somewhere in her distant ancestry.

'Lord Aidan,' she said, mockingly, then snapped at the startled Bethany, 'Sling your 'ook!' The girl couldn't get away fast enough, and Doreen stared after her with a thoughtful smile. 'To think that I was all dewy-eyed like 'er once.'

Aidan trusted her no more than he did any woman, but at least she was honest about her whoredom, whereas so many females pretended to be virtuous but acted like bitches on heat in secret. He was wise enough to understand that this was but a job to the majority of the streetwalkers, done through necessity not lust.

'How is it that you are here, at Valerie's party?' he asked, though possessed of that depression following sexual activity with the wrong person. He simply could not get Angela out of his head.

Doreen shrugged. 'I was asked along to 'elp out. Mrs Wallace an' me are old mates. She knows she can rely on me to do a good job. Is there anythin' you'd like me to do? I'm handy with the whip.'

Aidan stood up, towering over her tall though she was. 'No,' he answered, scowling darkly. 'I've had enough and shall take myself off to my club.'

'Really?' Doreen said, leaning forward till her breasts brushed his shirtfront. 'Nothin' at all? Not even information?'

His ears pricked but he remained wary. 'Regarding what?' he snapped.

Doreen wound sinuous arms around his neck. She smelt of spices wafting from a tropical desert island - exotic and bewitching, yet she was not the type that appealed to him - too confident and assured. 'Regardin' a certain young lady what's given you the slip,' she answered tantalisingly. 'Word is that you'll do anythin' to get 'er back. Is this right?'

'Maybe,' he replied, giving nothing away. He had moved in the twilight zones of big cities for long enough to know that it was best to keep a still tongue in your head and a hand on your wallet.

Doreen cocked a saucy eyebrow at him. 'I can tell you where she is,' she brought out.

Aidan's heart soared, but he kept a blank face. 'Indeed? And why should I trust someone like you?'

'You ain't got no option if you wants 'er.'

'How much?' Aidan conceded, though disbelieving. 'And what proof have you that it is her?'

Doreen fished down the front of her bodice and produced a crumpled piece of paper. She flourished it under his nose but kept a tight hold on it. 'This 'ere's a pawn ticket,' she said triumphantly. 'It's got 'er name on it... Angela Bayswater.'

'Where did you get that?' he snarled between clenched teeth.

'Took it from 'er pocket while she was sleepin'. She's stayin' with me an' my mate.'

'Give it here.' He made a grab for it but she dodged away.

'You can 'ave it when we've struck a deal. Let's talk cash, Lord Aidan.'

Angela was wondering what to do next. She had risen from the tumbled bed and dressed, possessed of that terrible lost feeling that weighed on her like lead - she was homeless, almost penniless, and had no idea what Tilly and Doreen had in mind for her. The idea of becoming a prostitute, like them, was anathema to her.

She heard a church clock strike eleven and peeped put of the grimy window. It was pitch dark and raining. The candle was guttering and she lit another from its stump. She was hungry, but investigation of the food hatch revealed nothing except a stale crust and a piece of mouldy cheese. She was almost tempted to return to Arthur Taylor's establishment. Surely Jacob would be home soon? She missed him more than she had thought possible. He was like the brother she had never had.

Suddenly she heard a rumpus down in the alley. It grew louder as whoever was arguing mounted the stairs. Tilly burst through the door, slammed it behind her and threw the bolt. 'You got to get away!' she hissed as a voice outside screamed at her and someone hammered on the door.

'What? Why?' Angela cried, leaping to her feet and grabbing her bag.

'It's that bitch Doreen. She's grassed you up to Lord Aidan. He's below, waitin' to get 'old of you.'

'Oh, my God!' Angela exclaimed, terror lending her wings.

Tilly thrust a chair against the shaking door and said, 'Out the window. The 'ouse next-door is empty. Get in the attic an' run down an' out the front door. Go on! Get movin'!'

Angela did not stop to think twice. She was on the slippery parapet in an instant, edging her way along to the broken casement of the deserted house. Dark, so dark and perilous, but panic drove her on. She dropped inside the echoing, empty room, found the door, the landing and the stairs and rushed down and down, tripping and part falling till she reached the hall. There she paused momentarily, listening, but it seemed that Aidan had followed Doreen and there was no one about. She was out of the door and along the alley like the wind and did not stop running till she had put several streets and the river between her and Friggle Lane.

A stitch was clawing at her side and her breath rasped in her throat. She paused, leaning against a wall. She had no notion where she was. London was an enigma to her and one dirty street looked much like the other. All she could be sure of was that she was far away from Aidan and the treacherous Doreen.

She had fetched up by the side of a tavern. Suddenly the door flew open and half a dozen men staggered out, shouting abuse and laughing and obviously the worse for drink. Angela tried to shrink into the gloom but one of them saw her.

'What's this?' he yelled and came towards her. He was large and brutish, wearing a shabby suit, a cloth cap and scarf. 'Look 'ere, boys, it's a girl! Come on, let's 'ave a look at 'er!' He lurched forward and she felt his huge hands digging into her arms.

'No!' she screamed. 'Let me go!' Her bag dropped to the road and the other men, hallooing like huntsmen, closed in on her. She was tripped and tossed on her back in the puddles. Someone jerked her skirt up and she felt cold air on her nakedness as the first man ripped at her drawers, pulling them down. She fought like a wild thing but it was useless; there were too many of them.

Feeling hands all over her, mauling her fork and belly and tearing at her bodice, she yelled and yelled, but the first attacker was already on his knees between her legs, erect cock out as he struggled to penetrate her. She tried to bring up her knee and jab him in the balls but one of his friends seized her ankles and held her legs apart. Her assailant's weight pinned her to the rain-washed paving stones. She could hardly breathe, her face buried in his dirty waistcoat, the foreign smell of him assaulting her senses.

'God dammit, will you keep still you bloody little bitch!' he shouted, having difficulty in maintaining his erection, his tool weakened by too much alcohol.

'Call yourself a man?' she mocked, though knowing it would only make it worse for her but unable to resist. 'What's the matter? Lost the lead in your pencil?'

'Shut up!' he bellowed, and fetched her a blow across the face that made her see stars. She could feel her strength draining away, and he was forcing his phallus into her, careless of making her pregnant or passing on some nasty disease.

Then, suddenly, the alley seemed to explode. He was hauled off Angela and felled with a single blow from an iron fist. A man loomed over him, a tall, commanding man. Angela got a quick flash of his walking stick raised in fury and, in that instant, it became a sword, the dingy light reflected on steel. The men backed off, turned tail and ran, and her would-be assailant dragged himself to his feet and followed them.

Her rescuer bent and helped her to her feet. 'Are you harmed?' he asked in a rich, rolling voice.

'Bruised, but that's all; they didn't succeed in their intention,' she said shakily, staring at him, impressed by his flowing black cloak lined with scarlet, and the fedora cocked at a jaunty angle on long dark hair. 'Who are you?' she added warily, hoping she was not about to jump from the frying pan into the fire.

He swept off his hat and bowed deeply, saying, 'Maximillian Devere, at your service. Actor manager of a small but talented troupe. We are performing at the hall that is part of and adjoins this hostelry. I'm lodging here, along with my artistes. Come inside and have a drink. You look as if you could do with a stiff brandy,' he said kindly, slipping the blade back into his swordstick. 'Just as well I arrived when I did. I thought those brutes were up to no good when they left the public bar.'

Angela was aching and battered, and not only physically. The actor was courtly and strong, he spoke well and reminded her of her own kind, long lost to her now. She instinctively trusted him, needing a knight-errant as never before.

What did she have to lose? she reflected, bending to retrieve her valise, but he was there before her, saying, 'Allow me,' and lifting it easily.

He offered his free arm and she slipped her hand into the crook of his elbow and, together, they entered the *Pelican and Garter*, inn combined with place of entertainment. A new phase had begun for Angela.

Chapter 9

It was like stepping into another world. The landlord of the *Pelican* was large, genial and a devotee of the theatre. He greeted Maximillian with an expansive smile, saying, 'Bit of bother outside, was there, sir?'

'Indeed there was,' the actor answered with a dramatic gesture. 'I rescued this young lady from a fate worse than death. Those ruffians were molesting her.'

'By God, sir, I won't have that,' the landlord declared, red around the jowls, his waxed moustache bristling. 'Point them out to me next time they dare show their faces in here and they shall be barred, sir, barred for good and all!'

He ushered them into the bar parlour and the sudden light and warmth and friendliness confused Angela. It took her a while to put names to faces after she had been introduced all round as Miss Angela Bayswater. She had never met thespians before, a stranger to this select breed of mountebanks who were respected, lionised and invited into the mansions of the great and powerful. They seemed to be classless, at home anywhere, leading a roaming life that took them all over the length and breadth of England, and abroad, too.

They made her welcome; a comedian, a juggler, an acrobat, a magician, ladies from the chorus line adept at high kicks, and then there was Max himself. He was a master of stagecraft, it appeared, as comfortable acting in the works of William Shakespeare as he was in melodramas.

'Can you sing and dance?' he questioned Angela as she sat beside him on the oak settle by the fire, and the landlord brought her over a balloon-shaped glass containing a measure of brandy.

'I have had singing lessons, and can play the piano. Dancing, too, was a part of my education,' she replied shyly, though feeling more at ease as the brandy slid down her throat and settled like a hot ember in her stomach.

'Then why are you wandering the streets at this ungodly hour?' he enquired solicitously, leaning towards her, and she liked the feel of his wide-shouldered frame next to hers.

He was a striking man in his thirties, his features having a foreign slant, with high cheekbones, a swarthy skin, and thick black hair that coiled in ringlets about his shoulders. He had flung back his cloak and wore a plum velvet suit beneath it, the narrow trousers thrust into soft leather knee boots that gave him a swashbuckling air. A silk cravat, a damask waistcoat, and frilled cuffs completed this outfit that singled him out as being far apart from the common herd.

'I have been the victim of misfortune,' she sighed, and proceeded to fill in the details, though omitting facts that she thought might be too shocking.

Max and his companions listened in silence, apart from the occasional sympathetic murmur, then, 'So you have nowhere to live, no money, and no means of earning any?' he asked quietly.

'That is correct,' she said, and started on a second brandy, losing her shyness, happy in the company of these interesting people.

Max appeared to be lost in contemplation, then he suddenly said, 'How would you like to join us?'

'You mean appear on the stage?' she answered his question with another.

'That's right. Of course, I shall have to give you an audition - which means hearing you sing and seeing if you have any potential for acting. You have the looks, my dear, and hopefully you'll also have the talent required.'

In his enthusiasm he gripped her hand and she was very aware of that firm grasp, surprised and even alarmed by the sudden rush of excitement that made her nipples stand out and her clitoris throb. 'Thank you, sir...'

'Call me Max,' he insisted, smiling with a flash of even white teeth. 'That is settled then. Tomorrow morning you shall tread the boards and I'll put you through your paces. Don't be alarmed. I can be a hard taskmaster, but promise to be gentle with you.'

'But where shall I stay tonight?' she asked, the sudden hope rising in her breast dashed by practicalities.

'Here, with us,' he proclaimed expansively. 'We having lodgings for a while, then we shall travel to our next venue in Cardiff. A touring company, you see, following the well-worn path of traditional strolling players... sometimes appearing in theatres, or music halls with acts suitable for vaudeville.'

'What is that?' she interrupted.

'It's a variety entertainment or a play interspersed with dances, and songs that are usually comic.'

'That's where I come in,' added the dour-faced person who Max had introduced as their 'funny man'. Angela wondered if it was true that jesters were often melancholy in daily life.

'Then there's burlesque. Somewhat coarser in content, mocking situations with grotesque exaggeration, showing a rather low form of wit. I give the public whatever it demands. My forte is serious drama, but I have to make a living though still striving to become a renowned actor like Henry Irving,' Max went on.

'It sounds exciting,' Angela said, but was having difficulty in speaking, her tongue seeming too big for her mouth. The warm fire, the feeling of safety, was making her as relaxed as a rag doll. She wanted to sleep very badly.

Max went into a huddle with the landlord, returning to say, 'He has no more rooms, I fear, and suggests that you share mine... no, don't be alarmed. I can occupy the couch. You will be quite safe, I assure you. We actors often double up if the accommodation is sparse.'

She trusted him and was by now so desirous of finding a corner in which to fall asleep that she did not argue. The other members of the troupe went to their own quarters, and Max led Angela upstairs. The room was softly lit and oak panelled, one of the best the tavern had to offer. The fire's ruddy glow added to the sensation of security and peace. All Angela could see was the four-poster bed and she dropped into its depths, pulled the quilt over her and sank into oblivion. She was hardly conscious that Max, true to his word, seized a blanket and pillow and settled on the couch near the hearth.

She was awakened by sunlight streaming in at the casement and Max standing by the bedside, holding a tray. Wisps of steam rose from a coffeepot and the smell of bacon and sausages reminded her that she had not eaten for hours. She sat up groggily and he smiled down at her, already washed and shaved and changed into yellow check trousers and a scarlet jacket. He was certainly a dandy, and she approved.

'I trust you slept well,' he said, the timbre of his voice tingling through areas of her body that should only have responded to touch. It was so beautifully modulated, so rich in tone, so restrained, whereas she was certain that he could be heard in the far reaches of an auditorium when the occasion arose.

'Very well, thank you,' she answered, aware that her hair needed brushing and that she was still wearing her black dress, even her shoes.

He seemed sensitive to this and suggested, 'Perhaps you might feel able to leave off mourning now. There are clothes in the property basket that might fit you, and more hanging in the wardrobe. Oh, don't worry; they aren't worn outdated garments, but simply articles that have been left by former members who have gone on to fresh fields and pastures new. Would you care to try them on?'

'I'd like to wash, if that is possible,' she said, sitting on the side of the bed and enjoying the breakfast he had ordered for her.

'So you shall. There is a bathroom along the corridor. I'll leave you to it, and then you may come and find me in the theatre. The landlord will show you the way.'

She was flattered by his concern, but a little disappointed because such a splendid man had made no attempt to storm her virtue. It would hardly have been a struggle - more a complete surrender. Angela found him as attractive as she had once found Aidan - still did if the truth was known, never fully able to shut her master out of her mind.

The bathroom was clean and provided with hot water that flowed from a gas-fired geyser. She found soap there and towels, and took off her clothes and had a strip-wash. Wrapping herself in a bathrobe that she found hanging on the back of the door, she returned to Max's room. Following his advice she rummaged through the basket and then turned her attention to the wardrobe. She found everything she could desire - satin underclothes, lace-trimmed corsets, diaphanous stockings; whoever had once owned them must have been a woman of taste. Though when she held them up against her nakedness and viewed herself in the pier-glass, it was to find that there was a certain racy quality about each garment.

A canister of scented talcum powder stood on the dressing table, along with perfume bottles and a range of cosmetics. She dusted her underarms, breasts and crotch, and then fastened herself into the tight stays, squirming round to draw in the lacing. Sitting on the stool she rolled the stockings up her legs and clipped them to the long suspenders. Watching her reflection was arousing, and she stared at her mound. Though part hidden by her bush, the labial lips pouted and her pink clitoris stood out, begging for attention. She touched it and the sensation was wonderful, and sighing she dipped her middle digit into a jar of face-cream and gently massaged the tip of her bud with it. Her nipples responded, poking above the low-cut corset, and she brushed across them with her other hand. Watching these lewd actions excited her even more. It was like seeing someone else doing it, a curious kind of voyeurism. Playing with herself was comforting as well as stimulating. She did not have to rely on anyone else for her satisfaction. Pleasure, pure and simple, was her goal.

She concentrated on her bud, rubbing it, circling the top, teasing and abandoning it momentarily, a feather-light touch all she would allow. Then she went to the other extreme, using pressure as she rubbed harder and harder till it tingled and she could no longer prevent an orgasm from sweeping her away. She plunged her fingers into her vagina, feeling the muscles contract around them as spasms of delight filled her whole being, and it was then that she longed for a huge penis to penetrate her, one attached to a powerful man. She closed her eyes and saw Aidan's face, but it was Max who walked into the room at that precise moment.

She shot up in her seat and hurriedly removed her hand and snapped her legs together, but it was too late. She could tell by his expression that he guessed what she'd been doing. He stopped and said, 'I'm sorry to disturb you. I should have knocked. Most remiss of me, but...' his eyes twinkled, 'I don't regret what I saw. Will you permit me to assist you?'

'In dressing?' she asked, thoroughly flustered as she could not help thinking that his cock was probably as large as Aidan's and why didn't she put it to the test?

'In whatever way you fancy,' Max replied diplomatically.

She pretended not to understand this innuendo and became very busy, stepping into taffeta petticoats and then a pale blue rustling skirt that fastened at the waist and, finally, a very tight and revealing bodice, lavishly ornamented with beads and lace.

'Absolutely ravishing,' Max enthused, sitting on the couch and clapping his hands. 'I can't wait to see you under the spotlight.'

She blushed at this compliment, but was also hugely embarrassed, aware of her scent on her fingers and sure he could smell it too. She started to dress her hair, brushing the long locks up into a coronet at the crown and twisting curls to hang down each side of her face. She turned to Max, posing with her head slightly to one side. 'Will this do?' she asked.

'Wonderful. You already look the part of a star. A touch of rouge, perhaps, a trace of carmine on the lips. The lights are strong and rob one's skin of colour, unless it is artificially applied. Here, let me show you,' and he gave her a lesson in stage make-up.

She was pleased with the result. Her eyes were emphasised, larger, brighter - and her cheeks and mouth were rosy-red. She sparkled, was radiant, and felt as if she had come home. The theatre! How lucky was she to have been found by Max and given the opportunity to embrace this life. What a heaven-sent chance to hide under a different persona! No longer Angela Bayswater.

'What name shall I adopt?' she asked Max, pirouetting round the room.

He chuckled. 'Well, my dear, we'll have to see, won't we? I'm sure we can come up with something suitably glamorous.'

Some of her confidence faded when at last she stood centre stage, a dazzling spot trained on her. A pianist sat in the pit, a flaxen-haired young man who was part of the troupe. The theatre was built alongside the public house and there was a bar at the back. Seats were ranged in rows and there was a balcony above. It was decorated with much gilt and red upholstery and had heavy curtains across the proscenium, just like a regular playhouse. Angela was impressed, and a bundle of nerves.

She had told Max what she wanted to sing and he'd gone into a huddle with the pianist. Within a short time the music was found and the first chords rang out. It had been one of her father's favourites and her eyes filled with tears as she recalled him begging her to sing it after dinner. Then she would accompany herself in the aria by Handel, from his opera *Semele*.

She took a deep breath and started, her voice growing stronger as she gained confidence. '*Where'er you walk cool gales shall fan the glade. Trees where you sit shall crowd into a shade.*'

Then the magic began. She forgot where she was or why, only conscious that this was right for her. She had come home.

Losing all account of time or place she was startled by the spattering of applause that rang out when she finished. 'There were cries of 'Bravo!' and 'Well done!' The thespians had gathered at the back of the auditorium to listen to Max's latest protégée. The landlord was there too, and several members of the bar staff. All seemed impressed and Max was positively beaming.

Father, you would have been so proud of me, she thought, but hot on the heels of this came another idea - and Aidan would be furious!

Max took the side steps to the stage in a bound, clasping her hands and saying, 'That was very good indeed. A tiny falter here and there, but this will yield to coaching. Now I want you to read this.' He thrust a script into her hands. 'It is the balcony scene from *Romeo and Juliet*. You shall be Juliet and I will play Romeo. Shall we begin?'

It was like a dream come true. Angela forgot that she was on a stage attached to a public house in a scruffy quarter of London, transported to Verona and becoming the fourteen-year-old Juliet falling in love for the very first time. She knew the play, having studied it with her governess, but now the words came alive, inspired by Max's perfect understanding of the Bard's poetry. The scene received further applause and, after she had performed a dance for him, Max pronounced himself satisfied with her budding talent and offered her a job. She was in the Seventh Heaven of delight.

They went to lunch in the inn's parlour and there discussed details, such as salary and billing and how she was to be presented when she made her debut. 'As an ingénue, I think,' he said, lighting up a cigar, the drifting blue smoke strongly reminiscent of her father's habit of indulging after luncheon. 'Yes, I can see it all. An artless, inexperienced and naïve young woman.'

'But I'm not exactly that,' she confessed.

'I know,' he replied, looking at her seriously with those melting brown eyes. 'But you haven't lost that air of innocence. We shall call you... let me see,' his brow wrinkled as he concentrated, searching his brain for something striking that would draw in the crowds. Then he snapped his fingers and his expression changed. 'I have it. Rose Trelawney, the Cornish Nightingale.'

'But I'm from Somerset, not Cornwall,' she pointed out.

'I know, dear girl, but it sounds more romantic.'

'I'm afraid. Supposing Aidan hears about it and comes to see the show. He'll recognise me.'

'No, no, he won't. I shall find you a long curly wig, turning you into a golden-haired enchantress, and I shall choose your wardrobe myself. You must be seductive but pure, wearing pastel shades and wide-brimmed bonnets that part hide your face, lots of flowers on stage and maybe a garlanded swing on which you can pose, showing a tiny flash of ankle, maybe. You'll be a sensation, or I'll eat my hat!'

'So this is a respectable family show?' She thoughtfully formed little pellets out of a bread roll and moved them around her plate.

'On the whole, yes, though the chorus girls do dance the can-can, but I insist they wear drawers. Some can-can dancers are nude under their skirts, you know, apart from stockings and garters.'

'I know.' Angela was recalling Valerie's party where just about anything went.

Max refilled their wineglasses. 'The comedian tells bawdy jokes and some of his songs are risqué, but all in all it is harmless enough. Come, you must practice this afternoon and I may include you in tomorrow night's show.'

She gulped, was stunned by the swiftness of events, but could do nothing but go with the flow, borne along by Max's enthusiasm and, the more time she spent with him, the more she was falling under his charismatic spell.

All too soon the moment came when she was standing in the wings, waiting her cue to go on. Max had devoted his time to coaching her and she felt as ready as she ever would be, shaking from head to foot as she listened to the uproar from the main body of the theatre. The dancers had pleased them, so had the magician and the antics of the comic, Max's dramatic monologue concerning a ship wrecked at sea had been well received, and now it was her turn.

He was announcing her assumed name, one she did not yet associate with herself any more than the fair wig that turned her into someone else. 'Ladies and gentlemen, it is my pride and pleasure to present the singing voice of the age. Rose Trelawney, the Cornish Nightingale, straight from a tour of Europe. Give her a big welcome!'

They did so, mesmerised by this tall, distinguished man in his faultlessly tailored evening suit who knew so well how to play on the emotions of an audience. They were putty in his lean, aristocratic, well-manicured hands.

Angela stepped out amidst a storm of clapping and cheering, smiling and dipping a curtsey as Max had shown her. The hall fell silent as the first chords of music rang out. Angela took a deep breath and started to sing. When she had finished cries of 'Bravo! Encore!' made the rafters shake, and they would not let her go till she had sung two more songs. After this she danced gracefully to a minuet and they were completely won over.

Max and she celebrated in his room later. He had ordered cold chicken and salad and bottles of champagne. Angela changed from her stage costume into a silk kimono, embracing the free and easy lifestyle of the thespians. No one seemed to worry about being seen in a state of undress. She put it down to the communal changing rooms and frequent close proximity during travelling. It suited her to perfection. She had always thought people too preoccupied with modesty, particularly the English who liked to 'keep themselves to themselves'. Not that she'd had much experience with Continentals, but assumed that the actors followed their example of greater freedom.

'You're enjoying the experience?' Max asked, lounging back in a wing chair and watching her as she removed the blonde wig, popped it on a stand and unpinned her own hair.

'Tremendously. They liked me, didn't they?' she said breathlessly, and her cheeks were still pink though she had removed the make-up.

'Of course they did. Who wouldn't?'

Before she knew it he was on his knees between her legs, gently easing them apart. She sat there as if rooted, unable to prevent him from peeling back her dressing gown and exposing her naked thighs and the triangle of silky curls between. She placed her hands on his head and pushed him away, but he resisted. 'Max... don't spoil it,' she begged, wanting to yield, *needing* to yield, but terrified of the consequences. Perhaps, once he had prised her secrets from her, he might no longer be interested and her career would be over before it began.

'Dearest girl, how could it do that? I respect you, adore you; I want to sanctify this moment by making love to you. Don't be afraid,' he murmured, and his voice was her undoing.

She no longer resisted and he carefully parted her legs as if unwrapping an infinitely precious treasure. She gasped and lay back in the chair, sliding forward to give him easier access. He inserted his thumbs either side of her outer labia, then parted the wet folds and exposed the inner pair and the thickening stem of her love-bud.

He was as expert at love as he was with declaiming words, playing her body like a delicate instrument; drawing rapturous notes from her as he caressed her breasts, cajoled her nipples and used his mouth and tongue on her clitoris. Passion surged through her and she was coming, the waves of feeling so intense that she cried out.

Max let her enjoy her second of bliss then he pulled her down onto the rug and, while she lay there, he stripped rapidly, the dancing firelight turning him red as a demon. His body rippled with muscles, his chest was darkly furred, his belly too, his penis like a lance rising from his groin. Angela held out her arms to him and he went to her, straddling her thighs, bracing himself on his arms as he lowered his head and captured her mouth, his tongue dipping and delving. She raised her legs and locked her ankles round his neck. He thrust into her again and again, his balls rolling against her perineum while she held him close, rejoicing in the sensation of his large helm filling her channel and stretching her inner muscles and jarring her cervix.

The logs threw off heat and scorched her skin, but lying there in front of it with him gave her the deepest satisfaction, yet there was something lacking. She dug her nails into his back and left long scratches hoping, deep in her psyche, that he would retaliate. She had become accustomed to being misused by men and found it hard to accept that this one was different, not wishing to own or enslave her, but willing to give her the freedom to express herself.

He was pumping into her hard and his penis jerked, portending his crisis. The movement of his hips became frantic and then she felt the gush of semen as he spent deep inside her. He lowered himself to one side, but his cock remained captive till eventually it softened and slipped out. Angela was soothed, healed and should have been the happiest woman alive, but there lingered regret that Max had not mastered her as Aidan would have done. He was, if anything, too good to her.

'There's person here to see you, my lord,' said Maurice, valet and general dog's body in Aidan's service. He was slim and dapper, his hair slicked back, a typical toady and Aidan despised him and would not have had him anywhere near him had he not proved to be so useful at spying. He also had a most enticing bottom and was not averse to showing it, sharing it and submitting it to chastisement.

'Who let him in?' Aidan barked, scowling darkly; his temper had not improved since Angela gave him the slip.

'The butler, sir. The young man was most insistent. Gives his name as Jacob Taylor, sir. Says he's on important business concerning Lady Angela.'

'Why the hell didn't you say that first? Show him in at once. My God, I'm surrounded by incompetents and idiots!' Aidan bellowed, making the china ornaments rattle.

Maurice backed towards the door, then scurried out. Aidan paced the carpet like a caged beast, hands locked behind his back. It was mid-morning, but he was still attired in his brocade dressing robe, the very one that Angela had borrowed on the morning after her deflowering. He had several others, of course, but liked to wear this one and imagine it folded round her delectable body.

Beneath it he had on black trousers, a shirt and waistcoat, was showered and shaved and booted, and it would be the work of minutes for him to don his coat and prepare to go out should this Jacob Taylor person have news of import.

He stared out of the window. From his apartment he could look down on the rotunda. It glinted in the sunlight and his gardeners were at work, keeping the lawns velvet smooth and tending the herbaceous borders.

A tap on the door and he swung round, barking, 'Come in.'

A young man entered, sturdily built and with brown hair. He was attired in a neat suit and carried a hat in one hand. There was something familiar about him and, in a flash, Aidan was transported back in time to earlier that year when he and Angela had gone riding on the very day her father died. There was a groom with them, and it would be unusual for Aidan not to notice a personable youth. He remembered the name, Jacob, having given him instructions to see Lady Angela safely to the manor house. Now he subjected him to a stern glare, saying, 'I know you. Weren't you a stable lad at Lairdland?'

'I was, sir,' Jacob replied, and there was no longer any deference in his tone. He spoke to Aidan man to man.

'Why are you here?' A suspicion began to take root in Aidan's mind, accompanied by anger.

'Where is Lady Angela?' Jacob demanded, standing his ground.

'I don't know, and anyway, what is it to you? Why are you in London and not in the country? How dare you come here in this impertinent fashion? I'll ring for my servants and have you thrown out.'

'Not until we've talked,' Jacob said stubbornly, and Aidan realised he could not intimidate him.

'It's nothing to do with you...'

Jacob stepped closer and Aidan's fists clenched. He had trained in boxing and was half a mind to give this rude young man a clout he would not forget. 'I left home and came to London after I'd heard that you brought her here,' Jacob said steadily, without flinching. 'My uncle owns a grocery shop and I live and work there. I found her ladyship at dawn, running away, terrified of you. I took her home to the shop and she stayed there for a while, looking for work. Then when I had to go on a business trip she vanished again. My uncle, Arthur Taylor, swears he knows nothing about her disappearance, but I've questioned a girl I know, called Tilly, and apparently she sought help from her.'

'Ah, and this Tilly has a friend... Doreen. Yes? A pair of whores. Fine company for a genteel lady like Angela,' Aidan said sardonically.

'You know about them?' Jacob expressed surprise.

'Doreen betrayed her whereabouts. She's a greedy bitch who'll do anything for money, and I mean *anything*. I went with her to persuade Angela to come back to me, but she fled.'

'And you don't know where she is now?'

'I haven't any idea, not that I'd tell you if I did.'

'You swear she's not here?' Jacob looked so grim that Aidan wished he had been carrying a revolver in his pocket.

'I don't have to swear. You'll have to take my word for it. I've not seen hide nor hair of her, more is the pity.'

'Why are you so keen to find her?' Jacob was no longer the groom who Aidan had once bullied. He was a man now, with money and a business behind him.

'Why are *you?*' Aidan remarked icily. 'I suspect our motives are the same. Both of us are cunt-struck. Ain't that so?'

'For an educated gentleman you have a filthy tongue, sir!' Jacob exploded, and Aidan could see the effort it cost him not to strike out.

'I'm allowed, as a member of the aristocracy,' Aidan sneered, then his attitude changed and he added, 'are you going to help me find her?'

'I'd do anything for her,' Jacob vowed. 'And if she wants to be delivered back into your hands then so be it. But that was not the impression she gave me.'

'Women are strange cattle,' Aidan observed, pouring himself a tot of whiskey. 'They say one thing and mean the opposite. As for Angela? I think Hamlet had it right when he said, "The lady doth protest too much, methinks".'

'I don't understand. How can she like you when you have ill-treated her?'

Aidan gave a smile and shrugged his broad shoulders under the damask robe. 'You don't know much about the fair sex, do you, Jacob? Now then, are you going to help me? Then you can ask her which of us she prefers... the rustic swain or the powerful master? Do you accept?'

'For her sake I'll do what is necessary,' Jacob answered stoutly. 'But if you lay one hand on her, I'll...'

'Oh, cool down, nothing will be done that she doesn't truly want to happen, you'll see,' Aidan assured him. 'Let's make a plan. Get those tarty friends of yours to assist. They won't refuse if they are paid.'

'I'm not so sure about Tilly. She has a kind heart.'

Aidan gave a bitter laugh and said, 'She's a woman, ain't she? One of the most mercenary animals on God's earth.'

Chapter 10

Angela had not realised when she crossed a bridge over the River Thames on that fateful night when she fled from Aidan, that she was entering a part of London almost separate from the central city. Not long ago the capital had been divided up into villages, now called 'manors', and the division remained. She could not have found a better hiding place. The *Pelican and Garter* was a popular watering hole, but out of the way. What happened within its walls would hardly make waves in Westminster, Mayfair, Soho or Cheapside.

The days passed, comprised mainly of hard work, for Max demanded a high standard from his artistes. The nights were spent in his bed where she learned what it was like to be held by a man who cherished her. She was already halfway in love with him. She watched the other performers and picked up tricks of the trade. The magician amazed her as well as his audience with his agile sleights of hand. The acrobats and jugglers were circus-born, the dancers skilled girls who trained under the eagle eye of their choreographer. She had once been a ballerina. Angela was her pupil too, and every time she appeared on stage her confidence grew.

As for the comedian? He was a trouper of the old school, never put off by hecklers, giving as good as he got, his timing perfect when he trotted out rude jokes and sang bawdy songs. He reminded Angela of a clown in his baggy trousers and sloppy jacket, his big shoes, red nose and comical hat. Off stage he was gloomy, always looking on the dark side. His dependence on alcohol did nothing to dispel this. Max advised him to give it up, but although he kept a tight ship he could not stop him, any more than he could stop his dancers from getting involved with admirers who wanted to take them out to supper in return for physical favours.

Angela discovered that she was developing her own following but was too shy and fearful to accept invitations. Max guarded her like a bullmastiff, warning her that the males in the audience considered actresses to be little more than whores, a reputation gained in the seventeenth century when women first appeared on the English stage, often ladies of questionable morals seeking a rich protector. Though they were now generally beyond reproach, mud sticks and the legend remained.

Angela was mostly afraid someone might recognise her and report in to Aidan. She wore a wig, it was true, and this might deceive beyond the footlights, but close up? She refused to take the risk, content to hide in Max's shadow. He too seemed to be delighted with her and, although they were discreet, word began to spread among the players. She had been with them a fortnight when, as she waited in the wings one evening she encountered one of the dancers, also waiting her cue to go on.

'A real pro already, aren't you, Angela?' she said sarcastically, a large girl in purple feathers and sequins who was showing a great deal of bosom and tweaking her nipples to make them stand out. 'Getting on like a house on fire, and with Max too, so I hear.'

'I'm beginning to get the hang of it,' Angela replied, adjusting her wide-brimmed Gainsborough hat, nervous as a kitten but knowing she would be all right once she stepped onto the stage.

'And finding out how *he* hangs, too,' the girl said, nudging her in the ribs. 'You aren't the first and you won't be the last, that is until his wife comes back.'

'His wife?' Angela stood stock-still, the orchestra accompanying the comic and the murmur of the crowd fading into the distance.

'Oh, didn't he tell you he was married?' the dancer said innocently. 'Well, there's a surprise! She's abroad at the moment with another company, but just you wait. She's a large woman with a spitfire temper. So be prepared for trouble.'

'He never said...' Angela muttered.

'Of course he didn't. But you just watch your arse.'

No more time for talk or to even think about this alarming revelation. The comic came off, returned to take another bow, then finally finished, reaching for a bottle he had hidden among the props. Angela's introductory music struck up and she was on.

They loved her, demanding an encore, and it was a while before she could escape to the backstage dressing room and collapse on a stool. She stared at herself in the mirror, the naked electric bulbs showing her how garish and sordid was this little space they all shared, and the falsity of her golden wig and painted face. Max! How could he have done this to her, if it was true? She couldn't wait to get him alone and confront him.

The chorus girls flounced in, chattering like parakeets, stripping to the buff, baring bottoms and clefts and nipples without the slightest thought for modesty. The air was rich with perfume and female essences. They hung around, fingering themselves or each other before changing into their own clothes, visions in stays and stockings, garters and frilly knickers topped by bustle cages and silk skirts and extremely low bodices. Angela was aware of their sly glances and wondered how many of them knew about her and Max and were laughing behind her back. It saddened her, for she had thought they were her friends.

He tapped on the door and they fluttered to him like moths around a flame, each jealous and vying for his attention. Even if it was true that he was married this did not prevent them from throwing themselves at him, Angela thought bitterly. Their sometimes spiteful attitude to her must be motivated by envy.

'Are you ready, my dear?' he said, looking over their heads to where she stood in her outdoor clothes. 'I'm meeting a gentleman in a restaurant in Stamford Street. He is taken with the show, and you in particular, and wants to discuss the matter of a private performance. I have promised him an introduction.'

She was instantly suspicious. He was fully aware that she did not want to arouse too much interest and the reason for it, so why was he doing this? Had he heard from his wife and wanted to get rid of her? 'Is this wise?' she questioned as he drew her towards the door. 'Supposing he knows Aidan?'

His curving black brows drew down in a frown and his eyes glittered. 'I hardly think this likely. In any case, I can't turn down such an opportunity. He'll pay well and it will be good for business.'

'Do I really have to come?' she pleaded, her hand on the arm of his velvet jacket.

'Yes, you are the bait, my dear.'

'But...'

'No buts. We are all obliged to do things we don't like if the occasion arises. Now stop being a silly goose. We shall be late. And be pleasant to him, above all things.'

'How pleasant?' she asked, her heart sinking.

He gave her a shrewd look, but seemed a touch uneasy, then replied, 'Whatever it takes, dear girl. Oh, by the by, wear your wig. He is expecting to meet a flaxen-haired innocent.'

'Is this really necessary?' she complained.

'It is. The success of our mission may depend on it. I'll help you,' he said.

So, within a short space of time her own hair was pinned closely to her head, the wig covering it and her hat on top.

The night was fine and they walked to the meeting place. *The Olympia* was not exactly on a par with the West End, where the *Café Royal* attracted the fashionable, witty and extremely rich, but it was a clean restaurant with a reputation for fine cuisine. Angela looked through the frosted opacity of the windows and, when she entered, was impressed by its décor. Walls painted with scenes depicting Venice, large gilt-framed mirrors, long red plush-covered banquettes and tables spread with the finest of white damask clothes. Here and there were statues of gods and goddesses, showing beautiful bodies but with carefully draped genitals, and the whole atmosphere attempted to transport the customer to Italy, and very nearly succeeded.

The waiters were attentive, clad in black suits with sparkling napkins over their left arms. The manager hovered on the balls of his feet like an overlarge stork, bowing and scraping and hoping everyone was satisfied. Mostly they were and *The Olympia* was becoming increasingly popular.

Max and Angela arrived first. 'We are guests of Sir Gerald Hastings,' he told the *maître d'*.

'Yes, sir. Certainly, sir. Come this way, sir,' the florid-faced individual replied, even more like a wading bird as he ushered them to a table and handed Max the wine list. 'Would you like to order a beverage while you wait?' he enquired, the absolute soul of propriety.

Max perused the list and made his choice. The manager bowed and signalled to the wine waiter who took over, selecting a bottle, uncorking it and pouring a small measure. Max sipped and pronounced it satisfactory and the waiter filled his glass and Angela's.

She was impressed by the way in which Max adapted to this situation. It was as if he had been visiting high-class restaurants all his life. Perhaps he had. She really knew very little of his past. She wanted to ask him about his wife, and was just screwing up courage to do so when several gentlemen entered the room.

Their leader waved his cane in greeting and led his companions over to join Max, who stood, bowed and said, 'Ah, Sir Gerald. This is your table, apparently.'

'And this is the oh-so charming songster, I presume,' Sir Gerald replied, and kissed Angela's hand. She was anxious to withdraw it but he hung on, smiling roguishly.

'Miss Rose Trelawney, from Cornwall,' Max said, without batting an eyelid.

Sir Gerald was a large man, not tall but heavily built. His superbly cut evening suit could not disguise the fact that he was running to fat. Two incisive lines stretched from the sides of his nostrils to the corners of his mouth and a greying beard formed a sharp wedge on his chin. He took the vacant chair next to Angela and pressed his burly knee against her thigh under cover of the tablecloth. She wanted to move but caught Max's eye and remembered his instructions. To her alarm Sir Gerald gripped her hand and moved it across so that it lay on the fly fastening of his trousers. Beneath it she could feel a large, hot swelling. She tried to ignore it and remove her hand, but he held on tightly and she was too embarrassed to make a scene, to say nothing of disrupting Max's plans.

'I greatly admire your singing, Miss Trelawney,' Sir Gerald said, and lifted a finger to toy with one of her curls,' and I particularly like young ladies with hair like fairy-floss. You are very pretty, my dear.'

'Thank you, sir, you are too kind,' she replied, hating herself for simpering, but this seemed to be what was expected of her, all part of the act.

'Indeed, y-yes, we agree, d-don't we, ch-chaps?' stammered one of his cronies, a weak-chinned individual with ginger hair plastered to his bony skull with verbena-scented oil.

'That's the ticket, Algie, old boy. Didn't hear you tonight, Miss Trelawney, but we'll take Gerald's word for it. He knows about these things,' chimed in another, handing his top hat, white silk scarf and opera cloak to a waiter who hung them on a coat stand.

Sir Gerald ordered champagne that arrived in an ice bucket, and soon corks were popping like miniature artillery. The wine frothed out, spilling into crystal flutes. The bubbles tickled Angela's nose, the sweet liquid trickling over her tongue and down her throat, and gradually Sir Gerald's insistence on pressing her hand into his groin did not seem quite so unpleasant.

The gentlemen were hungry, and soon snacks appeared: salad, prawns, oysters, canapés, washed down with more champagne. Sir Gerald was in an expansive mood, handing round cigars and generally acting the feudal lord. The circle around the table grew larger. She was the only woman, aware of male eyes, male faces, lecherous male smiles. It was flattering but made her increasingly uncomfortable. She looked to Max for support, but he was engrossed in conversation, singing the praises of his company. Tears burned behind her eyes. She wanted to lay her head down on the table and cry, but then someone topped up her glass. She drained it and felt better.

Champagne! She thought dizzily. When she was famous she'd have it for breakfast, dinner and tea.

She heard Sir Gerald say to Max, 'So, it's agreed then? You'll bring Miss

Trelawney and your dancers to my house on Hampstead Heath next Saturday evening, when you've finished performing at the *Pelican*. I'll send carriages, and it will be worth your while.'

'You don't want a juggler or comedian or magician?' Max enquired blandly.

'No, just the women,' Sir Gerald said, making no bones about it.

'As you say,' Max promised, and Angela despised him: he lost his power and arrogance when faced with a title and wealth, and the promise of gain.

With a final squeeze of her knee and a peck on the cheek, Sir Gerald left with his cronies, after telling the *maître d'* to add the bill to his account.

'Coffee, sir?' the man asked Max once the gentlemen had bundled into Sir Gerald's carriage and headed across the Thames and up West.

'No, thank you, we must be leaving. Ready, my dear?' And Max rose and assisted her into her wrap. He seemed so pleased with himself that she could not voice her doubts as to Sir Gerald's proposition. He was experienced in matters theatrical, and must know if his acceptance was wise.

In their room later they sat by the fire and he drank brandy and she was on the floor at his feet, resting her head against his knees. Then, emboldened by champagne, she tipped back her head and looked directly up into his face and asked, 'Is it true that you are married?'

She felt him start and saw the darkness that settled over his strong features. 'Where did you get that tale?' he said harshly, and his fist clenched around the brandy goblet.

'One of the dancers told me.' A bolt of fear shot through her and a pang of anguish, too. She could tell by his reaction that it was true. 'Why did you lie to me?'

'I didn't lie.' He was immediately on the defensive. 'The subject never came up.'

'Those clothes you said I could borrow. Were they hers?'

'Some of them,' he said grumpily. 'She's been gone a while, and we never got on well anyway. No need for it to make any difference to you and me.'

She sat up sharply. 'It's bound to make a difference. How can I trust you now? And may she not arrive at any time?'

He placed his hands on her shoulders and drew her close to him between his spread thighs. 'If she does, then she won't give a tinker's cuss. She has her lovers, too. We have a free and open marriage.'

If this was intended to mollify her, then it had the opposite effect. 'That's all very well, Max, but it puts me in an impossible position. I'm trying to rid myself of scandalous relationships. I want to earn an honest living, not be shunted from pillar to post at the whim of some man.'

He chuckled and pulled her closer to his crotch. 'That's what is so endearing about you, darling. Forthright and honest and I love it. You are my star, and I'll not let you go. My wife is ambitious. Once plain Charlotte Smith she has taken the name of Carlotta Guido. She is a soprano and sings with a touring opera company. She'll not be bothered if she finds out I've found solace in your arms during her absence.'

'And when she returns?'

'Don't worry. She may never appear, and if she does no doubt she'll be bringing along a train of boyish admirers. She likes her men to be young.'

His words soothed her wounded feelings. His body was so familiar by now, so warm and dear and he smelt so good. Her hand, that had been reluctant to play with Sir Gerald's penis, could hardly wait to touch Max's. He bared it for her and it was long and hard and swarthy-skinned, the shaft knotted with bluish veins, the foreskin rolled back round the base of the helm, which was darkly infused, mushroom shaped, and with a pearly dewdrop at its slit.

Angela submitted, holding the bobbing length of him and then covering the head with her mouth, beginning to suck. Her clitoris was throbbing, the gusset of her knickers drawn close into her crack. She rocked her hips in time to the slurping motions of her mouth, and the wet cotton fabric chafed her bud. He slumped low on his spine, pubis raised to extract every morsel of sensation from the feel of her lips on his cock.

Her jaw worked eagerly and her fingers teased his scrotum, cupping his balls and rolling them in her hand. She longed for him to touch her clitoris that was hard and throbbing with energy. Strange thoughts floated feverishly in her brain. She wished Max would tie her wrists, yet leave her with enough freedom to masturbate him. She wished, as often before, that he would thrash her, bruise her, and teach her to be his slave. But he was gentle though determined, passionate and manly, yet concerned about being a tender lover. He never dominated her, and she missed it. Whatever Aidan had taught her refused to be forgotten. There was a yearning inside her that could only be eased by violence.

Though Max was jerking in her stretched mouth she sensed that he wanted her vagina in which to reach his climax, but unable to hold out any longer he spent himself over her face. The opaque liquid ran down her lips and chin, lodged in her hair and dripped onto her breasts. She swallowed some of it, accustomed to the strange taste, and wriggled to let him know of her own need. He was a sensitive person and lay down beside her on the hearthrug.

His hand explored beneath her dress and lighted on the sliver of flesh that swelled between her labial lips. He clutched her mound in his palm and rocked it, while she thrashed and sighed and encouraged him to poke and probe her and stroke her clitoris. He knew exactly what she wanted and sucked her heated cleft while she squirmed. He rubbed her juices over her folds, wet and sticky and divine, ignoring nothing, running his fingers from the dark maiden curls of her mons to the puckered rosebud moue of her anal opening.

She cried out as she came, shaken with spasms. Max held her and, when she had ceased trembling, lifted and carried her to the bed. There he undressed her as if she was a baby, removed his own clothing and lay beside her, pulling the quilt over them and cradling her in his arms.

Aidan, she thought sleepily, who was he?

'Gerald is going on about a new singer he has discovered. He's throwing a party and she is entertaining,' Valerie said in a bored voice.

She lay on a massage couch in her bathroom while Julian, wearing a barber's apron and nothing else, plied a cutthroat razor to her pubic hair, removing every trace of stubble. There was a silver basin containing water on the table and a shaving brush covered in foam. He dabbed at her pink mound and applied a little more soap, then stretched the skin taut so that her clit stood like a tiny cock while he deftly tackled the area on each side and removed any stray hairs.

'Are you invited?' Aidan asked from behind a copy of *The Times* he was reading, sunk in the depth of a chair.

'Gentlemen only, I understand,' she replied, then gave a yelp and hit Julian. 'Watch out, you bastard. You nicked me. Look, it's bleeding. Lick it at once, soap, blood and all! I demand to come! You owe me that for being careless.'

Aidan lowered his newspaper and watched as Julian leaned over her and applied himself to his task. He could feel his cock hardening in response to the lewd sight of the boy nuzzling Valerie's snatch and the sound of her blows on his shoulders and her voice exhorting him to, 'Go on! Go on! Faster, faster! Oh, God!'

Julian's prick reared upward beneath his apron, and his bare arse was neatly criss-crossed with red stripes. Valerie had been busy. Aidan wanted him as well as her. Anything would have done at that fraught moment - a hand, a mouth, a backside, in fact any object that vaguely resembled an orifice into which he could thrust his virile member. But Valerie reached her zenith speedily and pushed Julian away, demanding that he finish shaving her.

'Tell me more about Sir Gerald's latest piece,' Aidan said coolly, controlling his cock and willing it to lie down.

'That's all I know,' she answered, almost purring under Julian's ministrations, lust sated for the moment. 'Saturday night at his Hampstead mansion. Can you get an invitation?'

Aidan shrugged disinterestedly. 'I don't see how. He and I have never seen eye to eye. He's a pompous ass, and fancies himself to be a connoisseur of beautiful women. A load of tosh, actually; he picks up some real old dogs.'

'Unlike you,' she said smoothly, looking at him from under her long lashes.

'Exactly. Didn't I choose you, my dear?'

'And that little runaway, Angela,' she reminded. 'Any news of her, by the by?'

'No, she's disappeared off the face of the globe,' he said tetchily, and his mouth closed like a rattrap.

'Might be worth investigating Sir Gerald's soirée,' she suggested, while Julian patted her dry. Her rosy mound looked sweet and fresh, the gold rings in her outer labia glinting invitingly.

'I'm not going to beg,' he snarled. 'But I'll send in a spy. Several of his cronies owe me a favour, but I doubt very much that she'll be present. More likely to have headed back to the country.'

'But you've tried there, haven't you?' Holding a silverback hand-mirror

Valerie was admiring her denuded cleft, knees bent and her thighs spread.

'Of course I've tried!' he snapped impatiently, throwing the paper aside and pacing the tiled floor like a caged tiger.

'Dear me, she did get to you, didn't she?' Valerie murmured.

'No woman "gets to me", as you so vulgarly put it,' he raged and leapt forward, unfastening as he did so and pushing her down.

Within a second he was on her and in her while she shrieked with delight, drummed on his back with her heels and encouraged, 'That's it, master. Use me, use me!'

'Damn right I will,' he muttered. 'And every bloody female who annoys me.' He started to come, pumping hard, and the more he used her the more Valerie enjoyed it, writhing beneath him like a demon woman.

Saturday night and the public show was over. The dancers were twittering with excitement at the thought of a private performance, but Angela had serious doubts. She retained her costume, stage make-up and wig, but added a long warm cloak. Max came to collect them and outside the *Pelican* stood two coaches, each with the Hastings crest on the doors. The drivers were seated on their boxes up front and liveried footman helped the ladies in and then took their places standing on ledges at the rear. The whips cracked and the vehicles rumbled forward.

'Ain't this a carry on?' commented one of the girls. 'Is that right you don't want us to wear any drawers, Mr Devere?'

He was sitting next to Angela, and gave a sardonic smile as he replied, 'Quite right. Sir Gerald wants a Parisian version of the can-can.'

'Lor', the dirty old sod,' she answered, and the rest chorused their disapproval, yet a thrill of excitement rippled through the plush lined interior.

'Don't come all girlish with me,' Max grunted, knowing his dancers and their outrageous views on such delicate matters. None of them were virgins. 'It's not the first time you've bared all. You'll get paid more for tonight than a week spent in kicking up your legs at the *Pelican*.'

'That's all right, then,' they trilled, rustling their silk skirts and flaunting fur wraps or ostrich feather boas.

Angela said nothing. She had a cold feeling in the pit of her stomach, helpless to do other than follow Max's instructions. At the moment she was decently clad in the underwear department, but no doubt would have to remove this bastion of respectability when they arrived at Hastings House. Fortunately her act did not include high kicks; she merely drifted round the stage with ballet steps and lovely arm movements. If this was all she was required to do things wouldn't be too bad.

Hampstead Heath was a fair distance, but they finally arrived, the coaches sweeping between wrought iron gates and up a long drive, finally halting outside a fine mansion with a stone façade and wings on either side containing pavilions. They were ushered up the wide, shallow steps and greeted by Sir

Gerald, then taken through the hall with its high ceiling, oaken beams and massive fireplaces.

'This was once a priory,' he explained as they descended into the depths of the house. 'And I have been careful to preserve the chapel and crypt and cloisters.'

'Ooh... creepy, ain't it?' squeaked the leading dancer, and Angela felt its oppressive atmosphere, too.

A strange place for a party, surely? It was the sort of venue that would appeal to Aidan and she hoped against all hope that he would not be there. It brought the dungeons of Compton Hall vividly to mind, but was even more sinister, having oppressive religious undertones.

The light was subdued, with sconces holding candles set at intervals along the stone walls. Braziers full of smouldering coals threw out heat, and there were sumptuous drapes and tapestries, divans and deep chairs, and a stage erected at the far end where once there had been an altar. A curtain was drawn across it and a piano stood on the floor to one side. Max had brought along his own pianist who was familiar with the musical routines. The dancers were shown to a dressing room and Angela detached herself from Sir Gerald and joined them.

He had been more than generous and there were sandwiches and coffee and wine in readiness for them. Angela peeped through a chink in the curtain and saw that his guests were starting to arrive. Aidan was not among them - not yet, at any rate. The pianist provided background music. Male voices rumbled and guffawed and footmen handed round trays of drinks. It was so convivial that Angela lost some of her apprehension. What could be more sensible, after all, than to turn this obsolete chapel into a small theatre? Sir Gerald was probably a patron of the arts, and maybe he would ask Max to put on a Shakespeare play.

More people came, and there was not a woman among them. Now the gentlemen were taking their seats before the stage and there was that buzz which always heralds an entertainment. The dancers were ready in the wings and, as the chords of their first number rang out the curtains parted and they pranced onto the stage.

'Have you removed your knickers?' Max whispered, standing close behind Angela as she watched. His fingers were exploring her bottom through her white lawn dress.

'Yes,' she hissed, none too pleased with this turn of events. She felt very vulnerable appearing in public sans drawers.

'Good girl,' he said softly, finding her ear and caressing the rim with his wet tongue. His hands slipped round and cupped her breasts, thumbs revolving on her nipples.

She could feel herself melting, the love-dew dampening her cleft and spreading to her inner thighs. The sight of the dancers added to her arousal. Their frilly skirts were whipped up and they brazenly displayed their hairy or shaven mounds, whirling to Offenbach's music, finishing with their backs to the audience, bending from the waist and flaunting their pudendum and arses. This caused a riot among the gentlemen.

If only this was all over, Angela thought. Then she and Max could slip off and return to the *Pelican* and their bed. Yet the budding star within her was keyed up and excited at the prospect of giving another performance. She loved the life and wanted to go on acting and singing forever. She had found her vocation, nobly born or not. With any luck and the right coaching she might soon be travelling the world, famous and sought after, Rose Trelawney, the Cornish Nightingale.

She heard the words being announced and was aware that Max was addressing the crowd and that the girls had retired to the dressing room amidst thunderous applause. Max held out a hand in her direction and she walked towards him under the blaze of spotlights. The cheering rose again and Max went off. The music started and she launched into her first song. This went well, at the start, and she was sweet and provocative, as she had been taught. She sang another sentimental ditty, and danced this time. Then suddenly two of her fellow performers rushed onto the stage and grabbed her by the arms. They were no longer dressed in their dance costumes, but wore black leather basques with suspenders meeting the tops of stockings, no knickers and laced ankle boots with stilt heels.

'That's it!' Sir Gerald shouted, seated in the middle of the front row of seats. 'Tie her up, the naughty minx. Virginal Rose, indeed! I hear she's not as innocent as she pretends. She needs punishing and I want you to make her yelp!'

'Hear, hear!' bellowed his colleagues. 'Give her a thorough trouncing, and then let us all have a taste of her!'

'Let me go!' Angela squealed, kicking out and catching one of her captors on the shin. 'Where's Max?'

'Shut up you stupid cow!' the girl cursed, giving her a hard slap. 'He ain't here. A messenger came for him and he went off. That's right, gal, put up a good show of fighting us. It'll please Sir Gerald.'

'Max! Max!' Angela screamed, refusing to believe he had deserted her.

The audience were in uproar, clapping and hallooing, and Sir Gerald, purple in the face, was on his feet, trousers gaping, rubbing his rather insignificant tool, which though erect was hardly formidable. The dancers were going among them, straddling laps, providing relief. Angela was shocked to realise they were little better than Tilly and Doreen, though slightly upmarket, yet still willing to sell themselves if the price was right.

A curtain at the rear of the stage was drawn back, revealing a wooden structure like a pillory. It was open. Angela was stripped naked and forced to stand close to this object and then bend from the waist. The upper half was closed, holding her captive, unable to move her lower torso, and her arms were drawn outwards and the wrists manacled. Her legs were stretched apart and her ankles tied. Her back was to the spectators, and due to her position her bottom was presented to them in all its rounded glory.

She stared at the curtain and waited in fear and trepidation, feeling the cold

112

air on her arse and vaginal cleft. It was awful to feel so helpless, so unable to defend herself and not to know which man came up behind her and used her as he fancied, for she was convinced that's what was intended. Max's perfidy was appalling. Bile rose in her mouth and she wanted to throw up. She swallowed hard and fought for control.

Her sense of hearing doubly alert she was aware of someone behind her. The two girls had vanished and she waited in an agony of suspense. Hands stroked her hinds and fingers pushed into her cleft, one working between her labial wings and stroking her clitoris, catching the sensitive little head as it poked forth. Angela could feel it responding to the moisture this unknown man was spreading from her vulva. It betrayed her aroused state.

The touch was abruptly removed. She strained her ears but all she could hear was the animal-like hoots and cries of the watchers, all goaded beyond endurance by the sight of her and the ministrations of the dancers.

Then, out of nowhere, she heard a swish and felt a burning sensation instantly recognisable as that of a leather thong landing on her skin.

She lost her breath and it landed again, and this time she shrieked. Her assailant whipped her mercilessly, and she sobbed and cried out and writhed in her bonds, but could not escape his wrath.

Blow followed blow and she was lost, rising above the torment of her flesh, entering a trancelike state, at one with he who was mastering her. It had a familiar ring - the way the lash fell, the pauses in between, the sound of his breathing. At last Angela gave up struggling, hanging in the pillory, the wood cutting into her waist, the manacles chafing her wrists, her head dangling.

It was then that the chastisement ceased. Cool balm oiled her reddened flash and dripped between her bottom cheeks, followed by fingers that entered her fundament and stretched it.

She clenched, trying to force them out, but it was useless. The fingers wriggled and penetrated, lubricated and widened the passage, then they were withdrawn and something else took their place.

She yelped and tried to tighten her sphincter but the object was already inside her by several inches. So big, so forceful, so familiar! There was only one man who had sodomised her. Aidan!

Her mind rejected it. Her body welcomed it, a wanton thing outside her jurisdiction. It was him. Every nerve and sinew recognised his cock, and the pain he was inflicting on her by forcing it into her deepest, most secret recess.

Then, as he sank in fully till she could feel his pubic hair brushing her backside and his balls tapping against her slit, her discomfort was transmuted into dark, searing, unnatural pleasure. She lifted her mound, grinding it into the hard wood, finding a knot at just the right height to contact her bud. Aidan, if it was him, pushed in and out and she clung to his length, closing her muscles round it, making him work for his orgasm.

Meanwhile her own crisis was coming, her clit sliding over the knot, thrumming and tingling until it spasmed and shockwaves flooded her. The man in her arse felt this and he too exploded, his creamy tribute jetting out, filling her anus and dripping onto the wood.

He pulled out abruptly and strode round so she could see him. He reached out and jerked off the blonde wig, the hairpins dragging at her scalp. Her own locks spilled down and he grabbed a handful, jerking her head up, making her look deep into his eyes.

'So it is you. The Cornish Nightingale, the songster Gerald has been boasting about.'

'Hello, Aidan,' she croaked, her anus hurting, her bruises stinging, her emotions in turmoil.

'Is that all you can find to say to me?' he growled, standing spread-legged in front of her, large and masterful and incredibly handsome.

'What else is there to say?' she asked. 'You must realise by now that I refuse to be your slave and wish to make my own way in the world.'

He snapped his fingers and the two dancers who had guarded her released her from her bondage and gave her back her clothes. But Aidan put out a hand and prevented her from dressing. 'No,' he said. 'I want to see you naked. I had forgotten how beautiful you are.'

Her legs were shaking and she needed to sit, but, 'How did you find out I was here?' she asked.

'Rumour about the new singing sensation intrigued me. I'm not a friend of Gerald's but I offered him Valerie in exchange for an invitation. He's always wanted her and the deal was done.'

'You have no scruples, have you?' she sighed, her spirits sinking once more.

'Very few,' he admitted. 'Now, get the rest of your things and come back to Temple Grove with me.'

'I want to continue performing,' she protested. 'I enjoy stage work.'

His smile deepened. 'We'll see. But I want you with me first.'

Angela did not trust him an inch. She must be as subtle as a serpent if she wanted to escape him. 'I'll get my cloak. Wait for me here,' she said, and picked up her garments.

Once in the dressing room she put on her clothes, gathered up her bag, stuffed the wig in it and swung the cape around her shoulders. Then she took another door, speeding down a passageway, up stairs that connected with the kitchens and out into the yard. She ran as if the devil was behind her, giving herself no time to reconsider. She wanted Max and her career, even though her whipped flesh and abused body hankered after Aidan.

On reaching the main road she hailed a cab and, lost in its solitary darkness, reviewed her situation. There was no doubt that Aidan would pursue her to the *Pelican*, but there she hoped Max would defend her, tell him that she had potential and demand that he leave her to pursue her career. Perhaps later, if Aidan regained his respect for her, there was a slight chance that she would permit him to woo her.

The *Pelican* was shrouded in darkness, but she had a key and let herself in.

She mounted the stairs that led to Max's room and opened the door. It was candlelit, and looked different. Several trunks and cases stood on the carpet.

'Max?' she called.

'What the hell...?' cried a female voice and she found herself facing a large, beautiful woman with tousled black hair who shot up in the bed, glaring at her. 'Max, who is this trollop?' Then her eyes narrowed and she leapt up, advancing towards Angela like a naked Valkyrie seeking vengeance. 'Ah, I see! You must be this Cornish Nightingale he's been fucking! My God, just you wait till I get my hands on you, lady. I'm his wife!'

Chapter 11

Angela was in a state of total shock. She had accepted that Max was married, but the sudden appearance of his wife came as an awful surprise. She stood there, her back to the door, and stared at the couple. Max was lying in bed looking tousled, disconcerted and ashamed.

'This is Carlotta, she came home unexpectedly, that's why I left the party,' he muttered, and it was the first time Angela had ever seen him at a loss.

'You abandoned me to Sir Gerald's mercy,' she snapped, unable to control her temper, tired of everyone pushing her around as if she was of no consequence.

'He owes you nothing, slut!' Carlotta stormed, aiming a blow that Angela dodged.

'After you went Sir Gerald had me stripped and tied to a pillory. I was forced to lean over it, clamped and restrained. My back was to the audience and I couldn't see the man who whipped and then buggered me, but I guessed his identity. It was Aidan. How could you do this to me?' she stormed.

'I'm sorry, I didn't know he would be there,' Max protested while Carlotta loomed over Angela, her voluptuous body, alabaster skin and mane of blue-black hair making her feel small and insignificant. This was indeed a formidable rival!

She could smell her, too - perfume, sweat, and female love juice mingled with Max's spunk that wafted from between her thighs. Her mat of public hair glistened with it. She raised a hand to strike Angela again, but Max leapt up and stopped her.

'No,' he said sternly. 'None of this is her fault. She didn't know I was married until today, and even then I wasn't sure if you'd ever return. She is talented... not as talented as you, my love, but her act is filling seats.'

'Sack her!' Carlotta demanded, her full red lips curved in a snarl.

'I can't do that,' he protested, and Angela was thankful that he had not dismissed her out of hand. 'She has nowhere to go.'

'That is not my problem,' Carlotta declared, and swung round on him. 'Why did you fuck her, Max? You could have listened to her sing, watched how she performed and probably given her a chance. But oh no, you couldn't control your dick!'

'And what about you and your boys?' he thundered, a vein throbbing in the middle of his forehead, his eyes blazing with fury.

Carlotta shrugged, every inch the diva though bare as the day she was born. 'That's neither here nor there. They mean nothing to me, but you are my husband.'

'They may mean nothing, but your infidelities matter,' he stormed. 'Why should I deny myself and remain faithful while you bed any youth that takes your fancy?'

'You know I love you,' Carlotta said, as if this explained her behaviour. 'You are the only one who has my heart. No one is as dear to me. You have accepted my dalliances in the past. We decided long ago that this was permissible if it enhanced my performance. I sing dramatic roles, full of passion. If I'm not with you I need to express my emotions in other quarters.'

'That's all very well,' Max replied, glowering at her. 'But the same should apply to me. "What's sauce for the goose is sauce for the gander".'

'Well, I'm back with you now. The tour is over and I shan't be needed again for six months. Rejoice, darling; I shall sing in your troupe and you can dispense with this little bit of folly,' Carlotta retorted, sneering at Angela.

'Be reasonable, my dove,' Max pleaded, stripped to the buff but still dignified. 'Would you turn a fellow artiste out on the street?'

'Damn right I would, if she's been usurping me,' Carlotta said imperiously, but her tone had softened and she was examining Angela from head to foot. 'Who is this Aidan person you spoke of, girl?' she asked.

'My name is Angela,' she answered stiffly, aware that the look in those black eyes was almost that of a man scrutinising his next amatory victim. 'And Aidan was my fiancé who jilted me when my father died, leaving me penniless and without a dowry.'

'An out-and-out cad, yes? A man without morals or principles, but he still attracts you. Don't deny it. I can tell when you speak his name. I'm a woman too, remember?' With every word she uttered Carlotta was becoming less fearsome and more human.

Angela hung her head. Her welts were stinging, her bruises aching, her arse sore, but yes it was true; Aidan still had a hold over her, devil though he was. 'This may be so,' she admitted. 'But I never want to submit to him again. He uses me as his slave. He refuses to marry me, yet won't let me go. I want to sing and dance and make something of myself. Max has helped me so much and I swear to you that I thought him single. I would never take another woman's husband.'

Carlotta sat on the bed and motioned Angela to join her. 'Don't cry,' she said. 'I'm not such a dragon, am I?' Angela winced as she touched her and Carlotta shot her a shrewd glance. 'He whipped you tonight, you say? Let me look. Take your clothes off, deary. Max, fetch that bottle of lotion from my case... not that one, dunderhead! The vanity bag.'

Angela was thankful that she was not to be turned out into the night. Carlotta seemed less threatening, and she hoped they would let her stay with the company though it was essential she moved soon, for Aidan would be on her trail. She had a little money saved, with which she had hoped to redeem the trinkets she'd left in the pawnshop, though it might be difficult without the ticket. She needed to acquire more wages from Max before she could branch out on her own and find another impresario who might give her an audition. She was stage-struck, and never wanted to do anything else.

Hesitatingly she undressed, feeling shy and inadequate under this gorgeous woman's appraisal. She stood with her back to her, one arm covering her breasts, the other cupping her *mons veneris*. She heard Max give a slow whistle while Carlotta tut-tutted.

'This Aidan knows how to handle a whip!' she exclaimed. 'A master at it, I should say. Is this how he gets his thrills?'

'He enjoys it, yes,' Angela admitted, shivering as Carlotta's fingers traced over the scarlet stripes and applied the cooling lotion.

'And you?' she questioned.

'I have grown to understand the mixture of pain and pleasure,' Angela whispered, her face as red as her bottom. 'He taught me well, and is my master. Yet part of me longs to escape him. I don't want to go back to him.'

'Then you need not,' Max put in. 'I will introduce you to Richard D'Oyly Carte who runs the *Savoy Theatre*. He's always on the lookout for suitable young actresses who can sing and act and meet the approval of that popular pair who write comic operas for him, Gilbert the lyricist and Sullivan the composer. Meanwhile, we'll have two divas here. You can perform duets.'

'But I need to sing arias,' Carlotta pouted. 'I'm an operatic soprano, don't forget.'

'That too,' he said placatingly, and Angela felt pity for him faced as he was with the dilemma of keeping both of them happy.

Once Carlotta had finished anointing the whip marks Angela took up her chemise and slipped it over herself, covering her breasts and partway down her thighs. 'Where shall I sleep?' she asked nervously.

'It's very late. I can't rouse the landlord now. Besides which, the inn is full,' Max answered, climbing into bed.

'Then may I use the couch?'

'Certainly not,' Carlotta rapped. 'You shall lie here, with us.'

'But...'

'Don't argue. There's plenty of room for three. And why should Max have had all the enjoyment of your perfect body. I want a share in you.'

Dumbfounded, Angela did as she was told, occupying the space next to Carlotta with Max on the far side. She had retained her chemise and held herself stiffly away from Carlotta's luscious curves, but the warmth was undeniable, and so was her curiosity. Was Max's wife of a similar persuasion to Valerie? Did she enjoy women as well as men? She resembled her somewhat, also well built and with a big bosom.

A single lamp glowed on the nightstand, and the tester bed was like a raft floating on the swell of an exotic sea. She had become used to it over the past weeks, looking upon it as *hers*, shared with Max. Now the dynamics had shifted: she was the outsider, allowed to lie in it with his wife's permission.

Carlotta was stirring, pushing her large bottom into Max's groin as they lay close, curled together like spoons in a cutlery drawer. 'Caress my tits, Angela,' she ordered, her voice husky with desire.

The situation was fraught but exciting and Angela responded. She started to run her hands over Carlotta's throat, and down to the opulent breasts. Carlotta raised herself a little, seized Angela's face and captured her mouth, her fleshy tongue poking inside, eliciting an instant response that took Angela by surprise. She moaned as that agile organ explored her gums and teeth and danced with her own slippery tongue. And, moaning still, she played with Carlotta's nipples, brown and crimped and rising from dark aureoles. They felt rubbery and instantly responsive, reaching even bigger proportions.

Carlotta released Angela's mouth and ground her hips against Max's erection. 'Lower, girl, lower,' she muttered, and seized her hand and guided it down to her curly pubes.

Just for a second Angela felt revulsion, and then this was superseded by interest as her fingertips delved into Carlotta's cleft, parted the labia and dabbled in the flow from her vulva. In doing so she encountered the end of Max's cock, inserted between Carlotta's legs.

'Ah, that's good,' he groaned. 'Rub it, Angela.'

'She is attending to me,' Carlotta objected. 'Do your work, Max, and spear me on your rod while she brings me off. Thus we can attain bliss together, beloved.'

He withdrew his tool from Angela's hold and Carlotta bucked and heaved as he slipped it inside her. She grunted her pleasure and dragged Angela's face towards her crotch. Angela lifted back the bedclothes so she might breathe. While Max slipped in and out of his wife from the rear Angela hung over her, slid her thumbs each side of the darkly furred slit and opened the pinkish labial wings. They parted easily, swollen and engorged, and Carlotta's plump clitoris crowned the slit, standing proud.

Fascinated by the sight of another woman's fissure, Angela dipped a finger in Carlotta's copious dew and stroked the hard nodule. It was like touching herself and heat blossomed inside her, and her own clitoris throbbed with need. The welts bestowed by Aidan had their own particular ache and she longed for him - his whip, his crop, his tawse.

Would Max make love to her when he had satisfied Carlotta? Or might the woman stroke her nub till she climaxed? Angela was too much in need to care.

Carlotta was shaking with the force of Max's entry and she growled, 'Slow down; give me a chance to come! Go on, Angela, suck me.'

He paused in his labours, making small movements, just enough to keep her on the boil, and Angela's desire made her lean forward, fingering the turgid little organ. Then, bewitched by the pungent odour that filled her nostrils, she stretched back the labia major and Carlotta's clit bulged. Angela dribbled saliva over it, massaged it, and unable to resist, placed her mouth over it and started to suck.

Carlotta stretched upwards, chasing the pleasure caused by those wanton lips. Max kept up with her, his penis buried deep inside her as he clamped her close with his arms around her and his hands firm on her breasts. Angela smiled within herself, a dark, satisfied smile. These people thought they had the better of her, but at that moment they were nothing more than her slaves. Like Aidan they mistakenly thought they were her masters, when in reality they were dependent on her skill and willingness to oblige them. Who was the dominator and who the submissive? One did not exist without the other.

This thought empowered her and she sucked greedily at Carlotta's bud, making her scream with pleasure, then gradually increasing the pressure till she felt her shake and jerk and heard her yelling as she reached crisis point. Max speeded up his movements, and as his wife came so did he. The juices flowed from both and Angela tasted them, salty and strong, then took her mouth away, drying it on the back of her hand.

'Oh... oh, darling... that was wonderful,' Carlotta crooned, to Max not Angela.

'Happy now?' he whispered, and they snuggled close together as if forgetting the third party in the bed.

'Ah yes, so happy. I love you, Max.'

'And I love you too, Carlotta.'

Then the silence told Angela they were asleep. Selfish bastards, she thought angrily, and turned on her side away from them. The entire world was comprised of self-centred people, she decided. There was no one she could trust or confide in or feel was a true friend. Except perhaps Jacob, but then there was his vile uncle to take into consideration. Maybe she'd go and see him; it depended on what Max and Carlotta decide to do with her. He had mentioned D'Oyly Carte, a renowned name in theatrical circles. If only she could be taken on by him!

'Why did you let her go?' Valerie asked, dressed to kill and seated by Aidan in a box at the *Royal Opera House*, Covent Garden, waiting for the performance to begin.

The great building was aglow, all gilt and crimson swags, drapes and deep carpeting, with evening-dressed, white-gloved attendants at the stalls and box entrances, or ushering the audience to their seats in the tiers. Outside its gas crescents blew in the breeze, the portico was a pool of light, every window gleamed and a rich yellow flood poured out from under its covered carriageway. Used though she was to going there, Valerie never failed to be impressed by the endless procession of carriages rolling up from the Strand, driven by coachmen in livery and tricorne hats, and cockaded footmen in buckskin breeches so tight that their packages were emphasised. They sat stiffly to attention at the rear with their arms folded across their chests.

Now, having fired her question at Aidan, she lifted her opera glasses and adjusted the lenses. She swept a glance over the crowd in the pit and stalls below, then across to others in the dress circle and those who had also paid dearly for one of the secluded boxes at either side of the stage, where they could see and be seen.

This was a gala night, and handsome, moustachioed men in tails and white waistcoats escorted ladies in silks and satins, with trains and low necklines. On their arms, fingers, corsages, and heads gleamed a fortune in jewels - rubies, emeralds, tiaras, ropes of pearls and diamond necklaces. The men brought their wives, sisters, daughters and mothers to such events, never their mistresses or whores. Apart from Aidan of course, a law unto himself, and in any case Valerie was well connected. She might be the subject of gossip and speculation, but no one could deny her, married as she was to the Honourable Dennis Gail.

Aidan smiled darkly and replied in answer to her question, 'Cat and mouse, my dear. My favourite game. I know where Angela is and can strike at any time. Let her sweat for a while, never knowing when this may happen.'

She put down the opera glasses and stared at him instead. His profile was just too attractive, as was the whole man. It was not fair that he could be so handsome and yet so devilish in his dealings with women. She shivered inside and felt her womb contract with lust. No matter what he did or how cruel he was, she could never resist him.

'So I amused that odious oaf, Sir Gerald, for nothing,' she complained sulkily, flicking open her fan and waving it. 'Dear God, he dressed up in one of his mother's gowns and had me cane him like a naughty schoolboy! His cock was tiny, even after I'd thrashed him, and then he had the bad grace to spurt all over me. The things I do for you, Aidan.'

'And you earn my undying gratitude,' he said, with a sincerity she knew to be false.

The conductor entered amidst polite applause, he raised his baton, the lights dimmed and the opening bars of Mozart's *Don Giovanni* stole across the auditorium. A magical moment, heralding a work of great beauty despite its theme of a licentious Spanish nobleman who tries to seduce every woman that swims into his ken, until he is dragged to hell by supernatural forces.

Valerie was distracted by Aidan's close proximity. They had the box to themselves, and the intimate atmosphere inspired her with thoughts of love. It was the kind of love portrayed in the opera - the violent destruction of innocence; similar to the sexual games she shared with Aidan. She wanted action, her blood racing as she willed the opera to be over so she might spend the night with Aidan, though not even sure if he wanted her.

As she sat there, eyes fixed on the stage, she was aware of his hand on her knee, though he, too, was concentrating on the singers and the unfolding plot. Valerie drew in a sharp breath as his fingers slowly lifted her skirt, encountered her silk-stockinged leg and went higher, his action hidden by her frilly petticoats. As usual Valerie wore no knickers, liking the freedom this afforded for a quick coupling with whoever she fancied at the moment, be it Julian, Aidan, Viola, Martha or any of her numerous sexual partners. She was a woman of fiery passions that refused to be quenched by anything less than the satisfaction of the senses.

The box was dimly lit and the spectators glued to the action on stage. Even so, the fact that they were in a public place excited her. She sat still, her fan in one hand, her programme open on the crimson velvet edge of the box. Aidan, apparently, was as absorbed in the plot as the rest, but his busy fingers reached her apex and gently stroked over her bald pubis, tugging at the jewels dangling from her folds. Not simple rings tonight, but diamonds, small, sparkling and perfect. She had worn them in anticipation of showing Aidan this latest addition to her very personal adornment.

She parted her legs slightly, giving him easier access to her treasures, and his silent exploration roused her to the point where she had to cling to her upholstered chair in the effort to control herself. The stage whirled. Aidan slipped into the motion she knew so well, then he suddenly pinched her clit and she came sharply, only just succeeding in restraining a yelp.

She felt him shaking with repressed laughter; hated and adored him in the same breath. Damned him, too. He was far worse than the reprehensible Don Giovanni and deserved the same fate, that of being condemned by the Devil to a fiery pit for all eternity.

Angela's life changed, but in a subtle way more than anything else. It obviously puzzled the rest of the cast to see Carlotta treating her affectionately. They couldn't make head or tail of it and there were mutterings.

The two singers rehearsed together, and Angela was taught several duets where their voices blended perfectly: hers lighter, that of a soubrette, while Carlotta had a heavier, more dramatic approach. But after a few performances Max shook his head and maintained that they were losing some of their audience; those who preferred naughtier shows, complaining that Carlotta had too serious an approach. They preferred the Cornish Nightingale on her own, able to weave fantasies about her, the charming young woman with whom they dreamed of fornicating. Carlotta took offence, labelled them Philistines and stamped about on her high heels.

Angela could see that they would soon come to the parting of the ways. Max promised to arrange a meeting with D'Oyly Carte, but the entrepreneur was a very busy man and had to be handled diplomatically. By now she had been banished to a single room on the top floor of the inn, and she was lonely, upset, and the future looked bleak. So one morning, free from rehearsals as Carlotta had commandeered the pianist, she boarded a bus to Soho.

She was tempted to wear a veil when going abroad, but refrained from doing so, afraid of drawing attention to herself. She had on a skirt and blouse of sprigged georgette, flounced and frothy and summery, with a lace scarf draping her shoulders. Her hat was a mere trifle, round as a pork pie and decorated with artificial roses. Her hair was piled up and she wore this example of the milliner's art tipped forward archly.

The weather was warmer now, trees blossoming under the blue sky where drifting clouds reminded her of woolly sheep. She felt a pang of homesickness. It seemed incredible that this time last year she was the cherished daughter of a titled noble without a care in the world, and soon to be married to the man she loved. Fate had an unkind way of having tricks up its sleeve and she had never ever dreamed that she would be in this predicament.

She thought of Lairdland even more as she reached the grocery shop with its impressive sign, bearing Arthur Taylor's name. For an instant she almost took flight, remembering that nasty man, but at that moment Jacob appeared at the shop door. He wore a smart dark suit, with a high-buttoned waistcoat, a gold watch-chain spanning the pockets, a striped shirt with a stiffly starched collar, and a bowtie.

'Lady Angela!' he exclaimed, blushing to the roots of his brown hair. 'What are you doing here? Without a chaperone, too.'

'Those days are long gone, Jacob,' she said with a wry laugh. 'I came to see you, needing a friend, if only to talk over the old days. Is your uncle in?'

Jacob frowned. 'He is, but he won't bother you. He'll have me to deal with if he does. Come in.'

'I'd rather not,' she said.

'All right, I'll get someone to hold the fort here. Shan't be a moment,' and he went back inside, appearing again very shortly wearing a bowler hat.

She took his arm and they strolled towards the park, where sitting on a bench she recounted her adventures. Jacob had matured, now given the responsibility of managing the shop, and she found him attractive with his wholesome clean features, honest eyes and infectious laugh. He had not lost his countrified accent and even this brought it all back to her - the village, the manor house, the time when everything seemed so enduring and secure.

'I went to see Lord Driscol after you scarpered. Thought perhaps you'd gone back to him,' he said quietly, and dared to take her gloved hand in his.

'What did he say?' The mention of Aidan made the fine down rise on her limbs.

'He's a cool customer, but was very angry that you'd run away. He asked me to help him find you, so I played along with it, hoping that if he heard anything he'd keep me informed.'

'And did he?' Angela leaned her shoulder against his, comforted to be able to speak with someone so normal. Actors and the like were all very well, but they did tend to exaggerate.

'I heard never a word,' Jacob said, his firm lips setting angrily. 'Of course I made enquiries, but didn't really trust Tilly or Doreen. It was her that led him to you. I kept my weather eye open, though, having the feeling that you'd turn up some time. Are you well? What can I do for you?'

'I'm well enough, and love being on the stage, but Max's wife thinks I'm stealing her limelight and I know she wants to be rid of me. He's going to introduce me to one of the big theatrical managers, and I'm waiting for this to happen.'

'Does Lord Driscol know that you're appearing at the *Pelican and Garter?*'

'I've an uneasy feeling that he does, but I've not heard from him. It's unnerving, and I'm wondering where he'll strike next... and when.'

'Perhaps he won't,' Jacob said, without conviction.

'I don't believe that and neither do you,' she said emphatically. 'I'm not sure what to do next. I can stay with Max's company till I get fixed up elsewhere, and it will be exciting if I'm taken on at the *Savoy Theatre*, but I admit to being nervous. I shan't know anyone there, and Carlotta won't encourage me to visit him or her. That's one of the reasons why I've come looking for you. I need a friend.'

Jacob was seated with his knees apart, his hat dangling between them and his head down. He appeared to be uneasy, and she felt a coolness emanating from him that she'd never been aware of in the past. He had been shy, but unable to hide his admiration. In fact she had worried because she could not reciprocate as he desired. Now she would have welcomed an advance on his part.

'I'll be your friend, milady,' he vouchsafed at last, and looked at her, his eyes shaded by thick lashes. 'But things have changed. You see, I went back to the village not long ago and who should I bump into but Bertha Marten. You know, the girl who used to be your maid. I told her all about you and where you were and that, and we got on like a house on fire, and well, to cut a long story short, we kind of fell in love. We're going to get engaged soon and she's coming up here to live and then we're getting married. She'll help run the shop, and it'll be mine when uncle pops his clogs.'

Angela felt as if a door had slammed in her face. It wasn't that she wanted Jacob as a lover, but had contemplated sleeping with him if he would protect her. Now she had missed the boat and he was Bertha's. She truly was on her own now. 'Congratulations,' she said, and meant it. Whatever life had in store for her she would face it by herself. At least she didn't have to see Arthur Taylor again. 'Has Bertha met your uncle?' she added.

Jacob seemed not in the least perturbed. 'Not yet, but she'll have him eating out of her hand, and he'll have to behave himself. She may look as if butter wouldn't melt in her mouth, but she has a razor-sharp tongue when she gets going.'

They parted at the park gate, and she reached up on tiptoe and kissed him on the cheek. 'Goodbye, Jacob,' she whispered.

'Goodbye, milady,' he responded warmly, but with a touch of regret, maybe for his lost dreams of what might have been. 'I'll invite you to the wedding. Is that all right?'

'I'd love to come,' and she turned and walked away. A door was closing but another would open soon, she was sure.

She turned off the main road into a quiet alley, a shortcut to the bus stop. Her mind was preoccupied. In one way she was glad for Jacob, but on the other hand felt the loss of such a devoted swain. She had clung to the notion that he might wait for her indefinitely, always there, somewhere in the background, ready to do battle as her chivalrous knight. Now she was forced to see him as he really was - a normal man who wanted to marry, settle down and raise children If only Aidan had been like him, or even Max. Men! They were put on earth to plague women!

The alley was deserted, surrounded on two sides by high brick walls. A slice of sky could be seen way up above the rooftops. She was very nearly at the end, anticipating walking out into broad daylight, when her ears caught a sound. Her heart started to pound and she hurried along. It had been foolish to come this way. The place abounded in pickpockets and she was carrying a handbag, an open invitation to have it snatched. She stopped for an instant. So did the footsteps behind her. She dared not turn round but broke into a run.

The stranger kept pace with her and then she felt a hand on her shoulder, sluing her to a stop. She was jerked round so that she faced her assailant. 'Aidan!' she gasped.

His smile was grim, his eyes bright and ferocious. 'You can't get away from me, Angela,' he ground out. 'No matter where you go or what you do, I'll find you and have my way with you.'

'Leave me alone,' she pleaded, though breathless with running and being suddenly faced with him.

He shook his head, his hair falling to his coat collar from under a black hat, wide-brimmed and rakish looking. He smelt good, his personal aroma and that of expensive shaving soap entrancing her. She felt as if she was sinking into him, longing to be absorbed and lose her own personality, even her soul, in the exquisite, agonising union that she dreaded yet hungered for.

He laughed, a low mocking sound, and pushed open a door to the right that led to a stairwell. He propelled Angela through. Steps wound down into darkness and others corkscrewed up into a pale streak of light entering from a narrow window above.

'Where are we?' she whimpered, while he lifted her skirt, yanked down her knickers and grabbed her bottom cheek, digging in his nails.

'In one of my warehouses,' he replied, and explored her flesh, remarking, 'You've not been flogged lately. Dear me, and you want it, don't you? Have you been fucking Max again? And what about his wife? Word has it that it's a *ménage à trois*.'

As if getting ready for action he took off his hat and hung it on a rusty hook. 'Keep yours on,' he instructed. 'It will make you look even more of a slut when I fuck you, like a sixpenny drab who sells herself against a wall.'

'That's not my style, you should know that as you seem so well informed about the rest of my life,' she retorted, stung by his mockery.

'Let us say that I'm keeping an eye on my property.' He chuckled and reached between her legs, squeezing her clitoris. She gasped, seeing him sneering at her, an intent look on his handsome face.

He pulled off her silk scarf and used it to tether her hands behind her, then turned her sharply and pushed her so that her knees hit a lower stone step and her torso rested on the one above. Her skirts were thrown back over her shoulders and she gave a smothered cry as she felt the burning impact of his hand on her buttocks, first one then the other in quick succession.

'There you are, dirty little bitch,' he grated, and smacked her again, harder this time till she writhed and wriggled but could not escape his mastery. 'That feels better, doesn't it? Don't try to pretend that this hasn't haunted your dreams and filled your mind while you played with yourself?'

As he spoke so his palm landed on her behind, harder still. She gave up struggling, tears running down her face and dripping onto the dirty stairs, despairing because every word he said was true and that she could never escape him, no matter how she tried. Her rear was burning and this heat penetrated her loins, making her vagina clench and her love-bud twitch.

'More,' she sobbed, losing every iota of self-respect. 'Punish me, master. I fornicated with another woman's husband.'

'And what else?' he asked, stern as a confessor, his stinging blows raining down.

'And slept in the same bed with them, while they copulated and I excited her breasts and cunny and brought her off.'

'You have been wicked, my child,' he said severely, and slapped her over and over again. By now Angela was mad with desire for him, her body and mind open to anything he intended to do. He paused in his chastisement long enough to unbutton his fly, then he parted her arse and wetted his cock with her juices and grasped her hair like a halter to give him better purchase. His member rammed into her so hard that she shrieked. 'Be quiet,' he hissed in her ear. 'Unless you want my workers to find us like this.'

His hand was beneath her, rubbing her clitoris as his propulsion in and out became quicker and more brutal. He was treating her like some streetwalker he'd just picked up. This sense of degradation, the pain in her hinds, the friction on her clit, and the pounding of his cock in her love-channel was preparing her to come.

The squalor of their surroundings, the smell of urine on the stairs, the damp walls and general neglect seemed right, reminding her that she was as nothing. His thing. His toy. Aidan was her master and could do what he willed with her. Her heart ached with love for him and her body was obsessed with the need to climax, blanking out her mind that stormed angrily at this treatment. How dare he? But as he drove his erection faster and faster so her orgasm was upon her, not in waves but in one mighty crescendo, like a volcano erupting.

She clenched around him, expecting his final surge, but he pulled out of her quickly, spun her round and, while she sat on the step, thrust his cock into her mouth.

It tasted of herself, with the addition of pre-come. It was huge and meaty, on the brink of exploding, and he held her steady with his hands on her cheeks, working her head up and down on that burgeoning tool. She heard him groan and felt that extra stiffness that heralds ejaculation. Then her mouth was filled to overflowing by the eruptions his penis gave forth, viscous fluid that got everywhere, on her lips, dribbling down her chin, wetting her hair. She had nothing on which to wipe her face.

Aidan withdrew and passed her a monogrammed handkerchief, then he released her hands and replaced the scarf round her throat. Just for a moment she imagined he was about to strangle her with it, but this passed as he freed her, rearranged his trousers, reclaimed his hat from the hook, opened the door and went to go out.

'Don't leave me here,' she begged, trying to tidy herself, scared of this dark, alien place.

'Why not? You obviously know your way about,' he said coldly.

'But...' words failed her, yet she wondered why she had expected anything from him.

He shot her a final glance, then said, 'I'm sure you'll find your way home, wherever that may be. The *Pelican and Garter*, so I understand. Goodbye, Angela, till next time.' And with that he disappeared from view.

Angela ran into the alley, but there was no sign of him. She did not hurry to cross the river again, meandering along the pavements, window-shopping. She caught a glimpse of herself in a glass-fronted emporium. It was amazing how prim she looked, not a hair out of place under that frivolous hat. No one would have guessed that the gusset of her drawers was wet with her own dew, that her buttocks stung, and the unmistakable odour of Aidan's spunk clung to her face and throat. If anyone came near her she was sure they would recognise it on her.

She passed unheeded among the shoppers, an ordinary lass who was bold enough to walk abroad without a companion. The morning was wearing on and she waited for the horse-drawn omnibus and returned to the *Pelican and Garter*.

She was met at the stage door by Max. 'Ah, there you are!' he exclaimed. 'We've been searching for you.'

'I went to visit a friend,' she said, alarmed by his urgency and deciding not to mention Aidan. 'Is something wrong?'

'Be careful going out on your own, dear girl, but there's no call for alarm. All is well. I bumped into D'Oyly Carte at the club over luncheon. Told him about you, and managed to get him to agree to giving you an audition. Tomorrow morning at ten o'clock sharp.'

'Oh, my goodness,' she whispered, gloved hand to her lips. 'What shall I say to him? What shall I sing? Oh, I can't possibly...'

'Of course you can,' Max said sternly, gripping her by the elbow and propelling her into the auditorium. 'You'll spend the rest of the day rehearsing. I've ordered the pianist not to leave his seat, on pain of death. Carlotta will help you. Isn't that so, my love?' and he stretched out a hand towards his wife.

'I'll do all I can,' the dark beauty replied, her expression a mixture of envy and the sincere desire to help a colleague, especially if it meant withdrawing her from her husband's presence.

Angela understood this in a flash but was too excited to care. The *Savoy Theatre* was prestigious. Its shows drew huge crowds, its principles were popular and famous, and it was not beyond the realms of possibility that she might one day be up there with them. Then indeed she could cock a snook at Aidan Driscol.

Chapter 12

There was a row about it, of course, but eventually Max talked Carlotta into giving permission for him to accompany Angela to the *Savoy Theatre* in the Strand. The weather was capricious, a wind blowing and drizzle making the streets muddy. It was a nigh impossible task to keep one's hem dry, as Angela soon found out.

They travelled by hansom cab - no such thing as a humble bus for Max. He liked to arrive in style, particularly when seeing someone important. The vehicle drew up outside the frontage and Angela stepped from it, saying, 'My, what a fine a edifice. It looks new.'

'It is. Carte had it constructed to his own design a few years ago. Did you know that it was the first public building to be entirely lit by electricity?'

She shook her head, very impressed, but was also acutely nervous. It was all very well being auditioned by Max, but this had been tempered by the fact that she was desperate and he fancied her. D'Oyly Carte was an unknown quantity. She had heard that he was strict with his cast, or rather the scriptwriter, W. H. Gilbert, was, and it was he who supervised the rehearsals of new operettas and put everyone through their paces, stars and chorus members alike.

'Carte won't employ anyone with loose morals,' Max continued as they arrived at the red painted stage door round the side. 'His female members, and the males for that matter, have to have an aura of respectability. Oh, you get the toffs hanging around, the young men about town, same as everywhere else. The girls may condescend to have supper with them at *Romano's*, or perform at private functions, but it's essential that they behave like well-brought up ladies. An inch or two of ankle is all they are allowed to show on stage, and this is enough to drive the men wild.'

'You know an awful lot about it,' she remarked, glad she had dressed modestly.

He gave her a lopsided grin. 'The theatre is my life, or hadn't you noticed?'

'Where shall I live, if I get the job?' she asked nervously, clinging to his arm and feeling a revival of sexual interest. It was lovely to have him to herself, without that pushy Carlotta's gimlet-sharp eye boring holes in them.

'"Don't count your chickens before they're hatched",' he advised, patting her hand that nestled in the crook of his elbow. 'Though I gather that Carte prefers his ladies to reside in sober, theatrical boarding houses. Shared with several others. When they become top of the bill they can usually afford to rent apartments, or even buy their own homes. Then they have more freedom of movement, but woe betide them if their names are associated with the slightest breath of scandal.'

'I find that reassuring,' she murmured, praying that she might get taken into the *Savoy* fold and be protected from predators like Aidan.

Max pushed open the door, and the first person to greet them was a man who stepped from his cubby-hole with all the precision of a guardsman. 'Can I have your name, sir, miss?' he asked, carrying a clipboard, pencil poised.

Max handed over the note he had obtained from Carte. It was in the nature of an entrance ticket. Then he took a business card from an inside pocket. It had gold deckled edging. 'I'm Maximillian Devere, the actor-manager,' he announced grandly. 'And this is Miss Rose Trelawney. We have an appointment with Mr D'Oyly Carte.'

Angela threw the man a bright smile; warm enough to be friendly but without the slightest hint of coquetry. She was sure she looked stylish but not over-bold, a soft grey chinchilla cape round her shoulders, her hat a froth of pink tulle and roses.

'Thank you, sir, my name is Enoch. I'm the stage door keeper. Anything you require please let me know. I'm on duty most of the time, but if not then my assistant, Wilfred, takes charge. Now then, I'll escort you to where Mr Carte will be waiting. Follow me.'

Stairs led upwards, but Enoch took them straight along a corridor, branched off into another, and crossed an area at the back of the stalls that had small round tables and bent-wood chairs, and bottles and glasses reflected in wall mirrors behind a highly polished mahogany counter.

'The green room is over there,' Enoch informed them, with a jerk of his thumb to the right. 'That's where the actors relax or entertain guest, and this here's the crush bar so as the punters can get a drink between acts. "Crush" is the right bloody word for it, if you'll excuse my language, Miss Trelawney. But there ain't no one in here at this time of day.'

The interior looked unfriendly and almost dingy. They walked into the main body of the theatre where cleaners were sweeping the aisles and dusting the red moquette seats. From backstage came hammering and the humping and sliding of scenery, male shouts and the occasional swearword. Angela was in a ferment of excitement now, though her stomach felt as if it was home to a hundred butterflies. She sniffed the air. It was reminiscent of the auditorium at the *Pelican*, a conglomeration of damp, the stale smell that a crowd leaves in its wake, used cigars, perfume and perspiration. It was in partial darkness, too.

'Ah, there he is!' exclaimed Max, spotting Carte centre front of the orchestral stalls.

'I'll take you over to him, sir,' said Enoch firmly, ever mindful of his orders.

Max stood back so that Angela might precede him and they walked down the side aisle and stopped at the row where Carte held court and observed what was happening on stage. With him were several assistants, including a woman in her thirties. She resembled a secretary, neatly dressed with a simple, upswept hairstyle and a business-like notepad on her lap.

Carte was forty-odd, with a pleasant face, shrewd eyes, dark hair and sideburns. He was hatless, and had a black overcoat with a velvet collar and lapels slung around his shoulders in an ostensive, devil-may-care way, very much the impresario. Angela tried a trick she had perfected when faced with scary people - she imagined them naked. Now she visualised Carte completely nude. His coat made his frame look wide, but maybe in reality he would be hollow-chested, with a rounded belly. As for his genitals? She mentally pinned a dick on him no bigger than a cashew nut, and a pair of infinitesimal balls. Big coat, big theatre, small cock!

Unaware of her mischievous thoughts he shot her a glance and nodded to Max, saying, 'Is this the young lady? What is her name?'

His female companion supplied the answer, checking on her pad. 'It's Rose Trelawney, Richard,' she said, and Angela noticed the flash of a wedding ring on her left hand.

Not another married man? she thought, panicking. I hope she's not as jealous as Carlotta.

Max bowed from the waist, giving the woman a dazzling smile. 'Good morning, Helen. Congratulations to you both. I've only recently heard that you'd become Mrs D'Oyly Carte.'

'Thank you, Max,' Carte replied, calm and composed. 'She's been my assistant for years, and it seemed sensible to tie the knot.'

Arrogant pig! Angela thought. His assistant, indeed! She probably ran the whole shebang! Why was it that men adopted this superior attitude towards women? If she wasn't so keen on forwarding her career she might well join those courageous ladies fighting to get the vote, to repeal the divorce laws and raise the age of consent to sixteen.

'Indeed, yes,' Max was saying, 'very sensible, Carte.'

And he was another one, Angela's thoughts raced. They had no idea how to make women feel worthy. Didn't they know that at one time they were goddesses - earth mothers - with temples and shrines dedicated to them? Where did it all go wrong?

'Shall we start?' Carte cut in. 'There's a lot to get through this morning. Now, Miss Trelawney, will you please give the pianist your music and take up your position on the stage. What are you going to sing?'

'Where'er you walk,' she said clearly. This song had been lucky for her before and she hoped it would be again.

Enoch took her to the wings and she was awestruck. The stage was much bigger than that at the *Pelican*, a fully-fledged arena with scenery and backdrops, footlights and arc lights and all the paraphernalia needed to complete the illusion and take the audience into a magical world. She felt dwarfed, standing under the spotlight's direct beam. This rendered the auditorium black. It always did, and it was a blessing. She could forget that she was being watched and give of her best.

The acoustics were splendid. She had never heard her voice sound so rich and full. She gained confidence and before she knew it the ordeal was over and the critical watchers were clapping.

'Well done,' said Carte from the darkness. 'What's your opinion, Gilbert?'

Angela edged forward and shaded her eyes. Now she could see that another man had come in and was standing near the aisle. A lean, sober-looking man with greying hair. Could it be the renowned Mr Gilbert who wrote the words for those amusing shows for which he and Arthur Sullivan were famous? Her father had taken her to see one of them during a visit to London, and she had never in her wildest dreams thought that one day she would be auditioning.

'Very nice,' he said flatly, displaying neither enthusiasm nor disapproval. He then addressed her. 'Can you dance, miss... eh, what's your name?'

'Rose Trelawney,' she answered clearly. It was now or never. 'Yes, I can dance.'

'Let's see you, then,' Gilbert replied.

The pianist struck up and she knew the tune. It was from one of his comic operas, a topsy-turvy farce about fairies and peers. She took off her hat and fur cape and went into a routine taught her by the ex-ballerina who coached Max's dancers. Like much of Sullivan's music it was gay and light-hearted, and her skirt floated around her, never showing more than her insteps and dainty shoes. She was transformed into a sylph with lovely arms and a supple waist.

'A bit too graceful,' Gilbert remarked dourly. 'The fairies in *Iolanthe* are much more clumpy, that's what makes 'em amusing, but she'll learn. Now, can we get on with the rehearsal please, Carte? Can't keep the cast hanging about,' and he indicated the people who had begun to stroll in, those fortunates who were already part of the *Savoy Theatre*.

'Come down, Miss Trelawney,' called Helen. 'We'll go to the office.'

The upshot was that Angela signed a contract for a trial period. She was stunned by the salary offered - two pounds a week! Why, even ladies' maids and butlers were paid less than that *per year!*

Max was a great help, insisting on studying the contract before she committed herself, then declaring it to be fair. Helen did most of the donkeywork while Carte offered Max a cigar and said little to Angela, except for one comment.

'You speak well, Miss Trelawney. Do you come from the upper class? Please, tell me, for I don't like my players to be secretive. All above board, that's what we require at the *Savoy*.'

'I was born into a good family, sir, but unfortunately my father passed away and left me nothing. The estate had to be sold. I came to London looking for work and Mr Devere very kindly helped me. I was taught to sing, dance and play the pianoforte during my schooldays. Trelawney is my stage name. I prefer to keep my anonymity.'

'Very well, I shall respect this. You seem a sensible young lady, and talented, too. Mr Gilbert was impressed by you.'

'Was he, sir?' Angela expressed surprise.

'Oh yes, I could tell. He's a man of few words, apart from the written ones, and a stickler for perfection. Although you'll be under the guidance of our director, Mr Gilbert insists on being involved in a new show, though he hides away on the first night. Sullivan, on the other hand, conducts at every performance, even though he may leave rehearsals to his second-in-command. He's got quite finicky about his music since the queen knighted him. He has always had aspirations to write grand opera.'

'Don't look so worried, my dear,' put in Helen kindly. 'You'll soon get the hang of it all. Who's who and what's what. We shall expect you to be here at ten o'clock sharp on Monday morning. I can give you the names of several landladies who already look after some of our girls.'

'Thank you so much for offering this opportunity to my protégée,' Max said, rising to his feet.

Carte smiled and also rose from the swivel chair behind his elaborately carved antique desk. 'I'm surprised that you are willing to let her go,' he observed, eyes twinkling as the two men shook hands.

'Well, you see, Carlotta has returned from her tour with the Carl Rosa Opera Company, and we don't really need two sopranos,' Max said smoothly.

Carte raised an eyebrow sceptically, observing, 'Especially one as young and beautiful as Miss Trelawney, eh, Devere? I recall that Carlotta is somewhat, how shall I put it? Fiery?'

'She is indeed,' Max conceded, and then changed the subject. 'I say, is it possible that I could take a look round your theatre before we go. I'm sure Rose will be very interested, too.'

'But of course, my dear fellow, Enoch will show you the way,' Carte said grandly, proud of his achievements.

Enoch conducted them through the dressing rooms, practice rooms and costume department, but it was rather inconvenient as the cast was in rehearsal and did not welcome intruders. 'I expect you'd like to see the under-stage area where many of the props are stored,' he said, and was then interrupted by the appearance of Wilfred, a keen young man who suffered from acne.

'You're needed up front, Mr Enoch,' he said, glancing nervously at Max and Angela.

'Right-o, lad,' Enoch rejoined. 'I'll be there in a jiffy.' He turned to Max and added, 'That's the way down to the props department, if you wouldn't mind going alone, sir. You can catch me at the stage door on your way out, unless Mr

Carte has an errand he wants me to do.'

'Shall we?' asked Max, with a sideways look at Angela as Enoch hurried off.

'I'd love to,' she responded eagerly. It was all too exciting, taking her breath away. She was actually signed up as an actress with this prestigious company! To add to this, she was about to spend a stolen hour in a secluded place with a man she found devilishly attractive. Just thinking about it made her whipped derrière smart.

The theatre had been constructed on a much older site, the cellars of which had become the foundations and useful repository. Stone stairs led steeply down, made extra wide to accommodate bulky pieces needed on stage. Bare electric bulbs illuminated it. The ceiling was arched and low. Max had to bend to avoid knocking his head.

Despite the activity taking place in the distance overhead, the music, the singing, the interruptions as choruses and action were repeated until perfect, down there it was tomblike. Angela could have been frightened had not Max been with her.

He took her hand and led her through the series of rooms, one leading from the other. It seemed that the items for scenes of each play were stored together. In one alcove were Japanese artefacts, in another seafaring gear, then castle interiors, and a multitude of things that could transform the stage into whatever period, time or place was demanded. Colours blazed and gilt sparkled; it would look even more splendid under the stage lights.

'Marvellous,' Max commented, looking round. 'Carte is in an enviable position.'

'You'll get there eventually,' she comforted.

'Shall I?' His face was gloomy. 'It takes money or a patron who believes in one.'

'Your turn will come.'

'Your faith in me is heartening,' he said and pulled her close, his heat penetrating her clothes and his. 'And this is overdue, don't you think?'

'Carlotta,' she reminded, placing her fingertips across his lips.

'She isn't here,' he said, and removed her hand, his mouth swooping down to kiss her with warmth and skill. Right from the start she had enjoyed the way he kissed, and she could feel herself melting, dissolving, wanting him to devour her. He pressed her against the wall, his muscular thighs grinding into hers and his hungry cock prodding her belly. She carried her hat and he combed his fingers through her hair, pulling out the pins and bringing it tumbling down. He held her away from him, studying her from beneath hooded lids, his mouth slack with passion.

'God, you're beautiful,' he said huskily.

'And you, Max, belong to someone else,' she reminded.

'Not at this moment,' he replied ironically. 'No one exists for me but you.'

He kissed her again, not her lips but her brow, her ears, her throat, and this drove her mad. His hands were at the front fastening of her dress, undoing the buttons and pushing it aside, then bending to fasten his lips on her nipples, sucking them through the thin silk of her chemise. Angela became limp in his arms, incapable of logical thought.

Oh yes, he belonged to Carlotta, but she had subjected Angela to embarrassing moments, always trying to humiliate her. She owed her nothing. And then there was Aidan, who imagined that he owned her. Angela closed her mind to memories of them. She wanted Max, inspired by being in the basement beneath the grand theatre, wanting to have him make love to her there, in this holy of holies.

He rucked up her skirt and petticoats, untied the tape bow that held up her drawers and eased them down, then combed his fingers through her pubic bush and tantalised that sensitive spot between her labia. Standing in his embrace with his wonderful fingers playing havoc with her clitoris, she unbuttoned him and took his stiff shaft in her hand, breathing deeply of the intoxicating odour of his arousal. He lifted his hips towards her touch, pushing his cock into her hand and she shivered with delight, the response echoing deeply in her sexual regions.

'I want you... now,' he whispered, keeping up that rapid friction on her hungry little organ.

'We can't, can we? Not here. Supposing someone comes down?' she protested, though feeling she might die if he stopped.

'Doesn't this make it more exciting?' he murmured, his breath caressing her ear, giving her goose bumps. 'What a performance we should give, you and I. Better than anything we might offer on stage.'

'You're wicked,' she chided half-heartedly, keeping up that frottage on his helplessly addicted penis. 'Where can we make love anyway? Leaning on the wall? I don't think so.'

He chuckled, and releasing his cock from her hand for a moment, guided her across to where a carved throne stood against a whitewashed wall. It had an oriental look about it, covered in Chinese silk. Max kissed her again, his tongue wooing her into submission, then he turned her gently and had her stretch across the throne. He lifted her skirts and completed the removal of her knickers. Angela was only too eager to comply, and he reached between her legs and kept up that steady rubbing motion on her hard nubbin. When she started to peak he lowered himself and guided his cock into her. Delight flooded her as she came, and he moved silently within her while her muscles tightened round his prick. Her heart was thudding furiously and she was glad he had taken her from behind, his lower body bumping against her welts, reminding her of her master's chastisement.

He was in no hurry, rocking to and fro, plunging in and then withdrawing so that only his tip remained. 'Oh, Max... Max,' she moaned.

He was superb, poising above her like an eagle over its prey, then thrusting into her again so that she almost yelled with the force of it. This excited him beyond endurance and he took her fast, his cock like some powerful piece of machinery, pumping and pumping until he threw back his head and barked his climax. She could feel every second of it, that solid spear piercing her very core as his libation jetted, bathing her in seed.

Even in that moment of ecstasy he did not forget to cup her mound and pay attention to her love-bud, bringing her down slowly, as an experienced lover should. She collapsed beneath him, prone across the Mikado's throne, willing herself to imagine that this might go on forever. But paradise is short-lived, as she had discovered, and Max kissed her cheek and removed his weight from her.

'I shall miss you, darling girl,' he said, in that beautifully modulated voice of his, one that could whisper intimacies or reach the very back of an auditorium full of people.

'But I can come back with you now, can't I?' she asked anxiously. 'Just until I find lodgings, that is.'

'I shan't turn you out, but it will be wise to get addresses from Helen and start looking straight away,' he said, tidying his attire. He didn't have to say more. Angela knew he was thinking of Carlotta and, as he was inexorably tied to her and wanted to save his marriage, so she must get out of his life as quickly as possible. What they had just done, enjoyable though it was, did not signify any permanency in their relationship.

But he was kind and considerate, nonetheless, helping her find her knickers, tidy her hair and rearrange her hat and cape, and then seeking Helen for addresses before escorting Angela from the *Savoy*.

Mrs Morrison was one of that stalwart breed without whom thespians could hardly have survived - the theatrical landlady. She was outspoken, stood no nonsense or avoiding paying rent, though she was tolerant of and extremely kind to those who had fallen on hard times - perhaps going through a period of 'resting' that meant they were not employed in their chosen profession at that precise moment.

Angela was intimidated the first time she met her, taken to her terraced villa in Woodgreen, not too far from the Strand and Leicester Square, by a member of the chorus called Elsie May. This bright, honey-blonde trouper had already done a year at the *Savoy* and was a mine of information. She lived under Mrs Morrison's roof.

Angela's mind was buzzing. She had joined the company on Monday, been introduction to the cast, the director, chorus master and choreographer. She was given a sheaf of music and the lyrics and told to learn it pronto. Just for a while she was to sit and watch and understudy one of the dancers in case she twisted an ankle or had similar bad luck. It was bewildering and heady and she was thankful to have been introduced to Elsie by Helen, who instructed her to look after the 'new girl' and help her find lodgings.

Mrs Morrison had hennaed hair and an opulent bosom, her figure laced into tight corsets, and she was wearing the latest in fashion, the actually physical work of running her establishment left to several servants. She discussed mundane matters like the cost of laundry, how many meals and when, rules about not bringing men into the house and a strict regime of lights out a certain time of night. Her boarders where given keys, but she wanted to be informed if they intended to be late. Angela was relieved, for she had feared that she might be nothing more than a bawd, expecting her female guests to whore for her. But nothing could have been further from the truth.

'It's not exactly a nunnery, and we're not expected to be novices,' Elsie explained when they sat in a teashop eating sticky buns after Mrs Morrison had said Angela could have a room. The first week's rent of three and sixpence (including meals, laundry an extra shilling), had to be paid in advance.

'I don't mind that,' Angela said, feeling safe for the first time since her father died.

'It doesn't mean to say we can't have fun. We are taken out to supper and invited to parties by the nobs, but keep our legs together. Those mashers aren't to be trusted, so never believe a word they say, just use them to climb the ladder of success,' and so saying, Elsie poured tea from a pot into china cups with blue rims and helped herself to another cake.

They were soon in possession of each other's history - not all, naturally, only what they chose to reveal, and Angela kept quiet about Aidan, but hinted at a broken romance. This seemed to satisfy Elsie's curiosity and they were soon fast friends. Their rooms at Chez Morrison were next to one another. Angela thought she might have felt lonely once she left Max, but her life was now so full as she learnt her trade. And there was always Elsie and the others to chat with and exchange views and gossip and fashion tips. The days flew by and she enjoyed every moment of it. Then she was deemed ready to start rehearsing.

The Yeoman of the Guard was playing six nights a week plus two matinees, and also Gilbert was drilling them to learn a new opera, *The Gondoliers*, due to open in December. Angela was taking part in the chorus of the former, and experiencing her first taste of appearing in public where the audience was nothing if critical. Any spare time she had was devoted to studying the forthcoming Christmas production.

She was too busy to dwell on Max, Jacob or even Aidan, though he still came to her in dreams and supplied fantasies for her self-relief. Not that there was much time or privacy for even this. Elsie was giggly about the young men who hung around; the Stage-Door Johnnies in their opera cloaks, silk toppers and silver-headed canes. She seemed to have no notion of lesbian love, and Angela did not enlighten her or recount her own dabbling in that direction. Both of them were as prim and proper as Mr Carte decreed.

The excitement of chorus work in the *Yeoman*, its setting that of the Tower of London, the Elizabethan costumes, the music and storyline, occupied her whole attention. She longed to be taking the leading female role, but knew she had a way to go yet. She had never been more content. Everything was wonderful, especially the camaraderie in the dressing rooms.

The greasepaint transformed her into someone else, with wide, blue-lined eyes, long lashes, rouged cheeks and lips. Any exposed parts were dabbed with wet-white (in reality a colour wash that was put on with a small sponge to give her a glow). Her hair was tucked under a demure coif, but the whole effect was charming. She radiated enjoyment and confidence, and this, besides her voice and dancing, singled her out from the rest. People were beginning to recognise her and ask questions as to her identity.

There was no word from Aidan. It was as if he had disappeared from the face of the earth. Then a new beau appeared, sending flowers that were delivered by Wilfred. The card inside said he was Lord Alfred Codford, and that he would deem it a great honour if she would permit him to take her to *Romano's*. She politely refused the first time, but kept the bouquet.

He was persistent, at the stage door the following night. More flowers, another request that she might at least meet him. She softened and permitted him to come to the dressing room when the other girls had left, and only Elsie remained.

'What shall I do?' Angela asked, her heart thumping. It was so long since she'd had contact with a man on a personal level. Too long, complained her body.

'Just see what he's like,' Elsie advised, skewering her hat in place with long, amber-headed pins. She nodded in the mirror, satisfied with her appearance.

There was a tap on the door and Wilfred poked his head round, saying, 'Lord Alfred is here to see you, Miss Trelawney.'

'Let him in,' Angela said, trying to assume that haughty tone used by the leading ladies.

In an instant a tall, thin young man with sandy hair and an open expression stepped through the door. He was elegantly turned out, wearing evening dress beneath his cloak and holding a top hat under one arm.

Elsie was impressed, Angela could tell, positively simpering as he said, 'Good evening, ladies. May I say how much I have enjoyed the show? Seen it five times, don't-cher-know? Whistling tunes from it all the time.'

'That's most gratifying. Thank you for the flowers,' Angela replied graciously, sizing him up and wondering what he really wanted, though it was not hard to guess.

He stood there, leaning elegantly on his cane and smiling as if she was a stunning revelation. 'Beautiful blooms for a beautiful lady,' he replied gallantly, and looked at her so admiringly that she was reassured. He did not seem like a town rake out for all he could get from a girl. Then he added, 'Dare I hope that you'll consent to come to supper with me? I have booked a table and have a cab on standby. I will deliver you safely to your lodgings later. I give you my word.'

Oh dear, she thought. Now what was she to do? But she knew that she had already made up her mind when she consented to receive him. She looked at Elsie and Elsie looked at her. There was encouragement in her eyes, as if to say: This one seems harmless enough.

Young, even boyish, Angela refused to listen to the warning bells in her head. It was time she had a break from work. There could be no harm in accepting him, surely?

'Very well,' she said and stood up, her skirts whispering about her, cape on and hat, too. 'Elsie,' she continued, 'would you be so kind as to tell Mrs Morrison I shall be late? Let her know that I've gone to *Romano's* with Lord Codford. I'll pop my head round your door when I return.'

'I'll do that,' Elsie agreed, and gathered up her outdoor things. 'Take good care of her, your lordship.'

'You can trust me,' he replied, hand on heart.

Elsie went off with several of her friends who intended to catch a bus home. Alfred gave Angela his arm and they left the stage door, nodding to Wilfred who was on duty that night. Angela rather wished that Enoch had been there, for he was an experienced judge of character and would have seen through anyone up to sharp tricks. He did not think much of these aristocratic gentlemen who tried to take advantage of the actresses.

It was a clear night, the lights of theatre land still burning brightly, and the streets were filled with people finding cabs or their own vehicles and going out to supper. Alfred walked down the road a little way, and there was a hackney carriage waiting for him, its cabby seated aloft, a rug around his burly knees and the reins held loosely in his hands. He clambered down and opened the door for his passengers. Angela climbed in first, followed by Alfred. The door closed, the driver climbed back to his box and Alfred rapped on the roof with his cane. They moved off.

It was then that someone spoke in a deep voice that sent chills down her spine.

'Good evening, Angela,' said Aidan.

'Dear God! You!' she cried, and reached for the door handle. 'Let me out. Driver! Stop! Stop!'

Aidan gave a deep, ironic laugh, and now she could see him, a dark, satanic shape on the opposite seat. 'He won't hear you, and anyway, he has his orders.'

She turned on Alfred frantically. 'What is this? You said we were going to *Romano's*.'

Aidan answered for him. 'Alfred is a friend of mine. I thought I'd play a little game with you. I doubted you would accept my invitation and he acted as a go-between. Don't be cross with him. You'll thank him later. Did you really think I would let you escape me?'

She shrank into herself, as far away as possible from either of these vile deceivers. 'I don't care what you thought. I'm happy how, doing what I love best. Leave me alone, please.'

'Ah, you have always been able to tear at my heartstrings, dearest,' Aidan answered mockingly. 'Of course I shall let you continue with your career. I'm proud of your efforts.'

'You've seen me on stage?'

'Oh, yes, and have every intention of aiding you. It isn't fitting that my mistress should be in the chorus. I want to see you as the star of the show.'

'That's up to Mr Carte, surely... and Mr Gilbert,' she protested.

'I'm not without influence in those quarters. Sullivan would understand. He has an eye for the women.'

He moved, leaning across and insinuating one hand up her skirt and pushing aside the froth of petticoats. His fingers slid across the taut silk of her stockings and under the lace hem of her knickers to the naked flesh above. Her spine tingled and her nipples ached. She wanted him to go further but was terrified of her own reaction. She felt him moving slowly upward, and knew that as soon as he reached his goal he would know by the wetness there how much his touch was arousing her.

She tried to tighten her thighs but he would have none of it, finding her pleasure point and stroking it. Angela trembled and could not resist opening her legs. He gave a low laugh and addressed Alfred.

'You see how eager she is, my friend? I told you this would be so when you doubted the wisdom of deceiving her.'

'Yes, sir, I do indeed,' and Alfred, who was seated beside Angela, leaned closer, trying to see her pussy, though the interior of the cab was only lit by a swaying oil-lamp.

'She denies it to the bottom of her soul, but can't resist me. Can you, slave-slut? You want a sound spanking, don't you? Can't wait to be punished. And you shall be. Oh, yes.'

'Where are you taking me?' she gasped, his words like fire and wine to her.

'It's a surprise,' he said, and she could tell he was triumphant, amused and in a high state of arousal. She wanted to grasp his cock, feeling its solidity through the black barathea trousers, but before she could do so he slipped manacles around her wrists and snapped them shut.

'There's no need for that,' she protested, denying that the cold metal felt natural, even comforting.

'I think there is, and I give the orders,' he said sternly. 'Now, stop talking.'

He placed a scarf round her eyes and thrust a ball-gag in her mouth. She was trussed and helpless, expectant and thrilled, yet there was the sharp edge of fear that added piquancy to her high-strung state.

He returned to his exploration of her cleft and she moaned into the gag, saw stars behind the blindfold, was swept aloft as he kept her hovering on the edge of a climax. Then, at the very moment when she strained to achieve release, he took his fingers away and left her suspended between heaven and hell.

The vehicle stopped. She was lifted, carried down the steps, and then hoisted over a broad shoulder. She guessed it to be Aidan by the smell of him, and the way in which he held her with an arm under her buttocks.

He was walking and she swayed, her head hanging down, her hair streaming, hat and pins lost in transit. Cold air. Sounds of footsteps and the jingle of harness as the cab retreated. Where was she? What was the bastard about to do to her? It was horrible to be robbed of sight and voice, and unable to struggle or defend herself.

Would he let her go eventually, or did he intend to keep her prisoner? She heard the squeal of iron hinges and knew by his movements that he was descending. It was colder still, and damp, and Angela was terrified.

Chapter 13

Down, down, then the footsteps changed as Aidan reached level ground. Angela hung there like a puppet, limp and helpless. It was a nightmare, or perhaps the life she had thought she was carving out for herself was merely a dream and this was the grim reality. Only Aidan could do this to her, stripping her of everything, humbling her, subduing her, and a part of her, that dark part that responded so strongly to him, rejoiced and could not wait for the next bout of pain-pleasure.

His footsteps echoed now and she sensed they had reached their destination. A cellar? A vault? This was the impression that played on her senses. She was aware that they were not alone, feeling surrounded. Aidan set her down. She grabbed at him, tottering blindly.

'You want to see where you are and meet your admirers?' he whispered in her ear, then took off the scarf.

She blinked in the dazzle of torchères standing near the rough stone walls. She had been right in her assessment. The place was a basement, or a dungeon. Another of Aidan's hideouts where he and his confederates could indulge the passions they carefully concealed from the outside world. They murmured amongst themselves as her beauty was revealed.

'I say, old sport, what a stunner!' exclaimed a colonel with a flushed face, military moustache and medals across the breast of his crimson uniform jacket. 'This the gal you had before? Thought she'd run away, what?'

'I have given her enough rope to hang herself,' Aidan replied loftily, and pinched Angela's nipples through her bodice. 'No matter what she does or where she goes, she'll always come back to me.'

'She thinks she's very clever, giving us the slip, but we know all about her, don't we, Maude?' said Valerie, appearing from the background wearing an oyster satin gown. Angela's onetime companion accompanied her. She was dressed in trousers with her hair slicked back, and was drawing on a cigarette in a slim jade holder.

'Hello, Lady Angela,' she said, blowing smoke rings in the air, acting the dashing dandy while Valerie watched her admiringly. 'Doing well on the stage, are you? And enjoying your lodgings with Mrs Morrison?'

Angela's heart sank. They knew everything about her. She felt trapped and unutterably miserable. Why could they not wish her well and let her go her way? She did not deign to respond, knowing that they had come to mock and abuse her. There were enough rods and whips hanging from racks for all to take their turn if they decided to flog her. Let them do their worst.

'Still haughty, I see,' Aidan said grittily, and took the gag from her mouth. 'Time to bring you down a peg or two. You're not top of the bill at the Savoy yet, and even when you are I shall remind you every so often that you're my slave.'

'Bastard,' she managed to mumble, and was rewarded by a slashing blow across the rump.

'Take your clothes off,' he ordered, and unchained her hands.

'Go to hell!' she shouted, and made to run, but the men closed ranks, laughing and applauding.

'The lass has spirit, Driscol, I give her that. A wild little filly,' the colonel guffawed, quizzing her through his monocle.

'What a challenge to break her,' Aidan answered grimly, and swung round to Maude. 'Strip her!'

'Yes, master,' she said, leaping forward and wrenching at Angela's buttons and lacing.

Valerie joined in and, despite her flailing hands and savage kicks, Angela was soon deprived of all her clothing, with the exception of her pink corsets. Suspenders made a frame for her pubis in front and her bottom in the rear, attached to the tops of her silk stockings, and she retained her high-heeled ankle boots.

The observers cheered and swigged back tots of whiskey. Several already had their cocks out, stroking them in eager anticipation of joys to come. Angela, feeling more exposed in her stays than she would have done if entirely nude, cringed back, attempting to cover her bush with her hand.

Valerie seized her wrist and prised her fingers away, while Maude grabbed her other hand so that she stood there fully revealed. The men were in a ferment. The colonel collared Aidan and demanded, 'You said you were holding an auction tonight. I'll bid for her.'

Aidan shook him off and brushed his coat fastidiously. 'What I said was, whoever fancies her can bid to be the second man to have her. I shall be the first, naturally.'

'I say, what a capital wheeze,' the colonel bellowed. 'Reminds me of my days in the West Indies. What a jolly time we had before the abolition of slavery.'

'I'll bid, too,' piped up Alfred, and the sheen of sweat on his brow enhanced his fresh complexion. 'Don't give a cuss about being the third, just as long as I can get my prick in her. She's a stunner and no mistake. And I shall be able to boast that I've had one of the *Savoy* actresses. That'll impress my friends.'

'You'll keep your mouth shut,' Aidan snarled, grabbing him by his lapels and pinning him to the wall. 'I don't want any of this to be public knowledge. If I so much as hear a whisper I'll get you, Codford, and you'll regret that you were ever born.'

'All right, old chap, don't be like that. I only thought—'

'Don't think... be your normal addle-pated self,' Aidan said acidly, and set him on his feet with a force that made his teeth rattle.

It was chilling to hear them squabbling over her like dogs with a bone, and Angela stood between Valerie and Maude and dreaded the next move.

Two black servants dressed as eastern guards placed themselves on either side of her. They were strapping men with fine physiques, bared to the waist, showing rippling chest muscles and mighty arms banded by damascened bracelets. One wore a turban and the other had a mane of ebony ringlets. Their emerald-green pantaloons drew the eye to the mighty packages nestling between their thighs. Valerie could not keep her hands off them, rousing those magnificent phalli and circling the tight discs of their nipples. They ignored her, immobile as rocks, arms folded and bare feet planted apart, awaiting their master's orders.

Aidan gestured and they seized Angela and lifted her onto an oblong central stand that was doubling as an auction block. Chains were attached to her wrists and the ends slipped into rings fastened to the wood. Her ankles were treated in the same manner, and she stood there in all her nudity, unable to hide or run away.

The cellar throbbed with excitement and the men gathered round. She looked down into a sea of faces, some young, some middle-aged and some old enough to be grandfathers, but each wore the same glazed expression. She was being adored as perhaps once the Mother Goddess was worshipped, but there was a huge difference. Then, in those past ages when the world was still young, she had been viewed with reverence and awe, and no man would have dared lay a finger on her, let alone force and ravish. Now, all Angela read in their eyes was desire - a desire to conquer and enjoy - to show her that they were the superior beings and she a mere vehicle for their passion.

Aidan mounted the rostrum close by, banged on the surface with a gavel and shouted, 'Let us begin, gentlemen. The only lot tonight is this beautiful Caucasian woman, well bred, well educated and talented. She is almost a virgin.' A derisive roar went up and he silenced it and continued. 'I can assure you that her only lovers have been men of consequence, and I was the first to wrest her maidenhead from her. So, where shall we start the bidding? May I say forty guineas?'

'Aye, start there,' the colonel shouted.

'Forty five!' declared an elderly statesman, devoted servant of Her Majesty.

'Fifty!' This came from Alfred, and Angela hoped that he might be the one to second Aidan in his possession of her. At least he was young and personable, while the rest looked what they were: a collection of debauched roués.

'Sixty!' chorused the colonel rashly. He approached Angela and, at Aidan's nod of approval, prised her lower lips apart and inserted a stubby finger into her divide. 'My word, Driscol, but she's soaking wet!' he exclaimed in delight.

The men guffawed and rubbed their pricks vigorously, while Valerie and

Maude opened the guards' pantaloons and got to work on their fully erect members. They stood there deadpan, neither moving nor responding while the women used their expertise on them. Then the one in the turban grunted suddenly and his spunk shot from him, landing on the colonel's highly polished boots.

'Goddamn it!' the colonel shouted, and brought his cane across the man's thighs sharply, its end cutting into his deflated penis. 'Lick it off, you dirty sod!'

The guard tucked his equipment away, sank to his knees, and applied his tongue to the task. The colonel lashed him with his cane but the man carried on regardless. When he had finished and the toecaps of the boots gleamed, he stood up and resumed his post.

'Well done,' Valerie crooned, and kissed his pointed nipples, that were darker even than his shining skin. 'Perhaps these gentlemen will let you enjoy your prisoner once they've finished with her.'

Angela shivered with loathing and longing. She was at a high pitch of emotion that bordered on hysteria. The colonel had been right in his assessment of her readiness for penetration. She could not bring her thighs together, but could feel the trickle of lubrication seeping from her labial groove. Her excitement had almost the same quality as when she stood on stage, listening to the thunderous applause as the final curtain went down. Then she was caught up in the warm wave of feeling emanating from her audience. She felt loved, truly loved and, in a strange way, the admiration and attention of this crowd of rakes had that same curious intensity.

She adopted the pose of an abject slave, thinking herself into the part, head bowed, wrists and ankles chained, and the colonel inserted two fingers into her pulsing depths while his thumb rotated on her bud. Aidan stepped behind her, raised his whip and delivered a cracking blow on her quivering buttocks. She yelled and shrank and lost the rising impulse to orgasm, angry and disappointed, raging against him, her flesh seared by the sting of the lash.

'Leave her be,' he growled at the colonel. 'You haven't bought the right to use her. Let the bidding continue. Stroll round her, sirs, and view that perfect rump, fleshy yet firm, ideal for spanking, and more. See how it glows from my chastisement.'

With a hand at the nape of her neck he pressed her down from the waist, bottom in the air, her anal opening and damp pudenda on show. She had no choice but to gaze at the floor, aware of movements behind her and fingers exploring her intimate parts. She cursed Aidan mentally, and railed against fate that had brought her so low.

Aidan was guarding his treasure fiercely, and after a while shouted, 'Enough! Stand up straight, slave.'

The auction continued, with more gentlemen joining in the bidding. At last Aidan brought down the hammer after pronouncing, 'Have you all done, sirs? Any more advances? No? Then she goes to Lord Fennes for two hundred guineas. Going, going, gone!'

This couldn't be true, Angela thought bleakly. She couldn't be bought like this. Aidan wasn't her owner - just her cold-blooded, ex-betrothed who betrayed her so dishonourably. This was England, not some uncivilised foreign shore. And as for Lord Fennes, she'd rather scrub floors than have him lay a hand on her!

He was certainly repulsive, a bent, bald-headed nobleman, impeccably dressed yet with a lined, sneering face and rheumy eyes that feasted upon her with undisguised lust. He had a walking stick on which he leaned, and his other hand was busy at his trouser opening, massaging a lean prick that dribbled pre-come. She wanted to beg Aidan to release her from his bargain with this disgusting peer, but knew it would be useless.

The colonel and Alfred were in second and third place, but Aidan had no intention of letting anyone near Angela till he had finished with her. Lord Fennes was smiling in lecherous glee as the black servants released her hands and feet and lifted her from the block. She glanced round for a means of escape, but Valerie and Maude were watchful and the crowd too great to break through.

'Come, our audience is waiting,' murmured Aidan in her ear, his cool breath raising goose bumps all over her.

'I can't, not in front of all these people,' she protested, but his hand was on her rump, weighing the curves, toying with her.

'It won't be the first time,' he reminded. 'If I recall correctly I took your virginity at one of my parties, and a photographer was there. Did I show you the prints? No? They were excellent. I'm sure Mr Carte would be interested to see them.'

'You wouldn't!' she gasped, horrified at the idea of such shameless pictures of her being laid on her employer's desk. What would Helen think? And Mr Gilbert? She would be dismissed out of hand, her career finished when it was only just beginning.

'Wouldn't I?' Aidan whispered, and his vulpine smile said it all. He was without scruples or mercy. There was nothing she could do, no argument that would sway him. Aidan was used to getting his own way on every issue, and it was this spirit of dominance that made him so irresistible. But she would have run from him if she could. She had much to lose now, whereas once there had been nothing save her self-respect.

'Set me free, Aidan,' she said quietly, not begging or imploring or tearful, but as one human being to another. 'Let me get on with my life. What harm can it possibly do you? Don't you want to see me successful?'

He stared at her coldly; an almost reptilian stare. 'Of course I do, my dear, but under my terms. I should get the credit for freeing you from your straight-laced background and putting you in the footlight's glare.'

'I don't belong to you, Aidan,' she pressed. 'I'm not your creature.'

He caressed her breasts in such a way that she leaned towards him, drawn like steel to a magnet. His smile deepened and his eyes were hooded as he responded, 'Aren't you, my love? Wasn't it myself who taught you all you know about passion?'

'And deceit and lies and pain and humiliation...' she added.

'You've enjoyed every moment of it,' Valerie broke in, bizarre and beautiful, teasing the men who were trying to touch her and using a birch mercilessly if they persisted.

'You're wrong,' Angela insisted, remembering oh-so-much. 'I wish life had worked out otherwise.'

'Too much talking,' Aidan said finally, and propelled Angela towards a couch spread with a damask coverlet, adding, 'time for fucking.'

He guided her down onto the heap of cushions, then lowered himself beside her and took one of her hands and placed on his fly. She could not control her fingers, tracing over the hard baton that lay behind it. There came a low growl from the spectators, and Lord Fennes pushed his way to the front, grinning down at the couple.

'By God, Driscol!' he exclaimed. 'Get on with it, man. My prick is near to bursting.'

'You'll have to wait, sir,' Aidan stated, leaving Angela momentarily to remove his clothes. 'She is mine and I may decide to keep it that way.'

'But I bid for her!' Fennes cried angrily.

'No money has been exchanged,' was Aidan's cool reply. 'Now, if you will excuse me I have business to attend.'

He braced himself, leaning across Angela, his hands wandering over her with a sensualist's knowledge of the female erogenous zones. She could not keep still under those arousing caresses. When he tired of this and stretched her across his knees and used his flat palm to spank her posterior soundly, she writhed and mewed like a kitten. Her buttocks were on fire, and so was her clit. By now she was blind to the stares and remarks, feeling the heat of his cock against her side, willing to endure his slaps if only she could have it within her.

The torches flickered, the brazier throwing off a blood-red glow. When Aidan righted her and took her in his arms and lay with her, all she could see was his chiselled features and burning eyes, his hair falling over his face as he bent to kiss her. She gasped her pleasure and her tongue responded to his. He raised his lips from hers and parted her legs, his eyes never leaving hers.

'You are mine, Angela,' he said huskily.

'Yes...' she breathed, all arguments forgotten.

'Say it properly,' he reprimanded, slapping her breasts,

'Yes, master,' she faltered, then added, 'don't give me to them, please.'

'I'll reconsider, if you show me how dutifully you've practiced your lessons.'

It was as if the two were alone on a mountaintop. Nothing was of greater significance than his fingers slipping within her, then fondling her nubbin till she came, shuddering and sobbing. He opened her legs and brought them up, and angled himself above her, his penis brushing the tip of her clitoris, rousing it again. He supported himself on his arms then thrust forward, his cock plunging into her wetness. She welcomed him, her legs tightening around his waist. The watchers were rustling and murmuring, but she did not care who saw her taking Aidan into her body. Cruel he undoubtedly was, but her ardour for him had in no way diminished, though she tried hard to deny it.

He penetrated her again and again, slowly at first, but she lifted her pelvis, wanting deeper and deeper thrusts, rubbing her clitoris on his pubic bone, seeking sensation after sensation. Her passion was rising again and she tightened her arms round Aidan's neck and ground herself against him, his shaft filling her completely. He lay prone upon her, crushing her with his weight, unconcerned about her discomfort - and this lack of consideration thrilled her. The more he thrust, hurting her with his savage intensity, the more she responded to his ardour, but his cock-root grinding against her clitoris was too rough and climax eluded her. Not so Aidan.

She felt his organ like a molten spear penetrating her tender depths. He moved faster and faster, the tension in him rising to breaking point. He shot his semen into her, and then buried his face in her neck for a moment, clasping her to him. There were cries of 'Bravo!' from his guests and he raised himself on one elbow and looked down at Angela.

'All this nonsense about being chaste and ladylike,' he mocked. 'You're a hot-arsed piece, and don't try to deny it.'

'I am what you made me,' she responded, the sudden rush of tenderness she had felt melting like snow in sunlight. He really was incorrigible!

'I merely brought to the surface that which lay in your heart of hearts,' he replied, and smacked her bottom before rising and covering his lithe form with a dressing gown.

Fennes was there. 'My turn,' he demanded, banging on the floor with his cane, then raising it and poking Angela.

She drew up her legs and curled into a ball, trying to hide her nakedness, her expression one of abhorrence. Aidan drew himself up to his full height and looked down his nose at Fennes. 'No man makes demands on me,' he drawled, very calm and cool, but Angela knew that when he was controlled, then he was at his most deadly. 'I regret, my lord, that the deal is off. I have withdrawn the merchandise from the auction.'

There were shouts of, 'I say, that's not fair!'

'You're a poor sport, Driscol!'

'You can't do that to a chap, not when his todger is in full spate!'

But Aidan ignored them, saying, 'She is going home now, gentlemen. Valerie and Maude and these two noble savages will take care of any little duties you want performed. Goodnight to you all.'

They grumbled but Valerie soon had them smiling, performing a dance during which she removed her garments one by one, and permitting the intimacies they cared to lavish on her, providing they paid in hard cash. Maude took the money.

Angela could not believe that Aidan was being merciful, but she did not question his motives, dressing quickly and allowing him to bind her eyes again and lead her to where a cab waited. He gave the driver Mrs Morrison's address, paid him, and removed the blindfold.

'Shall I see you again?' she asked from the darkness of the interior while he stood on the step. She hated herself for her weakness, but could never resist him. 'Will you come to the theatre?'

He shrugged, once more the suave aristocrat in his superbly tailored evening suit. 'You won't know, will you, my dear?'

'But you won't stop me acting?'

'No, I promise you that. I shall be with you again when you least expect it.' And he leaned forward and brushed his lips across hers, the chilly night air filled with the personal scent of his hair, and the musky odour of his body.

'What happened? Bit of all right, I thought, that Lord Alfred. Did he wine and dine you?' whispered Elsie, round-eyed as a fluffy barn owl when she answered her door to Angela's hesitant tap.

'No, he didn't,' Angela replied, still reeling from the night's experiences.

'Why? Look here, you'd better come in. I told Mrs Morrison what you said and she was fine about it, but we don't want to wake her up now, do we?'

'It wasn't Alfred's idea to take me out... well, not exactly. He's keen, but there was more to it,' Angela said, loosening her cape and taking off her hat.

'You look as if you've seen a ghost,' Elsie said, and slipped on her cotton negligee. 'Wait here and I'll pop down to the kitchen and make us both a nice cup of cocoa. Shan't be a moment.'

Angela sat in the pink basket chair and wondered how much to tell Elsie. She needed to talk to someone badly, but was not sure if this was the right choice of confidante. Maybe Elsie was too innocent to understand. She'd tone it down, she decided. Embroider the truth.

But when Elsie returned with two mugs from which rose wisps of fragrant steam, she found herself delving more and more into her past and the present situation. Elsie listened, eyes rounder than ever while she dunked biscuits in her cocoa and made little comment.

'Deary me,' she said when at last Angela had talked herself to a standstill. 'Well I never.'

'Are you shocked?' Angela asked anxiously.

'No, not shocked. I've been around, you know, worked my way through shabby music halls and had to say no to many a roguish stage director who thought himself in with a chance,' Elsie said, and her colour deepened. 'No one knows this, only you, but I'm courting.'

'You are?' Angela expressed surprise, and was a trifle envious. 'And who is it?'

'Ewart Reynold. He's in the male chorus. I expect you remember him. He's got red hair and blue eyes and is ever so handsome. We keep it a secret though, for Mr Carte is fussy and doesn't like the cast consorting, as it were. He's afraid he'll lose the girl if she marries, for chances are she'll want to start a family.'

Angela listened to this naïve chattering and doubted that Elsie understood a word of what she had been saying. Corporal punishment for the fun of it was outside her ken. She left shortly after and retired to her own room, and she had never felt more alone.

The feeling of isolation remained and deepened and Angela threw herself into her work. This gave her the greatest satisfaction of all and she shielded her mind against thoughts of Aidan. As for Max? He had faded into the background, although one night he appeared in her dressing room when everyone else had departed. He carried a large box of fancy chocolates, and looked debonair in a mulberry velvet suit.

'My dear girl, I'm so proud of you,' he declared, and she flushed with pleasure.

'Am I doing well?' she asked, having been promoted to a small speaking part.

'Top-hole, sweetheart,' he enthused. 'You're getting there, girl. Carte is delighted with your progress.' Then he stood behind her where she sat at the dressing table and placed a hand on each of her shoulders, staring at her in the mirror. 'And you? Do you miss me? Has anyone else stolen your heart?'

'I can't imagine why it is of consequence to you, Max,' she chided gently. 'After all, you are married to Carlotta. My love life has nothing to do with you. But yes, since you ask, I have seen Aidan, but only once. There is no one else. I keep myself to myself. It is wiser that way.'

'Wiser, perhaps, but not half as much fun,' he chuckled, his handsome face lighting up. 'And did he treat you with respect?'

She half turned, gazing up at him. 'Aidan is Aidan. Nothing more and nothing less. He beats me, uses me as his slave, and I love him for it.'

His strongly marked brows drew down in a frown. 'I can't understand you, Angela, but accept that this is a matter between the two of you. I am willing to enjoy what is left.' He bent and kissed her full on the lips and she enjoyed it.

'Carlotta?' she reminded as his hands pushed aside her kimono and closed on her bare breasts.

'Has gone to supper with several members of the Carl Rosa cast. She'll be touring again soon, and so shall I.'

'With her?' Angela relaxed under his touch, almost purring with pleasure.

'No, we're off up north for the autumn season, and then there will be pantomime, of course. I've been offered the part of the villainous magician in *Aladdin*. I shall get booed and hissed and it's quite delightful, with a standing ovation at the end of each performance.'

Max was looking at her intently and nature had not only endowed him with a beautiful voice, but the most arresting and eloquent eyes. Angela stopped questioning his motives, or her own, as he lifted her from the stool and sat her on the dressing table, scattering the boxes of dusting powder, greasepaint sticks and jars of rouge. She did not resist as he placed a hand on each of her knees and prised them apart. She wore nothing under the kimono. She closed her eyes and leaned back on her hands and felt him stroking her inner thighs and then

147

touching the curls that covered her mons. He caressed her slit, coaxing her to wetness.

His trousers were open and his large member jutted forth. She supported herself on one arm and used her hand on that warm, silky-skinned object. He stood between her widespread legs and continued to rub her clitoris, easing back the little hood, leaving the tip bare, wetting his fingers with her juice and massaging it delicately, taking her to the top of the mountain and letting her fly.

'Oh, Max,' she gasped, needing this desperately.

He pushed her back and eased her hips towards him, then thrust his cock into her and she cried out again in her extremity. Her inner muscles gripped his hugeness, the glans jarring against her womb as he gripped her and pumped steadily.

He was already close to coming and she saw his eyes glaze and felt that extra force as his semen gushed from him, filling her to the core.

He sighed deeply and held her close, legs locked around him, his cock still sheathed in her depths. She laid her head against his chest and was filled with regrets and what-might-have-beens. If only he wasn't married. If only Aidan hadn't acted like a cad of the first water. But she checked these thoughts; life couldn't be made of 'ifs and buts'.

'Shall we go to supper?' Max asked, slipping from her and wiping his cock on a make-up towel.

'You don't have to invite me out because of what has just taken place between us,' she said sensibly, slipping off her robe and beginning to dress. He helped her with the stay-laces, as competent as any ladies maid.

'That isn't why I asked you,' he said, standing back to view her in her corsets. 'I enjoy your company.'

'No, my dear Max, but thank you anyway. You mustn't make Carlotta jealous or she'll give you hell.'

'I'm willing to risk it,' he averred with a wide grin.

'No, Max,' she repeated. 'I have a hectic rehearsal tomorrow morning. I'm understudying for the lead soprano in the production due to open in December. I'll take a cab back to Mrs Morrison's and have an early night.'

He hugged her and said, 'I love you, Rose Trelawney.'

She laughed at him and replied, 'And I love you, too, Maximillian Devere, but...'

He sobered. 'There's the mysterious and perverse Aidan.'

'Not forgetting Carlotta,' she said, turning it into a joke.

'But we'll always be friends, eh?'

'I hope so,' and he accompanied her to the cab rank outside and even shared one with her, dropping her off safely in Woodgreen.

An event occurred that is the dream of every understudy. It was not a broken leg or twisted ankle that laid the lead singer low, but Mother Nature in all her wisdom deciding that this was the time when she should become pregnant. She was a respectably married woman, but nonetheless, was now troubled by morning sickness that made it impossible for her to carry on. So, as luck would have it, Angela was offered her role.

Nothing mattered any more but putting on a first-rate performance, and she practiced and perfected her art till the first night, when the thunderous applause told her that not only was *The Gondoliers* an outstanding success, but that she had become a star.

Her name and picture was in all the newspapers, on posters, in magazines and the stage door was swarming with well-placed suitors, all jostling for a glimpse of her and leaving flowers and cards that begged Rose Trelawney to accept their invitations. Angela thanked them politely but let it be known that she was something of a recluse. She had decided that she wanted nothing more to do with men; thrilled with her career and the standing it gave her.

Carte was pleased with her progress and modesty, but did suggest that it would be wise to indulge any truly influential person who might wish her to sing at a soirée. This was always beneficial to an actress's career, if carried out with dignity and professionalism. Angela took his advice and did just that, and very soon a duke was courting her. At the same time she heard down the grapevine that Aidan had announced his engagement to an American heiress. This news entered her heart like a poisoned barb, and she accepted the duke's invitation to entertain his guests after the show one evening.

He was staying in his stately town house in the West End, and sent his carriage to convey her there. It was a freezing January night and Angela wrapped herself in a fur stole. She had brought a pianist with her, and Elsie to act as chaperone. The mansion was brightly lit, distinguished guests arriving, and the door standing open with footmen ready to usher them in. Randolph, Duke of Thorndyke, grey-haired patrician and widower, greeted them in an entrance hall that was as large as a ballroom.

As an honoured entertainer Angela was welcome by the duke, who had his butler show her and her companions to an anteroom near the music saloon. There she took off her furs and prepared herself, with Elsie fussing round her and the pianist tugging at his shirt cuffs, running a nervous finger round the inside of his stiff collar and fidgeting generally. Before long the butler came to tell them that the guests were seated and it was time to begin. Angela walked to the front of the salon under the full blaze of chandeliers. She was applauded and stood by the black grand piano, while her accompanist shuffled music and set it on the stand.

The duke made a short announcement and a faint rain of applause met this. Angela wished the room were dark, like the theatre always was. There was just too much distraction - evening gowns that were the last word in fashion, men in uniforms and tailcoats, the flash of priceless gems and orders. They sat and stared at her and some raised their lorgnettes. She lost her nerve for a second, and then glanced at Elsie who was standing at the side, and at her stalwart pianist. When he struck up the opening chords of her first song she forgot everything except giving the best rendition she could.

As Elsie said later, 'You went down a storm!'

It was true. The elite audience loved her, white-gloved hands coming together and clapping. Because the D'Oyly Carte productions were so popular they requested that she give them songs from the Gilbert and Sullivan light operas, and she was only too happy to oblige. Her nerves were steady now and her ego blossomed under their praise. She was happy and at home, leaning against the shiny piano in a beautiful new dress, its deep pink complementing the name by which she was known - Rose Trelawney.

It was while she was beginning to give voice to one of these arias, that she saw a slight disturbance at the back of the salon as two late arrivals were shown to seats. Angela gazed to where the newcomers sat - an elegantly attired man and a rather plain but beautifully gowned and bejewelled woman - and thanked God that she was now a seasoned trouper able to carry on no matter what, for it was Aidan who was now staring at her relentlessly.

The applause rang out when she finished and Randolph held up his hand for silence and said, 'My thanks to Miss Trelawney. Perhaps she will be so generous as to entertain us on another occasion such as this. Now, supper is served,' and he indicated the damask-covered trestles to one side of the room, where footmen hovered, having brought in a cold collation on silver platters. The cutlery was silver, too, and the goblets were of Waterford glass.

Randolph offered Angela his arm and escorted her towards the tempting array. Everything was of the highest quality and she realised that she was hungry, yet dreaded approaching Aidan and his lady friend. Her progress was slow. It seemed everyone there wanted to meet her, but at last came the moment she'd been dreading; it had even occurred to her to feign a headache, make her excuses and leave.

Too late. The duke stopped by Aidan and said, 'So glad you could make it, Driscol, and your betrothed, too. How are you, Miss Symington? Enjoying your stay in England?'

She dipped a curtsy, big-boned, dark-haired and, as far as Angela could judge, in her late twenties. 'Sure, your Grace, I'm having a wonderful time,' she gushed. 'I just love your country. Everything is so *old!*' She turned to Angela, eyes shining with admiration. 'Your singing was angelic. I enjoyed it so much. Aidan must take me to see one of your shows.'

'Of course, my love,' he answered urbanely, and his eyes met Angela's, amusement in their depths. 'As my fiancée, your wish is my command.'

'Permit me to introduce you,' the duke continued, completely unaware of the undercurrents rippling through the ether. 'Miss Rose Trelawney, meet Lord Aidan Driscol and his betrothed, Miss Penelope Symington. She is from New York.'

Bully for her! Angela thought with a savage fury that amazed her. And for him, too. Was this the heiress he'd been seeking? God, she looked rich enough even for someone as greedy as him, but could he possibly be attracted to her?

Had he fucked her yet, or whipped her, or shown her his secret vices?

He was gallantly insuring that Penelope was settled at a round table with the duke and several other notables with whom she was obviously very impressed, and that she had refreshments and a glass of champagne. Angela knew there was unfinished business between he and her, and she excused herself and made towards the ladies' room. She did not have to look round to know that he had given Penelope some cock-and-bull story and was following her.

The corridor was deserted and, as she reached the door he suddenly grabbed her from behind and propelled her further along till he wrenched open another, flung it wide and dragged her inside. He reached for the light switch. They were in a storeroom. There were shelves containing household equipment for the use of the servants - buckets, brooms, mops, a pile of newspapers. It smelt vaguely of cleaning fluid.

'What do you think you're doing?' Angela hissed, furious at this cavalier treatment.

'I'm about to enter you,' he said, his teeth gleaming in the dim light of the single bare bulb.

Her heart leapt and her treacherous body grew weak and lubricious. Even so, she put up a fight. 'And what about Penelope?'

He grinned wolfishly and fastened his hands round her breasts, giving her such strong sensations that she wanted to fall into his arms. 'A nice woman... totally without malice and shrewd with it,' he said, and nibbled her neck, sending shivers right through her. 'She was introduced to me by a certain Mrs Smythe who specialises in flitting across the Atlantic Ocean arranging meetings between fabulously rich American heiresses and titled English gentlemen. Penny and I got on straightaway, and did a deal. We'll marry. She'll gain a title and her millionaire industrialist father will gain grandchildren to whom he has to give precedence when passing through doors. It will work perfectly.'

'And she knows about you, does she? She's willing to be your slave and submit to your desires?' Angela's heart was beating fast with anger and desire.

'Don't be silly,' he murmured lazily, his lips traversing her throat, his fingers baring her nipples and his teeth gnawing at them painfully. 'She will be a dutiful wife, present me with a couple of heirs and then busy herself with other things. She'll run my household efficiently and spend much time in New York, I suspect.'

'So, apart from selling yourself for her father's money, your life will proceed very much as usual.' Angela was trying hard to despise him, but was breathing in the arousing fragrance that was always Aidan; his unique skin and a certain pomade he used to control his hair.

'That's the general idea,' he confirmed, and before she knew what he was doing he seized a rope that lay on a bench behind them and wound it round her wrists. Now she was restrained, and Aidan took fire from the sight.

'You're a bounder,' she gasped. 'You don't know the meaning of the word honour. I'm sorry for Penelope.'

'Don't be. She knows the score and doesn't expect love. This is a business arrangement and once we've produced a couple of sprogs she is free to do as she likes.'

'And you'll carry on as you've always done. You disgust me,' she stormed, yet her pubis ground into his through their censorious clothing and she longed to plunge into the dark pit of sensation that he always offered.

Her arms were tied behind her and Aidan twisted her round and had her face the wall. Her cheek was pressed to the plaster and she waited with baited breath as he became silent. Had he left her there? But there had been no sound of the door opening. The possibility of someone coming in and finding them like that appalled her, but it was exciting, too. He moved and kissed her neck, after brushing aside the wispy tendrils that hung there. She turned her face to smile at him, but he was gone again, until she felt him lifting her clothes and baring her bottom.

His hand, then, was to be her punishment? She waited, filled with longing and fear, that terrible, potent brew that she had missed with Max. Then she felt an alien touch on her skin and heard him saying, 'So kind of the staff to leave their tools behind. This long-handled wooden spoon, for instance, will act as well as any paddle.'

He did not use it at once. Angela felt his hand on her, massaging gently, then raining down light slaps, and following this with an exploration of her cleft. Yet she was very aware of that which he held in his other hand, then without warning he brought it down on her rump. It snapped and stung and the heat was intense. She wailed and he stopped for a second, rubbing the crimson flesh. Then he whacked her with the spoon again, and again and again till she was on the edge of breaking. He drew back and the relief was unbearable - but inside she was screaming at him to go on.

'You want me to stop?' Aidan goaded.

'Yes... no, please.' She could not believe what she was saying.

'And I am your master, your Nemesis from whom you can never escape, punishing you for being a filthy slut full of unbridled passion.'

The spoon hit her so hard that she bucked and writhed, remembering not to scream lest she be heard from outside, though this was unlikely, the entertainment in full swing in the distance, voices, laughter, and someone playing dance music on the piano. Aidan brought the spoon down harder, and she managed to get free of his grasp and fling herself to the floor. What price her new and expensive gown now? Her bladder had failed her and she was wetting herself all over the rose-hued satin.

Aidan lifted her to a kneeling position, whipped up her damp skirt and spanked her with his hand. 'Dirty girl, now it is my time,' he said softly, and unbuttoned his trousers.

His fingers dipped into her and came out covered in dew. This he applied to his swollen cock then lifted her under her waist and positioned himself at her anal entrance. His erection, though slippery, felt enormous, but he eased in, inch by solid inch. She had never become used to or enjoyed this way of being fucked. Besides which, he had made no attempt to bring her to a climax. She hated him, wanted to expel him from her most private passage but he was too strong, too large and too close to his moment of rapture. Nothing could stop him now and even though she swore and berated him, he came in spurts, fluid jetting deep within her rear.

Without pausing he raised her till she was standing in front of him, his cock still buried inside her. He slipped a hand round to her pubis, parted her lips and rubbed her slippery kernel. She responded in spite of herself, and came in a fierce explosion of sensation that left her trembling and bearing down on the rigid object that still filled her. When she came to her senses she disengaged herself from him and replaced her underclothes, keeping her face turned away from him.

Her skirt had dark damp patches where she had urinated, and she needed her wrap to cover it as she made her exit from the mansion. 'Send Emily to me here,' she said icily. 'Give the duke my apologies, but say I am unwell and have had to leave early.'

Aidan stood there as if nothing untoward had happened. 'I'll do that for you,' he said. 'Good luck, Angela. You have Randolph eating out of your hand, and could end up a duchess.'

'And that would be what I deserve,' she replied haughtily. 'I'm as wellborn as he, and probably more so than you.'

'Spiteful,' he teased, then paused at the door, turning and saying, 'Will you come to my wedding?'

'I'll see you burn in hell first,' she said.

'I will make sure you receive an invitation,' he concluded, smiling wickedly, then bowed from the waist and stalked out.

Angela was the talk of the town, *The Gondoliers* a box office sell-out. The world was her oyster, and all the well-heeled men in it. There was talk of her joining the touring company and playing in America, but Carte did not want to lose her yet; she was too valuable an asset for the Savoy. By now she knew most of the repertoire, constantly practicing, constantly rehearsing, giving herself no time to brood or become involved with those most dangerous of creatures - men!

Randolph was a kindly man, and a lonely one. He had adult sons and daughters, and Angela sometimes permitted him to escort her to some of the smart restaurants that had sprung up in and around the theatres in Leicester Square. She found herself warming to him. He reminded her of her father and, a great admirer of the stage and all its works, had offered to become her manager, making certain that she was always given a fair deal. It was around this time that she left Mrs Morrison and purchased a villa in Finsbury Park. Randolph helped her through the transaction and she could hardly believe that she had saved enough money to buy it - two hundred pounds! He also accompanied her when she went to *Liberty's* to furnish it.

Elsie was married by now and living with her husband, Ewart. They, too, were doing well and being given leading roles. Then came news that shattered Angela's feeling of contentment and success - Aidan sent her an invitation to his wedding, due to take place at St Martin's Church, Westminster, a most fashionable and highly sought-after venue.

'Strange,' Randolph remarked when she told him. 'I was not aware that he knew you.'

'We had met before your soirée,' she told him. 'We come from the same corner of Somerset.' By now she had told him the truth about her father's death but had omitted Aidan's part in her history.

'Fine, well, in that case, perhaps you will allow me to be your escort. We can travel in my carriage.'

'Thank you, Randolph, I would like that,' she replied, smiling at him across the restaurant table whilst thinking that would be one in the eye for Aidan, if he realised that maybe she was about to take his advice about netting a duke.

It was summer again, over a year since her life had changed so drastically - for the better, as it transpired. She was at the height of her beauty, elegant, stylish, setting fashions in fact. Her female audience looked to her for guidance regarding the latest vogues. It was a heady feeling, but Aidan marrying rankled, and sometimes she tossed and turned in bed at night, burning with desire, giving herself relief, but it was never enough.

They arrived at the church on time, she and Randolph, and his coachman dropped them off and drove round to the rear to wait for them to be taken to the reception. The press and photographers were there. The crowd thickened, a swarming gaggle of women from all walks of life, all eager to see the bride and dream that it was them wearing a veil and a slipper satin gown, heading for a life of luxury instead of being downtrodden.

Angela walked in, imagining the whispers and speculation that went round the church. An actress on the arm of a duke! There was an air of anticipation. Young men in morning suits, white gardenias in their buttonholes, were acting as ushers. As she sat with Randolph, she could not help brooding on how it might have been if she was Aidan's bride.

She did not enjoy the ceremony, the music, the flowers and Aidan standing at the altar exchanging vows with Penelope. It had been cruel of him to invite her, and foolish indeed to have accepted and put herself through this anguish. It wasn't that she still loved him. She knew him too well for that, but her body, that perverse animal side of her, remembered his lips, his cock and, most of all, his blows. Even as she occupied the pew beside Randolph, surrounded by grand and snobbish guests, with many of Penelope's American relations among them, so her nipples ached under her chemise and her clit throbbed and she wanted Aidan with a lust beyond all reason. It was as if his whip had traumatised her bottom, the memory of it branded into her flesh for all time.

154

The service seemed to drag on interminably, but at last the wedded pair walked down the aisle, stood outside amidst showers of rose petals, and then led the coach and motor cavalcade heading for the reception. The whole event passed in a daze. Angela drank a little too much champagne and Randolph was charm itself, looking after her as if he instinctively guessed there was something wrong. The food was superlative, the wedding cake a shining example of the chef's art, and Angela was treated with respect, simply because the duke was escorting her. No one asked her to sing, and she thanked God for it. The music had already been arranged and a string quartet played beneath the shell-like roof of an alcove.

Speeches. Jokes. More wine. The cutting of the cake. Then dancing led by the bride and groom. 'Shall we?' asked Randolph, and guided Angela to the floor.

She held her head high and ignored Aidan as they joined the other couples whirling to a waltz. She could feel him looking at her, his eyes boring into her back, and she saw Valerie among the dancers, in the arms of Lord Alfred Codford. There were other men that she recognised from orgies in which she had been included as the prime cut. Such hypocrisy shocked her, yet she had expected it.

Randolph was called away to chat with some of his friends and Angela wandered out into the lush and beautifully tended garden. There was a small pool into which a waterfall splashed. It made her homesick and she wished with all her might and main that she might find herself at Lairdland.

'If you marry the duke he may be able to buy it back for you,' said a familiar voice from behind her.

'How did you know I was thinking of home?' she asked, unsurprised to find Aidan there.

'I know everything about you,' he said, and ran his fingers across the nape of her neck where her spine linked with her shoulders. She shivered with delight.

'Where's Penelope?' she asked, trying to be sensible.

'With her relations, rejoicing in being addressed as *Lady* Driscol.'

'Have you had her yet?' she asked waspishly, hating the idea.

He pulled a reproving face. 'My dear, of course not, she's a virgin and the alliance will be consummated tonight, on our honeymoon. Meanwhile, what about coming into the potting shed with me?'

'What?' she cried, her heart leaping traitorously. 'We can't, not at your wedding!'

But for answer he linked his arm with hers and led her along a bush-shrouded path to the headquarters of the gardener and his assistants, now off duty. The shed was adequate for Aidan's purpose, and he slipped the bolt behind them. Then he lifted her up onto the tool bench, despite her protest about damage to her gown, and there rummaged beneath her skirts.

'Oh, dear me,' he muttered, lifting his lips from hers. 'No knickers, Miss Trelawney? How vulgar.'

'I left them off deliberately,' she gasped, as he found her notch and started to

155

fondle her nubbin.

'For me?' he whispered, and the bulge in his striped trousers was huge.

'No, it pleased me to know that my arse was bare when I was with those toffee-nosed bitches in the church.'

He kissed her deeply, and then slipped down her body till he could kiss her lower lips, too. He licked and sucked at her till she was pulsing with pleasure, then he raised his face to her and said, 'I want to spank you, Angela, and I shall do so, wedding or no damned wedding.'

'Yes, *master*,' she whispered, and yet again surrendered herself to his will.

More from Roxane Beaufort

Forever Chained, also published by us and available as a paperback on **AMAZON**.

There were benches with holes in strategic places, a contraption that resembled stocks, a vaulting horse and a whipping post set in the middle of the floor, and racks of instruments; whips and paddles, canes and tawse, rods and birches. Iron rings had been hammered into the damp stone walls and several young women hung from them, chained by their wrists. A man in top boots and riding breeches was moving among them, his crop landing on their thighs, bellies and breasts. Their moans and sighs augmented the organ toccata.

As a student and a singer Stella is haunted by the vision of a beautiful man, Lazio, who is often in the audience when she performs, but it is not until she takes up residence in Troon Hall and visits a ruined monastery nearby that she meets him properly, and falls victim to those who made him a vampire.

A dairy that once belonged to Emma, her great-great-grandmother, tells of a trip to Venice where she and her friend Candice met the leader of the Nosferatu, Prince Dimitri. Candice fell in love with him and accepted the dark gift of eternal life. Emma was distraught, and spent years trying to contact this immortal girl who wanders in limbo, but died without succeeding and now expects her descendant, Stella, to unite them.

Dimitri's bizarre votaries seduce Stella, keeping her under restraint and subjected to their unnatural desires, but the love that links her and Lazio can be used to form a bridge between Candice and Emma. Shall Stella exchange blood with him and become a vampire, too?